The Overlife

A Tale of Schizophrenia

Diana Dirkby

Copyrights © 2023

All Rights Reserved

To the memory of my mother, Patricia.

Acknowledgments

I thank my spouse for expressing his pride in my decision to write this novel and for enabling me, with his support, to devote time to writing. My psychologist and psychiatrist helped me maintain good mental health while writing this work, even when the subject matter was challenging to put on paper. Their impact on my life continues to enable me to achieve my goals. The publishing team at amazon.com was supportive and professional, helping me through the complicated processes of proofreading, promotion, and the appearance of this book on the world stage.

Lastly, I thank my parents for all the positive experiences they brought to the strange child I was and the fact that I exist in the first place. We had a complex relationship, but that admission should take nothing away from its merits.

Table of Contents

Acknowledgments 5

Preface 1

1 - Sarah: Death 2

2 - Dancer 4

3 - Despair 24

4 - Dalaigh 30

5 - Sarah: Violation 38

6 - Unborn 39

7 - Sarah: Fear 41

8 - Marriage 44

9 - Robert 57

10 - Sarah: Illegitimate 62

11 - Piano 64

12 - Sarah: Photos 71

13 - Humor 73

14 - Sarah: Letters 80

15 - Thirty-Eight 82

16 - Watch 93

17 - Sarah: Thirty-One 97

18 - Propaganda 117

19 - Feivel 129

20 - Sarah: Thirty-five 136

21 - Education 148

22 - Friends 156

23 - Sarah: Cacophony 168

24 - Inappropriate 170

25 - Sarah: Disintegration 175

26 - Nature 176

27 - Sarah: Words 182

28 - Violence 187

29 - Police 193

30 - Sarah: Knife 196

31 - Divorce 200

32 - Bedridden 205

33 - Job 212

34 - Sarah: Thirty-Eight 215

35 - Remissions	233
36 - Acquaintances	244
37 - Diagnosis	251
38 - Cancer	256
39 - Death	263
40 - Confidant	265
41 - Sarah: Symbolism	281
42 - Poet	286
43 - Beth	299
44 - Herman	307
45 - Sarah: Self-diagnosis	312
46 - Psychologist	314
47 - Psychiatrist	334
48 - Trust	344
49 - Music	351
50 - Sarah: Overlife	356
About the Author	400

Preface

This book is not a scientific work nor a factual biography or autobiography. It is not a study of the treatment and mistreatment of those living with schizophrenia in a societal or geographic context. It is a private fictional tale based on authentic experiences with schizophrenia in my family. In particular, my mother's and my struggles with paranoid schizophrenia inspired me to write this narrative through the prism of a fiction novel. Any references to real people are fictitious. Other names, characters, and incidents are the product of the author's imagination, and any resemblance to actual events or persons, living or dead, is entirely coincidental.

The word *Overlife* in the title of this book is a noun derived from the verb overlive. In Collins English Dictionary , published by HarperCollins, overlive means *to live longer than (another person) or to survive or outlive an event.*

1

Sarah: Death

I am eleven. A strong force pushes me through a dark tunnel that eventually reveals two exits. Death is one of them, and hope is the other. Death is right in front of me, a vast gelatinous, pulsating face, ugly to behold and forever hungry. It sucks me towards its mouth, though I fight its pull. I am losing, facing my impending and inevitable elimination. Hope is a distant welcoming light, off to the left side of my vision. I try to move toward hope only to realize that death has paralyzed me. I experience the weight of the certainty that everybody dies.

When I wake up, I am sure I am dead, and the terror of the nightmare suffocates me. I heave and heave until I can again draw a regular breath. So, I am not dead, but I feel I am no longer entirely connected to the living.

I, Sarah, as did my mother, Jodie, live with the brain disorder paranoid schizophrenia, whose onset many believe has no optimistic Overlife, meaning the afflicted cannot overlive it with worthy expectations.

2

Dancer

Like me, my mother, Jodie, lived with the brain disorder paranoid schizophrenia and, as her condition worsened, became labeled by most people who knew her only as mad. Jodie considered herself, above all else, to warrant the label dancer.

Jodie was born in 1927 in Broken Hill, New South Wales, Australia, to her father, Feivel, and her mother, Edith. Feivel owned a car dealership. Her only sibling, Beth, was four years older and was born in Adelaide, South Australia. The family stayed in Broken Hill until my mother was three, when they moved back to Adelaide so Feivel could take over a new car dealership. Feivel and Edith settled in that city for the remainder of their lives.

Broken Hill was at the edge of the outback. Due to its importance as a mining town, it was prosperous and was sometimes referred to as *The Silver City* due to the silver ore discovered there. The nearest big city was Adelaide, over 300 miles away, so there was a sense of isolation in Broken Hill, underlined by its proximity to untouched vistas of extraordinary beauty in stunning colors like orange, red, and brown. It was home to exotic Australian wildlife, such as the emu and the kangaroo. It boasted gorgeous sunsets. It could also be a scary place. My aunt vividly remembered the terrifying dust storms occasionally covering that city. My mother was always proud to say she was born in Broken Hill, even though she never saw it again after age three. Her pride must have made an impression on me. I visited Broken Hill as an adult. I was impressed and thought it was closer to my mother's identity than staid old Adelaide.

Both parents were born in Australia, Edith in Melbourne, Victoria, and Feivel in Ballarat, Victoria. Edith was forty-three when she gave birth to Jodie. Indeed, Edith was born in 1884, and Feivel in 1894. To have a husband so much younger was unusual at that time. My maternal grandmother was the youngest of fourteen siblings, her parents being distinctly Victorian. The values of that era, especially concerning sexual behavior and the shame of dissolving a marriage, were passed down to my mother. Then, by continual brainwashing from an early age to me. I was born in 1957, destined to be consistently behind the times in sexual etiquette.

Jodie and Beth each had basic ballet lessons for a year when they turned seven. It was their mother's idea. She believed some ballet was good for her daughters' deportment. At age eight, their ballet training stopped, and each child celebrated by attending, the following Christmas, a performance of The Nutcracker put on by one of the ballet companies in Adelaide. Each year afterward, their parents ensured the little girls saw a Swan Lake and a Nutcracker performance. The score for both ballets is by Tchaikovsky. The two ballets are famous and a staple for anyone who seeks an education in classical ballet. Jodie and Beth found the performances entertaining, but they did not make them fall in love with ballet.

Jodie and Beth were both slim and graceful, my mother being the tallest. "I was the gangling one in the family," she would say, "before I rounded out to slender and stopped growing at five foot five." Jodie had curly black hair, a generous face with prominent features, and round dewy black eyes. Her Mediterranean looks enthralled me; growing up, I wished I could be as beautiful as my mother. When I stopped growing, I was about three inches taller than Beth at five foot six, but I resembled her in my light build, mousy brown hair, and compact looks as if there had been a shortage of material when we were formed. Only our eyes differed. Beth's eyes were sky blue and almond-shaped, mine a much darker blue and the same shape as Jodie's. Beth and I were far from ugly, but our facial expressions didn't have the dramatic range of my mother's.

Jodie was conservative in her dress but always looked good in her clothes. She didn't compromise on shoes, underwear, and pajamas for herself and me. She would say, "Good shoes are so important. We are on our feet for a large part of the day. People outside the family do not see our underwear and pajamas, but they are next to the skin, making them our most intimate attire, and therefore crucial for our dignity." When she went out, my mother used only a few basics of makeup: foundation, face powder, and lipstick. She told me, "The idea is to make the skin on your face look more uniform and to give a bit of color to the lips. A woman doesn't need more than that." I applied these lessons in adulthood, except I never wore lipstick.

Jodie and Beth received an excellent formal education. Like many young women of that era, they left school at fifteen and continued their cultivation at home. The primary tutelage came from Feivel, who was incredibly erudite for someone mainly self-schooled. Edith was primarily concerned with transmitting moral values and teaching her daughters how to run a household. I saw photos of their home in Adelaide. It was a large, stately ranch house in a middle-class suburb.

When Jodie was sixteen and Beth was twenty, they both found a reason to love ballet. My mother told me the story. "We learned about a small ballet company in Adelaide from the advertisements for its performances in the newspaper. We were curious, as the programs contained items we didn't know. Rather than dancing complete ballets, each program consisted of excerpts from several ballets. This group of dancers called themselves The Wayville Company after the suburban location of their studio and performances. Beth and I attended some shows after nagging our parents for the tickets. The first ballet excerpts we saw were from Stravinsky's Firebird, written for the 1910 Paris season of Sergei Diaghilev's Ballets Russes company, with choreography primarily due to Fokine. At another performance, we saw some of Les Présages, a relatively new ballet choreographed by Léonide Massine to music from Tchaikovsky's fifth symphony. Except for Tchaikovsky, none of these gifted people had been on Beth's and my radar."

"What's more, the performances by The Wayville Company were athletic, passionate, and technically beyond perfect. We still needed to encounter such an approach to ballet in our lessons and the Nutcrackers and Swan Lakes we had so far seen. The female dancers were not delicate underweight fairies whose limbs looked like they might break at the slightest touch but solid muscular bodies that could still convey fragility and project powerful emotions. The male dancers were equally impressive with their high leaps, athleticism, and forceful acting. We both were so excited by these dancers that we felt we must begin to dance again too. That reaction worried our father. He was not enthusiastic about ballet as an activity for girls who marry well."

Their father gave in. In 1943, the same year Beth and Jodie discovered The Wayville Company, they entered the ballet school associated with it. Feivel paid for his daughters to have lessons there. My mother told me about this start in professional-level ballet. "The first step was the ballet lessons. A gifted male dancer called Wally owned the company. He organized his dance school as part of his company's activities."

"Through four years of grueling hard work," Jodie told me, "I made rapid progress to corps de ballet standard by twenty, as did Beth at twenty-four. In some sense, it was harder for Beth because she was older than me. We knew we had started serious ballet training too late to be soloists. Our goal was to maintain our level as part of the corps de ballet so that we would at least belong to an important wing of the company. As it happened, The Wayville Company did not have enough corps de ballet for many works, hence the idea of dancing excerpts for the programs. Expanding the ranks of the corps de ballet was a genuine help to Wally's company. He had enough soloists. We always used recorded music rather than worry about live music."

For the critical question of financing The Wayville Company, Jodie explained, "Wally charged a fee for his lessons, which were a major source of the income needed to set up the ballet performances. The performances were not free for the public, but the ticket price was low.

Wally's ballet school was a success; he had to turn many people away as he insisted on being the only teacher. Any person who wanted to be a company member first had to pay Wally for lessons. He only accepted students fifteen or older, so, for most, Wally wasn't their first teacher. Wally's school was the only conduit to the ballet company, so even with that age restriction, more than enough people wanted to learn ballet with The Wayville Company. If a student showed little potential after some training, Wally would ask them to leave. At the other end of the spectrum, when he felt a dancer had reached their full potential and danced well, he waived his fee. He then invited them to work for his company as full-time dancers, soloists, or in the corps de ballet. A handful of dancers often crossed between these two levels, depending on the choreography. Wally shared with them the company's profits from lessons and performances. For choreography, Wally either used a well-established version or asked his talented choreographer, Sasha, to develop a new one. Wally still needed financial help with the company wages and the material for the costumes and sets. He relied on the support of wealthy balletomanes who admired The Wayville Company. Each year they contributed money without which we would have gone under!"

"Many of the behind-the-scenes members of Wally's studio, who were not dancers or choreographers, volunteered their services in making costumes and simple scene sets. They worked at a real job and spent their spare time helping Wally. They did it out of love for the ballet."

"Indeed, the passion for ballet was the motor that kept the company and its performances going. Wally took no money for himself from the company's profits. His parents were both deceased but had left him a house and enough money well-invested to enable him to lead a modest life without working. Ballet was his reason to live, and he was fortunate to have the means to dedicate himself to it."

I once asked my mother, "How do you know so much about how Wally managed to keep his company going?" She replied, "Wally shared the financial situation with everyone. He knew it was precarious, with, at any given time, no assurances he could make it work for more than another year. He wanted everyone to know, so no one was under any illusions about their future in his company. Somehow, for me, as a young person, our precarious financial status only drew me to the company more, as I found it exciting and bohemian."

My mother was impressed with how Wally moved, "Wally could dance faultlessly, without warming up and still in his street clothes," my mother would often tell me. "He knew everything about dancing ballet and its history. He spent hours with me, coaching my dancing and sharing ballet anecdotes." My mother felt that Wally was giving her special attention as a dancer with potential and a young lady with a sharp intellect. What she didn't realize, Beth told me when I was in my teens, was that Wally made everyone feel special.

When my mother was about twenty-two, Wally suggested she move to Sydney, Australia, to spend some time in a ballet company founded by a Russian immigrant, Rya. This company was on solid ground financially. Wally visited Sydney a few times a year to connect with Rya. Wally thought that exposing Jodie to a real Russian would broaden her outlook on ballet. Despite the prominent influence of British ballet on Australian ballet, Wally credited the Russian ballet companies as having the best dancers. Jodie picked up on this preference and never deserted it. "The British stars dance nicely," she would say to me, "but not with the Russian schools' powerful technique and uninhibited expression. There is a lot of variation, nonetheless, within Russia. The Bolshoi Ballet has a different style from the Kirov Ballet. The former is more athletic, the latter more lyrical." I never cross-checked my mother's narration. That she thought so was enough for me.

Wally, not my father, was my mother's first love, and she fell hard! Yet, Wally had bad news for Jodie. She told me, "I was deep into loving Wally when he told me he was committed to the choreographer, Sasha. That shocked me, as Sasha was male." My mother could not accept Wally's choice and remained convinced she was the right match for him. The fact that he loved a man conflicted with her moral education, but she loved Wally no less for it. Jodie told me how Wally explained the relationship to her, "What binds Sasha and me is partly our common background. We grew up as only children in the same suburb of Adelaide, and our parents knew each other. Sasha's parents named their son after his Russian grandfather. My parents named me Walter, but everyone calls me Wally, which I prefer. Both our households were well-off, and both sets of parents are now deceased, leaving Sasha and me a home each and enough money invested for us to live without working outside ballet. Sasha and I are devoted to ballet. Our parents first took us to ballet performances when we were about six. They let us go into ballet at around seven years of age when it was evident that we loved it. Our parents strongly encouraged us to maintain our friendship when I emerged as a dancer, and Sasha spent hours on choreography. They knew that we were ever such nice boys (a euphemism at the time for gay), and they wanted to make sure we linked up with someone of the same social class. They hoped we would be discrete, which is not how things turned out, but they were right that our common background and love for ballet would create a lasting relationship."

Ultimately, the desire for a home and children tempted Jodie to stop pursuing the idea of Wally and marry my father, Dalaigh, in 1951 while she was still with Rya in Sydney. Through his left-wing political views, Dalaigh had a lot of friends in the artistic world and met my mother at a party Rya hosted. Jodie assumed the marriage would not stop her dancing, and Dalaigh seemed to agree. She wanted to have at least one child but did not see that goal as an obstacle to being in a corps de ballet. However, as soon as they married, my father denied my mother all hope that he would agree to her continuing ballet. In fact, as her husband, he was never anything but cruel about my mother's interest in dancing. I once heard him comment to Jodie, "You weren't that good as a dancer. Nowhere near the level of your sister Beth." My father's discouragement shocked my mother as there had been no hint of it before they married. She left ballet a few months into her marriage in a desperate attempt to please her new husband. Her friends in the ballet were worried and remarked to my father. "Why did Jodie so abruptly stop dancing? What a waste!" He was unmoved. I understood as an adult that the issue was about control. Often my father took a stand against something my mother loved. It was usually a power play designed to bully her into submission.

Beth, in the meantime, also left ballet at about the time my mother married. She was the only daughter left in Adelaide who could run the home for her mother, who needed full-time help due to her descent into depression in her forties.

Even after her marriage, Jodie never fell out of love with Wally. When he visited Rya, he often met with my mother for coffee and provided sympathetic support to her. She developed significant health problems during this period. Wally was so worried about my mother's health that he once walked into my parents' apartment unannounced to see if my mother needed help. My father was out. My mother repeatedly told me about this visit, starting when I was about eight. "Wally turned up dressed as a woman," my mother told me, "He was in disguise to fool your father lest he came home and caught us together!" Later, in my teens, when I asked Dalaigh's opinion of that visit, he said, disgustingly, "I heard about the visit though I wasn't at home for it. Wally was a cross-dresser, Sarah! He probably hadn't had a chance to change clothes before he dropped in to see your mother." However, as a younger child, I believed my mother's version.

My mother frequently talked to me about ballet, starting when I was about six. She instinctively knew how to subdivide her narration so that a small child would enjoy it and, more, fall in love with ballet. This education was updated and grew as I aged when my mother felt I was ready for the information. She resurrected for me the ballet world she had to leave behind. I adored that world she created, which remains with me. Through sharing what she knew about ballet with her appreciative daughter, she strove to keep ballet alive in her mind and to maintain her label dancer.

My mother would dance for me, as best she could, many excerpts from famous ballets while she narrated what was happening. Like so many ballerinas, Swan Lake was her favorite, and she knew all the dances from it. She told me which were complex and which were only seemingly so. "The Dance of the Little Swans, or Danse des petits cygnes, from Swan Lake is much more difficult than it appears," she would say, "the four swans involved have to work as one with no room for error. This unity involves the footwork and holding hands." She would hum the music for that dance and do her one swan version.

My mother told me, "Australia boasts a dancer born in South Australia who built an international reputation. Sir Robert Helpmann was born in 1909 and strongly influenced Australian ballet. He made an extensive career in the United Kingdom, which included partnering with the legendary Margot Fonteyn. He had many talents, including being a brilliant actor and choreographer."

One of Jodie's loves was the British film *The Red Shoes*, which appeared in 1948 and featured Helpmann in an important role. One of the central ideas of the film transfixed her. Namely, a ballerina's red shoes took control of the wearer and forced her to dance according to their will, eventually leading to the heroine's death. Jodie was also attracted to the ballet Giselle, in which the eponymous dancer goes mad and dances herself to death following a romantic betrayal. What appealed to my mother in these portrayals was the overwhelming urge to dance. She identified with the heroines as someone who, given a chance, would willingly give ballet her all. She repeatedly expressed her feelings about these ballets and others like The Firebird, which attracted her to Wally's company. She needed someone to know, someone who would understand. I did follow her. I knew, from about age six, that she would do anything to raise me in her way of thinking.

She bought me a book about dance, and we often went through it together. She would sing and dance the ballet highlights in the book with no self-consciousness.

Jodie knew the history of ballet well and shared it with me. She informed me, "One of the most famous dancers ever, Nijinsky, was a member of Diaghilev's company for part of his life." Another dancer who worked with Diaghilev and my mother idolized was Anna Pavlova, who died four years after my mother's birth at forty-nine. In Australia, a cake named for Pavlova remains a staple. It's a meringue topped with cream and fruit. Jodie's Pavlova was always delicious!

My mother didn't teach me ballet or enroll me in a ballet school. Even at six or seven, we knew I was a clumsy child since I had great difficulty with gymnastics and other sports. I grew into an awkward accident-prone adult. Nothing my parents did was at fault; I am just like that. To try to teach me ballet would have been a lost cause.

My mother shared several photos of Wally's company on stage and behind the scenes. She told me about the people photographed and the dances they would perform. Some featured the corps de ballet. My mother would clarify while pointing at a photo, "This dancer is Beth, and the one beside her is me." The pictures from behind the scenes were mainly from dressing rooms showing dancers putting on makeup for a performance. Wally was in one of them but scarcely recognizable due to heavy makeup for classical Indian dance. That type of dancing was rare in Australia, and Wally had made it a company specialty. "It was so exciting to learn Indian dancing from Wally," my mother told me, "we all had to work hard to master enough of this dance form to make an acceptable performance. Wally had studied Indian dance for years, so he was a wonderful instructor."

As my mother went deeper into psychosis as she aged, she became increasingly attached to Wally in the web of the world she tried to weave to match her symptoms. Gradually, in her mind, my father, not Wally's homosexuality, became the obstacle to her first love. After all, she could have been dancing without my father, even with a child to rear. Without my father, she could have had Wally in a dress.

3

Despair

About six years into her marriage, but before my mother knew she was pregnant with me, she visited her parents and Beth. They lived together in Adelaide, Australia. She was deeply depressed by her already unhappy marriage. An essential factor in that unhappiness was my father's lack of desire to have children, something my mother wanted. She had no surviving children yet. She had lost her first baby in about 1953 due to an ectopic pregnancy. The fetus tried to grow in one of my mother's fallopian tubes. An operation to remove the fetus and save my mother's life left her with only one ovary. She was afraid she might not be able to conceive again. Despite her aversion to divorce, she intended to leave my father for good. My father hadn't tried to stop her, even though it would hurt his reputation at work. His company expected its married employees to stay married.

On arriving in Adelaide, my mother learned from Beth that Wally had recently prematurely died from lung cancer. The news hadn't reached her in Sydney before she made the trip, so it was a shock. My mother was overpowered with grief and started visiting Wally's grave daily. She planned to join him by taking her own life.

When remembering that time, my mother would tell me, "I felt a distinct physical pull towards my dead but beloved Wally, and only suicide made sense." These feelings were overpowering, and Jodie felt she couldn't share them with her family, not even Beth, who had known Wally. She expected some glib remark at best. Beth understood Wally's homosexuality; she had always discouraged Jodie's love of him.

My mother's extreme attraction to death frightened me in her story. When she told me about that visit, I was too young to realize that she was already, then, at thirty, sometimes paranoid with a resultant poor grasp of reality. I would, in my turn, go on to have nightmares about death trying to overpower me. I understood more about Jodie's mindset at thirty only when I was older and had more information about that visit to Adelaide from Beth. In particular, during that same visit, Jodie became hostile to Beth, falsely accusing her of several misdeeds, and their relationship never fully recovered. Beth herself was an extreme personality, inclined to religious fanaticism and with few friends. She was not, however, an unlikeable person. She was kind, engaging, and always told the truth as she saw it in the fairest terms.

Jodie noticed a change in her parents' home atmosphere compared to the period before she left for Sydney at twenty-two. This new ambiance added to her fears and despair. When I was about eight, my mother told me, "Beth was starving our mother and trying to drive our father mad. All our mother would get to eat was bread and tomatoes. She planned to poison our father once our mother was out of the way." As often with psychiatric delusions, there is a grain of truth that helps to make them seem real. Near the end of that year, 1957, Edith died of pernicious anemia, and Feivel died three days later of a heart attack. By then, his relationship with Beth had soured as he blamed her for distancing Edith from him in her final months. So, my mother expanded on reality to arrive at the delusion that Beth murdered her parents. Despite my mother's continual retelling of it, I never accepted this accusation about Beth, even as a small child. Beth had begun to write to me when I was six years of age, and I reciprocated. The relationship by mail went well.

Then, during this stay in Adelaide, when Jodie was suicidal, she discovered she was pregnant with me. Having already lost her first fetus, killing her second one was not an option, so suicide went out the window.

My mother told me that Feivel remarked, "I was so worried about how thin and sad you looked when you first arrived to visit us. It looks like you're putting on weight. You even seem happy!" When my mother told him she was pregnant, he said, "Please don't return to Dalaigh. He's no good! I can help you raise your baby."

Despite her father's advice, Jodie became determined to repair her marriage. There was no place within her moral compass for raising a child without both natural parents present. My father welcomed neither my mother nor me back home. Jodie's pregnancy with me brought her back to Dalaigh, who was already celebrating her disappearance from his life.

Why didn't Dalaigh leave Jodie and the fetus that I was? The reasons were complex. In the late 1950s, a healthy nuclear family was a plus for the image of my father at work. He had by then advanced to store manager for a large chain of department stores. My mother was quite capable of losing my father that job if he tried to end their marriage against her will. Dalaigh knew it. Dalaigh was still physically attracted to Jodie. Dalaigh's love for Jodie also engendered emotional ambiguity. It was there, but he had thought it easier to do without it than to base his life on it. Against his better judgment, he took us back in, hoping, like my mother, for better years ahead.

Jodie always told me that she would have died by suicide without her pregnancy with me during that trip to Adelaide. It was surprising information to give to a small child, but all I felt was pride in my part in saving her. It's a gift to think that your conception helped someone find a reason to live.

4

Dalaigh

Before meeting my mother, the last thing my father, Dalaigh, wanted was a marriage and children. Unfortunately, for all concerned, that never changed. Marrying my mother was the only way to draw close to her due to her Victorian morals. My father must have loved her when they married to take on a life he didn't want, but that at least included my mother. My parents told me when I was too young to hear it that their marriage was a child of their sexual attraction to each other. My mother forbade sex before marriage, so Dalaigh had to take on that institution to get my mother into bed.

Like my mother, Dalaigh was born in 1927. His birthplace was Kent, England. His parents' marriage failed around 1936, shortly after Dalaigh's family immigrated to Perth, Western Australia. Dalaigh grew up in Perth with his mother and her three sisters. He was his mother's only child and an unhappy one, by all accounts. He joined the Australian Navy at the end of World War Two, then settled in Sydney when that war ended.

Dalaigh shared some of his childhood misery with me; the stories were pretty grim and depressing. Dalaigh's father was violent in the build-up to abandoning his family and making himself untraceable. "He used to beat me," Dalaigh confided, "and I never knew why. After he left, I had a complicated relationship with my mother and aunts, especially my mother. She learned to sing growing up and began working as a singer in Perth. She was out most nights singing in rather seedy places. She went through boyfriends like someone with a cold goes through tissues. She often brought them home, and that made for a sordid environment when she did so. By contrast, my aunts were puritanical. I'll never know how they tolerated sharing a house with my mother. Probably, they needed the money my mother earned to get by. All of us were Catholic, and my aunts were strict church adherents. They were also addicts of some of the peculiar fashions. One of these was loving the child actor Freddie Bartholomew who was three years my senior. His film *Little Lord Fauntleroy* came out in 1936 when I was nine. On formal occasions, my aunts went overboard and dressed me for several years in a copy of the suit of clothes Freddie wore in that movie. There was no love for me in this attitude, only love for Freddie."

The lack of love is what most hurt my father. "My aunts rationed everything in the pantry," he told me." We all had our separate butter dishes and were allowed one small serving per meal. It was difficult for me as a child to understand why I could not have a second serving of butter if I had no more butter from the first serving. For them, they were teaching me to be thrifty. It came across as a lack of care to me."

"For all her behavior, my mother was a snob," Dalaigh often told me the story for which this was an introduction. "My father may not have been a good man, but that was no excuse to despise the whole working class of northern England into which he was born. Before we left England, I remember my mother insisting I have a bath as soon as we returned home to Kent from visiting my father's relatives up north. She told me you never know what you may pick up from such people." I am sure some of these memories fueled my father's left-wing politics, despite his brief and lousy relationship with his father.

Dalaigh was extremely good-looking, like a matinee idol, but with morals closer to a film villain. He bore a striking resemblance to the English actor Dirk Bogarde, as I was to discover in my teens from watching the 1963 movie *The Servant*. I appreciated the similarity in that film of the character portrayed by Bogarde to my father, especially in his behavior and ability to manipulate others. My father was incredibly manipulative, and I was one of the few to see right through him. It was petrifying how he could maneuver within a situation. I have watched the movie many times as Bogarde's performance is pure genius. It still bowls me over. My father's social views are close to Dirk Bogarde's character

Hugo Barrett. That character has the idea to level the class distinction between himself and his employer by simply taking over his life. He successfully dominates his employer psychologically and intends to move into his house more as an owner than a servant, bringing along a few like-minded friends. My father would have approved. The rich owed the poor the right to move in and take over, a sort of anarchy. That my father did honest work was my mother's influence. Without his marriage, my father would have *Barretted* someone for sure!

Before his marriage to my mother in 1951, Dalaigh was a drifter, going from odd job to odd job and spending his spare time hanging out with artists of all types and petty criminals, as some reliable people confirmed to me many years later.

My mother told an anecdote from when she was first dating my father. One night, they were walking in one of the more sleazy parts of Sydney when a small group of men armed with knives tried to mug them. My father said, "Don't be silly; it's me, Dalaigh," The muggers apologized and backed off. I ran the anecdote past my father once. He said it was accurate.

Despite Dalaigh's preferred lifestyle, he let my mother help him find steady work. He worked for many years for a chain of large department stores, and he was good at his job, even though we were always worried about money for reasons I will never fully understand. I say we because he constantly shared his concerns about money with my mother and me, even though what he said made no sense.

He was obsessed, for example, with the price of yogurt, a food he disliked. My mother considered it a staple, so we had yogurt in the fridge most days. There would be frequent angry fights between my parents about yogurt. My father would go ballistic, shouting, "We are not in an income bracket that allows the private consumption of a product that smells so awful." My mother would retaliate with much more coherent logic, "It's not that expensive compared to ice cream and much healthier," but nothing helped. Eventually, they would tire of it for the day, and my mother and I went on eating yogurt.

Despite the constant propaganda from my father that we were on the edge of poverty, he worked hard at a regular job for about twenty years, from before my birth until I was about seventeen. My mother did not work, except briefly when I was about twelve. She had to leave that job as, around that time, I was constantly ill.

Considering the hurricane of my mother's mental deterioration, it was not easy for my father to live with us. I sided firmly with our mother in most of the arguments between my parents. My father had no committed ally in his immediate family. It's no crime that he dreamt of escaping us. My mother was a well-cultivated and highly intelligent woman with a dominating personality. It was sometimes lost on others that my father was also extremely clever and knowledgeable. My father passed on a lot of valuable insights to me. He found most of his material in shrewd observations of other people.

Despite the negative aspects of our relationship, my father and I did spend some peaceful time together when he had a chance to tell his own stories. I often wondered if he and my mother had such conversations. His favorite anecdotes originated in his trip to China with the Australian Navy at the end of World War Two. "By the time my ship reached China," he used to say," the war was over, and the main task of my boat was sweeping for mines. I spent much time on dry land and fell head over heels in love with a Chinese prostitute I met. I wanted to bring her to Australia, but she wouldn't leave China." My father never fell out of love with China or his girlfriend there.

5

Sarah: Violation

I am twelve. My mother and I have locked my father out of our house. My mother emits red light from her hands, directed at me. She commands me to keep looking at the light as proof that I am not betraying her. I am paralyzed by the light. I keep trying to look away so I can move, but my mother's pull is too strong. Suddenly, the red light dims, and I force myself to follow with my ears a noise at our back door. My eyes catch up, and I see my father outside the door banging his head against it. He has the head of a ram, not a man, and will beat it on the door until he can get in, take me apart until I die, and eliminate my mother.

I woke from what was another terrifying nightmare during my preteen years.

6

Unborn

My parents conceived my only sibling in 1953. The baby tried to develop in one of my mother's fallopian tubes, an example of an ectopic pregnancy. That fetus never knew the world outside my mother's reproductive organs. Jodie left it too long to see a doctor, and by the time she found a good obstetrician, she was dangerously ill, suffering pain and bleeding. She told me, "Your father was incredibly unsupportive, and that's one of the reasons I didn't see a doctor as soon as I felt something wasn't right. He said I was a hypochondriac who would cost him a fortune on doctors if let loose. I blame your father for the pregnancy going wrong. He returned from China with venereal disease and didn't see to it before the pregnancy. The venereal disease can increase the likelihood of an ectopic pregnancy."

When I questioned my father about my mother's story years later, he said, "That sounds about right, but I don't bear any guilt about it!"

The doctor who treated my mother was alarmed. My mother had grown painfully thin. Her clothes were shabby. Her doctor told her, "No one is looking after you. Please be careful." Luckily, the operation to remove the fetus was successful, and my mother did bounce back physically rather quickly. However, she was devastated by the dual psychological hits of losing her first baby and feeling my father's indifference to the baby and her suffering.

This whole story was one of my mother's often repeated monologues, and I am sure her urge to overshare fed into the nightmares I frequently experienced around the age of eleven and twelve. However, it was far from the only cause of my bad dreams.

7

Sarah: Fear

My father met my birth with anger. One of my first memories is of my father throwing me across a room in a fit of rage, then trying to get me to stop crying so my mother wouldn't know. I was three. At about that age, I began to stutter, and that impediment can still resurface.

At seven, I was terrified of leaving our house on school days. I had been the new girl so many times due to our multiple moves required by my father's job. I was excellent at my schoolwork. My situation wasn't a recipe for popularity for a girl in the 1960s in Australia. My mother told me to conquer my fears and go to school. I was terrified at home as well, but at least at home, the struggle was more predictable. Facing all these fears caused so much overload that it physically paralyzed me and often made me late for school. I would tell my mother,

"I have a kind of frighten-ish feeling!" My mother wrote a note to my teacher describing my feelings about school, but the teacher read the letter aloud to the class, and everyone laughed at me. I nonetheless threw myself into my schoolwork and intellectual challenges more typical of older children.

In my mind, at that age, I identified my father, Dalaigh, as the source of my fears at home. He was resentful of my existence as my mother's pregnancy with me brought her back to him when he was celebrating a likely release from his marriage. He would constantly threaten me with violence and act on his promise occasionally. I preferred to be physically hurt than to be psychologically terrified. My father was eating away at my sense of security, big chunks at a time. He also had too few verbal boundaries when it came to physical matters. Dalaigh repeatedly made fun of my whole body from the time I was about eight.

Yet, when I was three, this was the same father who looked forward to meeting me at the front gate where I waited for him every day to return from work. He would lift me from the gate and give me a warm hug. Then, we would walk into our home together, slowly, as we both knew my father's mood would change as soon as he walked in the door.

8

Marriage

What went so rapidly wrong with my parent's marriage, and why didn't it definitively end sooner? I heard my mother's and father's countless contradictory analyses of that union over the years.

As the adult I am now, I understand better the complexity of their situation. They married in 1951, both at twenty-four years of age, in Sydney, far from their families. My mother's family was in Adelaide, and my father's in Perth. They had no immediate family with which to share their situation. This distance from their parents mainly affected my mother, as my father wasn't close to his mother.

When I was about twenty, my aunt, Beth, began to offload a lot of repressed resentments over my mother.

She told me that Jodie had significant psychological problems growing up. "Already in her teens, Jodie was disturbed. She was always making up untrue stories and pretending to be someone else," Beth would tell me, "She wound Feivel around her little finger so that he would worry about her every mood. She was often agitated and verbose. Only Feivel was able to get through to her. She sidelined her poor mother, Edith, and I am sure it hurt her. At one point, during her visit to Adelaide in 1957, she thought I was starving our mother, Edith. Your mother harmed our mother and me significantly with her sweeping false accusations."

I understood the dilemma was not sibling rivalry but a wish for another type of sister. Too often, the reaction to psychological and psychiatric problems can be a wish the afflicted didn't exist in the first place. Beth's stories fit with Jodie's eventual diagnosis of paranoid schizophrenia. My father had no experience with psychiatric issues, and I suspect that dealing constructively with my mother when she had such problems was beyond his comprehension and ability.

The friends Dalaigh made before his marriage said, "Don't marry Jodie! She lives in a fairy tale!" Before he married, Dalaigh had no clue how sick my mother would become.

My father only took us once to Perth to meet his mother and aunts when I was about six. He had no intention of us all becoming close. My mother didn't enjoy the visit. My paternal grandmother spent much of it describing in detail why England was far superior to Australia, even though she had no intention of returning there. My grandmother complained, "There are no deck chairs on the beaches here in Australia, unlike in Britain. Oh, and that awful stuff, Vegemite, why do you give that to your child, along with that foul yogurt? Your daughter is most ill-behaved. She doesn't know her place." In short, her mother-in-law frowned on everything Jodie was striving for as a wife and mother. The inevitable rift between Jodie and my paternal grandmother added to the isolation from familial resources that can help bind a married couple together.

I believe the primary failure in my parent's marriage was due to the false premise they each harbored whereby it was possible to change another person simply by highlighting your contrasting morals. I have made this mistake many times myself, and I know how fruitless it can be to try to win someone over to your view of the world by talking about what is evident to you.

I accepted my parent's separate stories of how satisfying their sex life was during a significant part of their marriage. For my father, I was an unwanted child who got in the way of my mother being on tap for attention and its physical manifestation. My mother did not blame me for the fights over sex my parents inevitably had during their marriage wars. Even though their sexual relationship was pleasing to both my parents, even that enjoyment was squashed under the heel of exploitation to win a point.

For Jodie, I had saved her from her suicidal impulse to follow Wally to the grave. In her mind, that qualified me to be an ally in her marriage, someone who would always defend her point of view. In that, she succeeded, although I did enjoy moments alone with my father when I could be more sympathetic to him.

For example, my father didn't share my mother's classical tastes. He preferred more blue-collar ones that supported his left-wing views. I was an appreciative audience when I could get away from my mother, and my father was less threatening. My father introduced me to songs such as *Little Boxes*, written and composed by Malvina Reynolds in 1962, and *When The Boat Comes In* a traditional British folk song. I loved these songs; they are my fondest association with him. *Little Boxes* is a satire on suburbia and the conformity of the middle class. *When The Boat Comes In* is about a boy waiting for the fishing boat to come in. He dances to his father and sings to his mother. I especially like the version sung by Alex Glasgow. My father thought of it as a working-class song.

My parent's marriage was not all downhill. There were periods I remember when they seemed to regain the enjoyment of doing things together, which encouraged both of them. When we lived in Clareville, on the Northern Beaches peninsula of Sydney, my parents borrowed money to buy a block of land on nearby Scotland Island. I was in my mid-teens. They planned to move there and build a house. Given my father's insistence that we were paupers, I have no idea how they managed that debt. Still, the acquisition rekindled a feeling of adventure for my parents. Scotland Island was largely undeveloped then and inconvenient as you could only access it by boat. My parents found the idea of living there a promise of a romantic new start.

Conditions would be different on the island. Garbage collection wouldn't be as frequent. My father began rehearsing for the move by squashing used food cans so they occupied a smaller space in the rubbish tin. We visited the island many times. It was strikingly unspoiled and beautiful.

My parents never seemed to talk about how I would fit in. I would have had to go part of the way to high school by boat. Then, something broke again in their marriage, and my mother got cold feet about the idea. Maybe she thought the isolation on an island could be dangerous. Dalaigh was genuinely disappointed when my mother insisted they back out of the plan. I felt bad for my father. This aborted idea had been a natural booster of his happiness. Suddenly, it was gone, probably for no good reason.

"Here I have been, squashing cans and planning for a new life," he complained, almost in tears, "This move to Scotland Island was a real chance to repair our marriage."

Even though they all failed, such plans for starting anew helped to keep resuscitating Jodie and Dalaigh as a couple. They made them hope for what proved impossible in their relationship. They were in stark contrast to the vicious periods of war between them.

Dalaigh added to my crimes the nuisance of my existence whenever my parents had some idea to improve their marriage. Such plans were strictly a two-person deal. My father was annoyed I complained about Scotland Island's inconvenience for school. He blamed me for my mother's abandonment of the idea, which was completely unfair.

Over the years, my father made many attempts to leave us, both planned and impromptu. My mother fought hard to blackmail him into returning from the planned abandonments. The impromptu ones were usually only a way for my father to express his unhappiness at something my mother said to him. I remember one time he was roasting a duck when he argued with my mother. He declared he was walking out for good. He exited the front door only to appear at the back door about fifteen minutes later. "I forgot about the duck," he explained. We all laughed, even my father.

Despite their marriage's long unhappy periods, there was love between my parents, an affection that helped bind them together and made it difficult for my father to leave us without my mother's consent. Beyond her threats of losing my father his job, and her willingness to embarrass him wherever he went when he did walk out, I believe they both felt a sense of loss when they faced the possibility of dissolving the marriage forever. That basic love helped my father to decide to return after the many times he left us, except for the final time.

I saw the positive bond woven between my parents in the little things. When I was five, I had a nasty accident.

Some loose wires protruded from a power plug at home. Australian electricity runs on 220-240 V and 50 Hz. My mother always begged my father to get rid of the wires as they were dangerous for me. He never did so and laughed at her concerns. I got so sick of the arguments that I decided to try an experiment to see who was right. Early one morning, I sat on the floor and took up the loose wires. I pushed their ends against my right-hand index finger. I received a terrible electric shock and had difficulty disengaging the wires. As a result, the current burned my finger badly. My parents were not yet awake. I rushed into their bedroom to tell them what I had discovered to find them fast asleep in each other's arms. They looked so in love and at peace. Despite being only five, I decided my burn wasn't as bad as waking my parents from their embrace to a day of possible arguments. When they finally woke up, they both felt terrible about my mishap. My father fixed the wire problem. Doctors made house calls in those days, and the doctor who treated my burn gave my parents a hard time. "You could have killed your daughter by leaving wires like that within her grasp." I still have the scar from the burn, but it reminds me more of my parent's moment of a fond embrace than the pain of electrocution.

There were many examples of love tokens as we were a present-giving family. In particular, we always gave gifts for birthdays. My parents treasured them independently of what was happening at home. Each such present had an associated precious memory, and they wanted to keep those alive no matter what. My mother had a jewel box with a ballerina that my father gave her early in their marriage. She admired it every day. My father had a wine bottle stopper my mother had given him, which had a transparent glass cube at its top with dried Australian wildflowers inside of it. All those gifts meant something permanent. Each was an expression of hope. Although the concrete hope of a happy marriage never eventuated, the feeling of hope associated with these gifts did survive.

I wasn't a neutral participant in my family. That I always sided with my mother, was unfair to my father, and made him feel isolated at home. For all that, after each of our two-person conversations, my father would say I was the only person he could talk to without any inhibition. That lack of holding back often exposed me to material I was too young to understand, but I did my best.

Some of the stories about me as an infant were common to my father and mother. They both told me that, to stop me as an infant from getting hold of objects within my reach, my parents put me in an empty room alone for several hours at a time. They would put a few toys in the room with me. When feeding time came around, they would put me on a high chair in this room and place my dinner on its tray. I would immediately start throwing the food at them. Their solution was to give me my meal and flee the room as quickly as possible. Both parents told me I would settle down after they left and eat what I hadn't thrown.

My parents told me I had terrifying temper tantrums as an infant and small child. My mother's solution was to lock me in a room until my anger subsided. She told me that the fits were so extreme that I convulsed. Her method must have worked, as the tantrums subsided when I was about three years old. As an adult, I have a temper, but I mostly manage to contain it within myself. It's the only emotion I experience frequently. Taming that beast has been a big part of my growing up.

The modern viewpoint espoused by many mental health advocacy groups is that blame should not be introduced in discussing mental illness. Over Jodie's lifetime, the family blamed my mother for many bad situations. Her sister accused her, and her husband vilified her. Many of my father's friends took his side. These assessments were unfair, as my mother often tried extremely hard to do her best for herself and those she knew. I extend this notion of blamelessness to include what went wrong with my parent's marriage and any part I played in it. We all could have tried harder to make our lives happier and better fitted to lasting family relationships. But the direction of that effort wasn't destined to be that of a feasible cure. Jodie, Dalaigh, and I, each in our way, repeatedly journeyed in the direction of insanity we couldn't control. Jodie and I were clinically mentally ill, but my father's situation drove him to act destructively, not because of a psychiatric problem but because of the conditions he had to handle being so far from what he desired.

9

Robert

My mother and father both made friends with a poet, Robert, who would go on to make a successful career. Robert was fifteen years older than my parents. He was born in 1912 in Wollongong, New South Wales. As a layperson, he developed a passion for preserving Aboriginal languages and would travel all over Australia, trying to record as many of them as he could. He would then share his findings with professional linguists with the same interest. He was deeply sympathetic to Aboriginal welfare. As a poet, he believed his best way of helping was to focus on how they spoke. The term "Aborigine" is offensive to many as it's a word associated with colonial racism. I use it because all the people in this story used it, including me, before I knew better. Less offensive than "Aborigine" are the terms "First Nations," "First Peoples," or "Indigenous Australians."

My mother told me how they intersected with Robert, "Robert was part of the artistic circle I frequented before our marriage. Robert was fond of ballet and had many friends who were dancers in Rya's company. That's how we met. Your father was courting me by then and became friends with Robert through me. The three of us often went on backcountry hikes overnight, carrying frozen steaks that would defrost in time for a delicious BBQ. After our marriage, we maintained our friendship with Robert until about 1960, when we moved from Sydney to Bega for your father's job. Robert did visit us a few times in Bega. Robert did a lot to broaden my horizons, and he was a charismatic person. Robert and I were becoming close due to our long conversations about common interests. We looked great as a couple. Dalaigh got jealous. He made Robert unwelcome, so our friendship ended."

My mother told me that, just before they ceased being friends, Robert had tried to persuade her to leave Dalaigh. He knew of the difficulties in my parent's marriage. "Let me take you away from all this," Robert had said. My mother felt that divorce and becoming a single mother, with or without Robert's friendship, was irresponsible and amoral. She knew Robert would never marry her nor be faithful. She was flattered, though.

There is no doubt that, like Wally, Robert understood how my mother loved intellectual topics. For example, they had long discussions about famous Russian authors. My mother told me that Robert said, "I will never forgive Tolstoy for what he did to Natasha in his novel War and Peace!" My mother explained, "I was somewhat hurt as Natasha ended up marrying and having children as I did. Robert was making fun of my worldview. Well, he was a womanizer and would likely never marry."

Robert did many private readings of his poems for my mother. Years later, my mother would do them for me, starting when I was about eleven. In her imitations of Robert's poetry recitals, she was uninhibited. She would always be standing and adorned her recitations with exaggerated gestures. The essential part of Robert was then present in our home. I realized later that the time she spent as Robert was keeping a precious memory from her earlier years intact. For some reason, she did not want to see Robert, I presumed due to my father's hostility to him, and I was the only person she felt would appreciate how much she missed him. More than that, she wanted the oral history of her friendship with Robert stored in my brain, as she was struggling mentally and afraid of losing the fine detail of something she held dear.

The Australian Aboriginal people, at least as many non-aboriginal people understand it, call the beginning of time The Dreamtime. In this era, the Spirits determined how the aboriginal world would evolve for the different tribes, giving them a Dreaming. This Dreamtime has a beginning, but no end, so it remains relevant to aboriginal spirituality today and in the future. One of Robert's poems began:

"*We all dance on someone's grave,*

We dream on someone's nightmare..."

It refers to the British colonists of Australia, the most powerful of whom did their utmost to turn the aboriginal Dreamtime into a bloody nightmare. And now, many white Australians live the good life on top of the graves of murdered Aborigines whose surviving descendants are still struggling to preserve their Dreamtime. My mother's passion for reading the entire poem was not an act. It resonated with a chord of shame in her heart too.

Listening to my mother do Robert was no hardship. The poems were genius, and my mother's performances were wonderfully entertaining. She made the lyrics even better through her interpretation of them. At about the age she brought Robert into my world, I was writing poetry myself. She offered me a front-row seat in a great class on how to proceed. My mother gave me a book of Robert's poems with his handwritten notes in the margins. I still have it, and I treasure it.

10

Sarah: Illegitimate

Around the time I turned eight, my father stoked his resentment about his marriage until it burned white-hot. It wasn't as simple as just leaving us and suing for divorce. My mother had her weapons; one was the threat of seeing to it that my father would lose his job if he left us. Another was the threat of tracking and humiliating him at his new location.

I was physically afraid of my father. He often threatened me with violence and sometimes acted on it, though I was never seriously hurt. My fear was complicated by the beginning of puberty when I was about eleven and twelve. I began to feel sexually threatened by him without understanding what that meant exactly.

At this time, Dalaigh repeatedly brought up my mother's trip to Adelaide when she discovered she was pregnant with me. He said the timing of my conception showed he wasn't my father and I was illegitimate. He claimed I was the product of an affair between my mother and Robert. He grew fond of this accusation and stuck to it in the following years.

However, my mother also talked much about Robert, and I had come to love him.

So, Dalaigh was wide of the mark. Though he hurt my feelings by saying I was someone else's daughter, if it had to be accurate, then Robert was a great choice!

11

Piano

Due to my mother's passion for it, we always had classical music in our home in the form of long-playing records and concerts broadcast on the radio. As I was to learn, my mother was a gifted amateur pianist, especially considering she had only a few years of lessons as a child. She was a natural.

Before having a piano in the home, but after much exposure to piano music, I began showing strong reactions to pianos at age seven. Music stimulated my mind and body, and I was physically deeply attracted to pianos. I vividly remember going into music shops when we were out shopping and making a nuisance of myself by sitting at a piano and trying to play. I pestered my mother constantly about getting a piano for our home.

My mother somehow persuaded my father to buy me a Jesse French piano for my eighth birthday, despite his complaints that we couldn't afford one. My father always gave gifts at birthdays, not only to us but to his friends, which may have helped my mother's cause. Then, when I heard her play, I realized my mother was musically talented. She played well and was my first teacher and did that well too.

She stressed control in playing notes. "You have to develop strong fingers by doing technical exercises. Only that way can you control your touch and play soft or loud at will, not to mention the transition between the two. Staccato is not hard to master, but legato, or playing continuously, is. In all the contrasting ways of touching the piano's keys, command of touch has to be a factor." She introduced me to the dreaded Czerny exercises for technique, especially his five-finger studies that always made me feel I had three fingers on each hand.

My mother taught me piano and music theory for about a year. Then, after again winning an argument with my father over the cost, she hired a well-known piano teacher, Eric, for me in Newcastle, Australia, where we lived at the time. My mother's lessons were terrific, as Eric told me when I started with him. Eric was also big on the correct touch on the piano. He insisted on more technical exercises than my mother had recommended. I was skeptical. In my child's mind, I was sure that practicing well the non-technical compositions was just as good. After all, with enough practice of the pieces you relished, your fingers would have to rise to the occasion. Despite our differences, I loved my piano lessons with Eric.

As with everything I did, I worked ferociously. That pleased Eric. I remember Eric's niece had the weekly lesson before me. He made her stay back one day to hear me play. "Now, the way Sarah plays," he told his niece, "is a result of practice. Please start working." Eric had a ruler to hit you if you made an error. I don't think it was any help whatsoever to anyone. In any case, I was rarely a victim of this punishment.

A year or so later, we were back in Sydney. At that point, my father refused to pay for my piano lessons. My mother and I were shattered when he acted on this plan. The piano, and my progress playing it, had been something my mother and I shared that was free of all the difficulties we were both having at home.

My mother lamented, "But you were doing so well, Sarah! Your father controls the money. There's nothing I can do." Then, she broke down entirely and sobbed for about an hour. I was also upset and frustrated, but my self-pity retreated when I saw how much more acute my mother's feelings were.

Again, my father's excuse for cutting short my musical education was money. We couldn't afford it. However, even then, I knew the reason was the war between my mother and father. Our supposed poverty was merely a way my father had to control us over money. My mother and I had drawn closer together over the piano. My father wanted to drive a wedge between us. My mother did her best to keep teaching me, but the wind was out of her sails, and she mainly let me go on to work with the piano by myself.

My mother continued to play. She loved the romantic era of music from the 1800s, especially Chopin. I didn't directly experience the emotions I presumed were expressed by the music, but I saw them beautifully displayed in the mirror that was my mother. I understood the music through her and what she felt when she played it. I cared about structure, not emotion, and my mother encouraged me to follow my reaction. So, we went on together, without lessons, but with a mutual appreciation of how well we played.

My mother exposed me to great musicians' recordings, especially pianists. She always ensured that whatever my interest, I understood what it meant to be a genius. She wanted to convey the difference between being bright and working well instead of being singularly gifted. It was a great lesson. Her method did not upset me and, when I was older, helped me to make many compromises about my future. With each decision involving a so-called sacrifice for me, I tried to be realistic about what I could attain if I instead followed my potential to its limits.

When I was about eight, my mother introduced me to live concerts. She put a great deal of thought into how to educate me but not overwhelm me with this step. She decided that one half of a show was enough for a child of eight. She chose to take me to hear, at my first concert, the famous soprano Elisabeth Schwarzkopf. She paid for the tickets out of money she had saved from food shopping. I found the whole experience immensely exciting, and half a concert left me hungry for the second half, which we missed. This reaction is the one my mother was hoping for me. As I got older, my mother and I would go to whole concerts together when we could afford it. She spent a lot of time choosing these musical experiences so that they were high quality yet not intimidating. So, I may not have advanced much on the piano, but my mother was determined to foster my love for music, even if it meant a few bland meals, so she could finance the venture without my father's help.

I was a fortunate daughter in so many ways. Overall, I owe the most critical aspect of my sensory life, listening to music that moves me, to Jodie's infectious passion for her musical world. She was expressive around the house when we were alone, conveying her excitement for her favorite recordings, often dancing and singing along with them.

12

Sarah: Photos

Throughout my childhood, I didn't have many friends. It didn't help that we frequently moved around New South Wales due to my father's job and not within the same city. However, the primary cause was that I didn't have much rapport with other children.

However, I built up an imaginary world full of children and adults with whom I did have empathy. I collected every photo my family owned, including past school photos. I would spend hours alone in my room making up fictional stories about the people in the photos. The stories became more and more elaborate and were quite a challenge for my memory. I played with photos this way for about ten years, from age five to age fifteen. I stopped because my stories suddenly fell apart as they no longer seemed sustainable in the world of the adult I was becoming. They faded away.

There is one photo I will never forget, though I have no idea what happened to it. My mother gave it to me. It was taken by a professional street photographer when Jodie and Dalaigh were courting. They were a handsome couple, and they looked happy. I hoped so much that was the case, that they at least enjoyed some genuinely good times together.

Around age twelve, I developed an imaginary friend. A group of popular kids was teasing me at school. My home was unhappy, and I was getting some of the blame. In desperation, I invented someone who, I felt, understood me even better than my mother. I chose my deceased maternal grandfather, Feivel. My mother talked every day about Feivel's virtues, so this friend was valuable not only in my eyes but in my mother's eyes. Feivel could withstand the storm of these years of my life. I relied on Feivel's approval and strived to be a better person and a good student because he would be proud of me.

13

Humor

One of the greatest gifts my mother bestowed on me was a sense of humor. It helped us negotiate the stigma we endured due to mental illness being part of our lives.

The sweeping adverse reaction of so many to schizophrenia can drown the subtleties of someone living with this disorder. Talking about a psychotic disorder and a sense of humor in one breath may seem out of place. No one can deny the torment and destruction wrought by a relapse into paranoid psychosis. However, even at its worst, schizophrenia can be more livable thanks to some simple things. The more critical tools of medication and therapy may be necessary and powerful, but they shouldn't hide gentler and more modest means of relief. My mother and I used to exercise, listen to music, and watch classic films, to name a few, to help us through the worst times. However, none was so valuable for us, as a pair, as humor. It didn't have the profound effect on me individually as music did, but it could bring sunshine into the shared situation with my mother, and my dark episodes endured alone. I still rely on it to soften the blow of living with paranoid schizophrenia and people's reactions to it.

White Australia was a colony of Britain. Growing up in Australia, this cultural identity was still predominant among the white population, including many who had immigrated to Australia from continental Europe. Most of the humor my mother and I appreciated was British humor. The source was on records Jodie owned and broadcasted on the radio and TV. Sometimes, when you are afraid and liable to do something stupid because of your state of mind, a funny skit can deflect you.

For example, Jodie might go on about the evils of government and how they were watching her. I could deflect her delusion by our recording of Peter Sellers called Party Political Speech, which is a brilliant satire on colonial politicians. We relied on a steady diet of the famous Goon Show on the radio, with episodes like The Fear of Wages, which was a pun on the title of the movie The Wages of Fear (1953). Listening to it, we could both see the funny side, and hearing it, my mother often let her fear of being watched drop for a few hours. Like many goon fans, we loved imitating the characters' voices, done by the three goon performers, Spike Milligan, Harry Secombe, and Peter Sellers (again!). The Two Ronnies on TV was a considerable resource of relatively short skits, for example, the one making fun of university professors (Open University Lecture). The lewd aspect of many of these skits is part of British humor. It is not offensive to any honest person raised in Australia. We sometimes must remember that other cultures take such language literally and take offense. A skit that may seem objectionable to an American may seem mild to a British colonial.

A pertinent example is The Plumstead Ladies Male Voice Choir. The two Ronnies are in the choir, dressed appropriately in drag and gossiping to the music of the songs the choir is singing. Despite its sung dialogue being full of innuendo, it has helped me through some paranoia, and it helped my mother through several rejections by former friends. After all, weren't they like the gossiping Plumstead choir? We loved classic movies and the skit of Peter Cooke and Dudley Moore about movie stars (In the Pub) where they claim famous actresses romantically pursue them.

We also enjoyed American and Australian humor but had less exposure to it. We watched American comedies on TV, like The Beverly Hillbillies of the 1960s, and enjoyed them. We loved the skits of Shelly Berman, like The Department Store Window Ledge, where he tries to tell the people in a building across the street that someone is hanging outside one of their windows. He is shuffled from person to person on the phone until they find the right department to deal with the emergency. One Australian comedian we liked during the mid to late seventies was Garry McDonald. He played the satirical character Norman Gunston on TV. We loved Barry Humphries, creator of Dame Edna Everage, another satirical character with a long history, and, again, dressed in drag. British and Australian humor have a lot of satire and parody in their make-up. We loved Anna Russell, who was born in England and ended her life in Australia. She was a singer who did a brilliant satire on famous operatic works.

My mother loved Charlie Chaplin but seemed more interested in his life than his work. She followed the news of his family in detail and seemed to talk herself into believing she belonged in it. The fantasy helped her forget some of the marital problems plaguing her and her increasing loneliness. It was one of many fairy tales I had to follow to keep up with her. I needed to be sure that it didn't lead her to try to see a live Chaplin. It didn't.

The purpose of these comedians was to make you laugh, not to encourage you to abandon your moral standards to take up cross-dressing and lewd sexual banter. I am, by nature, a conservative person in my behavior, with my only departures from that norm being during periods of severe schizophrenic relapse. Yet, I am not offended by such humor. It's a matter of cultural upbringing. At the same time, what makes me laugh, and what I recommend as polite and considerate behavior are significantly different.

We also had a brand of humor only between Jodie and me. As the people in Jodie's life gradually deserted her because of her symptoms, we often found a way to laugh at such people and restore our sense of dignity. To chase after them was not an option, as the rejection was usually a result of Jodie going too far in her attempt to convert someone else to her reality. So, having a healthy laugh about them was not a wrong choice.

My mother could be hilarious all by herself and, especially when I was a young child, knew how to make me laugh. She would do funny dances, a satire on ballet. She would tell and retell jokes passed down from her father, who must have had a great sense of humor. She was generally disrespectful to social climbing and pretentiousness, what her father used to call cheap notoriety! In her world, what mattered most was to be genuinely worthy in deed and thought without considering where that placed you relative to others.

The whole family enjoyed the humorist Frank Hardy (1917 – 1994). My parents admired his politics, as Hardy was a communist deeply critical of how Australia treated its native population, the subject of some of Hardy's serious non-fiction. His fictional funny books, with personalities like Billy Borker and Truthful Jones, were tall tales parodying Australia. In most stories, one of these characters was spinning a story in a pub. The teller lengthened the yarn so the listener would keep buying him drinks!

For most of our shared existence, Jodie and I found something to laugh at every day. During the darkest times, that sometimes proved difficult, but those were the periods during which my mother was mainly in bed. Once we were alone, I became skilled at deflecting her torment by recasting her worries in lighter terms, pushing to the amusing if I could. Of course, it was only a temporary fix, but a beneficial drug nonetheless.

14

Sarah: Letters

As a child, I was a prolific pen pal. In those days, the means of communication with those far away, apart from the telephone, was by written letter. I often miss those days. I put a lot of time and thought into each correspondence. I mailed it and then had to wait for the letter to reach its destination to imagine a reaction. At that point, my pen pal read my letter and usually proceeded to put much care into the response. Then, there was the excitement of waiting for the reply. The process could take several weeks, or even months, depending on where my pen pal lived and how much haste versus effort they put into their letter. My grandfather, Feivel, had a younger brother Herman, who lived into his eighties, and we corresponded regularly. I also exchanged letters a lot with Beth. My high school organized pen pals for us in France and

Germany so we could practice our languages. I loved all of it! I still enjoy receiving letters and parcels by mail. The modern electronic version, email, has fantastic advantages. Yet, it misses much of the romance and appreciation of the effort of the old handwritten letter days.

After schizophrenia kicked in, the word letter played a predominant and different role. During every relapse, I have difficulty keeping the letters composing a single word together. In my mind, they are flying around independently of their rightful place. Every letter of the alphabet stands for a fluid message from those who have access to my thoughts. In my mind, that's just about everybody when I am at my sickest. So, thought insertions from others into my brain have a tremendous scope to put together letters how they choose, often mimicking my inner fears. Usually, I feel these inserted thoughts are, in particular, pushing me to suicide. However, they have never succeeded far enough to force me to attempt it.

15

Thirty-Eight

According to my mother's sister Beth, my mother, Jodie, had psychological problems since her youth. My father, Dalaigh, and others who had known my mother since her teens and early twenties complained about her issues. These included paranoia and an inability to accept reality.

People criticized my mother, with zero scientific knowledge about mental illness. A typical stigma plagued Jodie. She was to blame if there was any fault in a situation involving her since she was mentally unstable. I was next in line, propagating her errors in supporting her. Only my mother appreciated my efforts to help her. In everyone else's eyes, I was ruining my life by so doing and not aiding my mother. I have no idea what they viewed as the correct approach—it may have been dumping her in a ditch by the roadside. They ignored all that was worthy and delightful in my mother's interaction with the world as she perceived it. Some reservation about interacting with a mental health consumer is natural, but to write them off completely is on par with drowning unwanted kittens. The stigma that a mentally ill person is entirely to blame for anything going wrong in their life and that they are dangerous to know is ubiquitous but rarely accurate. Such fear mostly brings out the ignorance and cowardice of the person exercising stigma.

There was a noticeable downturn in Jodie's mental health when she was thirty-eight, me being eight. We lived in Newcastle, New South Wales, a city north of Sydney. It was one of the places where we lived for my father's work. His employers chose the house and took the rent out of my father's wages, per their usual custom.

Over our lifetimes, my mother and I had a sequence of significant relapses, each worse than before, leaving us unable to recover fully. It is not always true that psychotic relapses only occur in one's teens and twenties and that schizophrenia somehow gets better with age. Some doctors deny stress as a trigger for a psychotic relapse. Still, my experience is that stress has played a significant part in inducing my relapses, and it did likewise for my mother. Nonetheless, what we considered to be stress differed widely.

When I was eight, my mother's father, Feivel, had been dead for eight years. He died shortly after my birth. His wife had died a few days before him. My mother had led my father to believe that Feivel was well-off. She did so to heighten her father's achievements, not realizing that Dalaigh would take it so seriously. It took Feivel's lawyers until around my eighth birthday to declare probate on his will due, they claimed, to the extreme complication of his financial situation. Eight years to announce probate. Eight years after my birth. My father, Dalaigh, was waiting to come into what he thought would be a lot of money from Feivel, some compensation for his unhappy marriage. My aunt, Beth, spent eight years looking forward to a reward. One over and above the house her parents left to her. She looked after her parents until their death with no marriage of her own. During those eight years, everyone connected with Feivel had a chance to imagine more of his wealth going their way than was realistic to expect.

Nothing I heard in the family gossip about Feivel's riches translated into a certainty that he was extremely wealthy. Not even my mother's tales implied such riches. It's true that he did well selling cars for much of his life and won a lottery at some point. He also gambled, mainly on the ponies. He was extremely proficient at gambling, researching, and relying on inside information about jockeys and horses. He made money that way, although I am sure he lost a fair bit also. He had enough income to send his two daughters to top private schools. However, none of these factors assured he had a lot of money to spare for his will.

Feivel disapproved of Dalaigh strongly. My mother told me Feivel had even hired a private detective to look into my father's character and was worried by what he uncovered. My mother told me this story when I was about twelve. "Your father was hanging around with criminals," she said, "and my father was distraught. He pleaded with me to leave your father." I replied, "Whatever my father's faults are, the stage of associating with criminals seems to have been over for at least ten years." I didn't understand that sometimes disappointments and judgments remain even when they cease to have relevance, something especially true if you live with schizophrenia.

When Feivel's legacy was finally available, it was cash-poor. He left my mother no money, but she received some of Feivel and Edith's possessions. She told me they were all small keepsakes that she didn't want to share and expose to Dalaigh's disappointment and disdain. Nothing was left to Beth apart from her parent's house, although, before he died, Feivel had helped Beth get a job in a bank whose manager he knew. It was more than enough to support her.

My father was furious. "Where is the money you told me your father had? You can't tell me he sent you to fancy private schools, and you lived in the best suburbs, but that suddenly, one day, the money disappeared! We need that money. We're going under in debt."

My mother gave the will much thought and confided in me, saying, "My father complicated his financial affairs, including spending a lot of his money before he died so that no one would get a decent inheritance. He was upset by my marriage to Dalaigh and worried about Beth's eventual marital choice. He feared what such spouses would do to gain my inheritance and Beth's." To my ears, even at eight, the story sounded outlandish. At the same time, my father was dangerously interested in a legacy. My grandfather left me a small trust, about AUD 600, for my adulthood, with my mother as trustee. My father got all that money from my mother within two weeks of the gift landing in her bank account. I can still hear my father's bullying. "If you don't hand Sarah's money over to me, I will leave you. What good are you anyway? Do I have to knock some sense into you?" he said with a hand raised, ready to hit my mother. My mother caved in. I remember her going to the bank in tears to sign the forms to hand the money over to

Dalaigh. I tried to tell my mother that, as disappointing as it was for me not to get a gift from Feivel, it wasn't all that much money. "One day," I said, "I will make my own AUD 600!"

A lot happened to my mother's sense of reality at thirty-eight, not only because she harbored delusions but even more because her actual situation became clear. Her psychosis firmly set in when the disappointments piled on at a pace she couldn't handle. I learned later from Beth that this downturn in her mental health was not her first, but it was the first one I was old enough to feel with her fully.

The degree of Dalaigh's anger over the lack of inheritance from Feivel shocked Jodie. It was unexpected, and liquidating the meager amount left to me was traumatic for her. It didn't help that my aunt Beth, also angry about Feivel's will, visited us for several weeks then. I remember her shouting, "What happened to all that money?" Dalaigh developed a crush on Beth that she reciprocated. They made no secret of their feelings. I firmly believe their love was emotional and not physical, but the damage to my mother was immense. It was a cruel truth that had no place in her vision of marriage. The stigma against my mother's mental health struggles was developing. Even if someone in her life maltreated her, they could blame my mother for creating the conditions whereby anyone sane would pardon such acts against her.

Then, there were our precious dogs. We had two golden labradors. All the family was deeply attached to them, especially my mother. A neighbor complained about our dogs being outside, "Your dogs make too much noise! They jump on the fence, and my children can see their teeth. It scares them!" The campaign to browbeat my mother into keeping the dogs inside except to relieve themselves turned vicious. "We'll poison these dogs or run them over with our car if we see them again off a leash!" These nasty people attacked another part of my mother's equilibrium. There was no room for debate. My mother caved in and began shutting herself up in the house with the dogs, except to walk them. She shut me inside with her, except for allowing me to go to school and piano lessons.

Within a few months of enduring all this added worry, my mother became psychotic. I understand that now. However, at the time, at age eight, I had no clue why she had changed, and I tried to keep up with her. Deep down, I knew she was struggling, but I did not know how to push back constructively, so I went with the flow as that seemed to support her the best. At eight, as a working assumption, I believed my mother was right about everything.

What added to my confusion was that many aspects of my mother's love and care for me remained. Her attempt to reconcile her disappointments through tall tales didn't stifle all of the best of my mother. She still cared about my legato on piano and prepared nourishing meals at mealtimes. She retained her sense of humor when she took a rest from remaking history.

It was difficult for me, a loner by nature, to sustain friends. My mother had been a great hostess to two girls my age from school, but she asked me to stop inviting them home when her mental health took a downturn. I still saw these friends at school, but the friendships cooled off when I told them they were not allowed in my home. My mother sustained no friendships in Newcastle. That made my job as confidant essential to ease her loneliness.

When we moved, for my father's job, to Sydney from this home in Newcastle, my mother went out more. As a consequence of the move, we ended up in one of the scenic parts of Sydney with beaches, and she would go out, usually with me, to appreciate the outdoors and to help me shop. She demanded my companionship for most of her day. I did go to school nearby, and during those hours, my mother rarely left our home. Even with the time spent outdoors and her enthusiasm for it, she was mainly shut up at home. Her mental state did not improve much. My parents were entering the worst time in their marriage, so the pressure on my mother to cope with it didn't let up. However, the flora, fauna, and beaches of the part of Sydney where we lived were good for her and me. They also helped Dalaigh find ways to relax, usually without us, as he made friends he would meet at the beach.

16

Watch

About a year after probate on her father's will, my mother surprised me with the gift of a pocket watch that belonged to Feivel. I had just turned nine. Her father gave it to her to celebrate my birth. He mailed it to her the year I was born, shortly before his death. It was a 1957 Russian-made beauty that Feivel received as a gift from a grateful friend. He helped this man start a successful car dealership in the early 1950s. There was an engraving on the watch that read, "To my friend Feivel from Dieter."

Until then, my mother had kept the watch from both my father and me. Now, for a year already, Jodie had been distraught at the loss to Dalaigh of her father's AUD 600 put in trust for me. She wanted to give me something else from Feivel to compensate and to show me her pride that Feivel had been so generous to his friend Dieter. My mother told me, "You must hide the watch from your father and never speak of it to him, as he would surely sell it if he knew where it was." We decided to hide it in the chest of drawers in my bedroom. We covered the watch with a pile of cotton handkerchiefs.

I loved the timepiece, which was in complete working order, and was excited to hold it in my hand and admire its appearance. I looked at the watch most days when I was alone in my bedroom, then carefully hid it under the handkerchiefs. About six months after receiving the gift, I discovered it was missing. I started crying loudly, and my mother came into my room to find out why. "Grandfather Feivel's watch is gone," I blurted out. "Are you sure?" my mother asked. "Take a look yourself, Mummy," I answered. My mother searched the entire chest of drawers, but the watch wasn't there. We checked the rest of my bedroom with the same result, and my heart sank further as I knew I had not misplaced it.

"Your father has taken and sold it, Sarah," my mother said in a way that I knew excluded discussion.

Nonetheless, I asked, "But how? I never spoke to him about it!" My mother responded, "He must have searched your bedroom while we were out. What a horrible thing to do!" My mother wouldn't hear of any other explanation. I confronted my father with the accusation. His defense was, "First of all, I didn't know you had the watch, and second, if I had found it and sold it, I wouldn't tell you." My father was angry, not because I suspected him, but because I had received something of value from a man who left my father nothing in his will.

In my nine-year-old mind, my father was the culprit. At that age, to cope with my mother's mental instability, I acted on the hypothesis that everything she said was true. I knew my father was capable of the accusations she levelled against him, but deep inside, I allowed for the fact that he may not always be guilty.

Feivel's timepiece never reappeared, so I told myself something irreversible had happened. The pride I felt in my maternal grandfather for helping a man who needed a foot up was intact. My mother had achieved her primary goal despite the disappearance of the watch.

What I failed to perceive at that age was that my mother was molding Feivel into a central delusion of her increasing paranoia. She would tell me a story of his greatness daily, and she said it well. Listening to her talk about her father was one of the best parts of my day. Feivel became, also for me, an influential and pious person who looked after his friends. At this stage, her imagination was relatively harmless. Only later, when she tied Feivel's life to her persecution, would her fairy stories show a dislocation from reality that would adversely affect her.

17

Sarah: Thirty-One

At thirty-one, a real estate firm employed me in one of their agencies near where I lived. I rented a studio in Dee Why, a suburb of Sydney about ten miles from the city center, where I lived alone. I had worked for the agency since shortly after I left high school. Currently, there were five coworkers in all, four of whom met with potential clients and sold or rented properties. I was one of two workers who organized the office behind the scenes. My job involved self-taught skills like keeping records, filing, and basic accounting. Since I had joined them, I only worked part-time from 12:00 pm to 4:00 pm, Monday through Friday, an arrangement that had, at its outset, enabled me to spend significant time with my mother. The agency had not offered me a full-time job. I did not buy or sell property, and my work involved little contact with the customers. I enjoyed it, and it was well within my capabilities. My salary, which had kept up with inflation, was adequate for the simple life I led.

My coworkers were pleasant people. I was closest to Lucas, a single man with whom I had a platonic friendship and who was most successful in moving property. We went out to eat together once a week. Lucas would talk about the highlights of his work week, and then we discussed our interests unrelated to work. We loved classical music and films, as well as taking long walks. After our meal, we always took a constitutional.

The other colleagues were women. Our boss at the agency was Amelia, but I did not get to know her well. She was about ten years my senior. Amelia strutted in and out of the office with the most critical clients seeking to buy or rent our most expensive property. Amelia was a workout devotee, which had left her with a slim but muscular figure. She had dyed her hair platinum blond, and she wore expensive clothes. I had the most contact with Lucy, who worked only in the office like me. She worked a full day. She ate lunch early, so we would often share a pot of coffee after she returned to the office from her eleven o'clock midday meal, and I was getting started with my half day of work. Lucy was about my age. I thought her round figure and face were attractive, despite the view at that time that skinny was best. I was chronically underweight. I admired her fullness. She had a fantastic mop of untamed curly blond hair and light blue eyes. Lucy, having worked in the morning before I arrived, usually had a list of tasks that she asked me to spend my afternoon finishing. It worked well. Most days, I accomplished what Lucy had requested, and I had the comfort of knowing I was genuinely valuable to her. I did not socialize with her outside the office as with Lucas. She liked to forget about work once she finished for the day, so none of her friends were from the real estate agency. She, in any case, was married and had three young children who kept her busy.

I had made a handful of female friends through a girls-only book club in Dee Why. We met once a week on a Saturday for morning tea at 9:30 am, always at the same restaurant. The choices of books were imaginative and engaging. They were voracious readers. We would spend about an hour discussing books over our cakes and coffee and then stay an extra thirty minutes to gossip over refills of our coffee. I did not see any of the members of the club outside the meetings.

Every Sunday afternoon, I volunteered for a few hours at a food bank attached to a local church. I didn't attend the church services and had found out about the bank from a member of the book club. They were happy to have me help out. Again, I did not seek to see any of the other volunteers outside the time I spent at the bank.

Apart from these acquaintances and my friend Lucas, I had only one friend, Enoch. I had met Enoch, who lived nearby, by chance, in an art gallery in the city. He was incredibly erudite about painting and loved to share what he knew. Enoch was openly gay and sometimes brought a boyfriend along on our regular dates at museums. Both Lucas and Enoch were nice-looking. Lucas's parents were Norwegian; he had soft blue eyes, blond hair, and a well-built physique. Enoch was Jewish and had dark brown curly hair. His black eyes were like my mother's, little pools of water that could hide anything in their depths. Enoch was fragile, making him look like he was emotionally vulnerable.

I walked unaccompanied one night after work to my studio. Out of the blue, two men mugged me. They covered my eyes and mouth and pushed me down onto the ground. They held me there for at least a few minutes, long enough for me to fear they would harm me physically. Suddenly they took my purse, which didn't contain much money and nothing else besides that, and ran off. I then saw a man get out of a car who offered to help me. I gathered he scared off the muggers. I thanked him but told him I was OK. He drove off, and I went home.

I was not OK. I was frightened and shocked to my core. When I reached my studio and went inside, I knew I would be terrified to go out again.

Lucas lived close to me. I telephoned him.

"It's Sarah," I said, "two men mugged me today, and it's shaken me."

"Are you hurt?" asked Lucas.

"No," I replied," and not much poorer either, as I only had AUD 20 in my purse and nothing else. However, I know I will be frightened to go out again."

"I'm coming over," he insisted.

"Thank you, Lucas," I said, relieved.

About half an hour later, Lucas knocked on my door.

"Come in," I said, "I am making tea if you want some."

He joined me in drinking chamomile. We talked about what had happened.

"I know it's illogical, Lucas. There's almost no chance I will come to further harm from anybody, but I know I won't be able to go to work tomorrow. I will be too scared."

"Why don't I walk with you to and from work until you feel better," Lucas suggested. "It's not even inconvenient for me as I live close to you. I will accompany you daily while you shop after work."

"Thank you, thank you! You are so kind, Lucas! How will you get away from work, though?"

Lucas reassured me, "As you know, I finish work at 4:00 pm like you, as I arrive early at 8:00 am. Therefore, I can walk you home. I can take my lunch break from 11:00 am to 12:00 pm and walk you to the office to start your work afternoon at noon."

We talked some more while Lucas tried to calm me down. We both agreed there was not much point in reporting the mugging to the police, as I didn't get a good look at my muggers and couldn't identify them. When Lucas was sure he had *reassured me, he left. He told me to call him anytime if I needed to talk.*

Lucas and I teamed up for about a fortnight, after which my fear of being alone outside my studio subsided. I was nonetheless nervous within myself. I thanked Lucas and told him I would be OK to venture outside my studio alone.

Then, I suddenly felt better and went into a somewhat manic state of over-confidence at work and over-excitement everywhere else. It was forceful enough to get some people's attention but controlled enough not to worry anyone. Lucy did not like the new me, and our relationship became uncomfortable within a few days. Lucy had always prized her role as the principal organizer of a well-run office. She told me I was behaving like I had excellent ideas to replace her methods.

A few weeks into this borderline manic reaction to the shock of the mugging, I woke up one morning and turned on the radio. I was amazed to realize that the ABC (Australian Broadcasting Commission) radio channel I usually listened to was talking to me exclusively. The radio voice was making fun of my situation and judgments, predicting my life would end badly. I began to feel afraid. I turned off the radio but could still *hear it. Some entity was bugging my studio for sound, of that I was sure, and tracking my every physical move. I had been frightened to go out because of the mugging. By contrast, now my home seemed impossible to endure, so I was there as little as possible.*

As I walked around the streets of Dee Why, everything seemed to be bouncing, and I had whisperings in my ears. I kept seeing people I knew were not in Dee Why but were visible to me nonetheless.

One of the terrifying experiences was the impression that my brain was no longer my own. It registered thought insertion by arbitrary someone when I looked at them. Namely, I thought this or that person was dropping thoughts into my brain against my will. I believed I could reply by silently broadcasting my response. All this without speaking to the person or even being close to them physically. It was like the experience of hearing sounds that didn't exist, except that, unlike the experience with the radio, the process was taking place in silence.

I had no idea what was happening to me. I thought the world had suddenly changed and that everything I was experiencing was evident to everyone else. I was being singled out and judged for crimes I didn't understand, except that the most significant outrage was that I existed.

The fear of staying at home increased, so I sat all night on park benches for about a week and even spent a night when I locked myself in a public toilet trying to protect myself from all sensory stimuli. I then decided to visit Enoch. I couldn't think logically, and in my mind, Lucas was only a help for keeping me in my studio, not helping me to be outside of it. Enoch was at home and let me in.

"What's the matter?" he asked.

"I don't know," I said, "I am suddenly afraid to be in my studio. It's dangerous there."

Enoch had confided many of his secret thoughts to me during our friendship, some quite outlandish. He thought it was now his turn to help me with irrational fear. "You can stay here until you feel better," Enoch offered. He didn't ask any questions, and I said little. Enoch was kind, letting me sleep and tending to all my meals. After a few days with him, I felt better and strengthened enough to return to my studio.

Despite the long experience with my mother, I failed to realize I was sick in much the same way as she had been. In turn, my mother never accepted that she was ill. Doctors call this anosognosia, or lack of insight, a symptom of severe mental illness that impairs a person's ability to understand and perceive their condition. For example, your brain may not be able to process naturally what your senses tell it. My mind was working overtime to process my suddenly drastically different sensory world. Yet, the conclusions it reached had little to do with reality. I thought that my world was suddenly on its head, something everybody knew. The general judgment was that I had lived past when I should have died. Suicide would be a good solution; I felt that's what everyone wanted. I was not suicidal, so though these impressions were devastating, I didn't act on them.

After Enoch's help, my studio, though still bugged for sound in my mind, became less threatening. After all, I felt everyone had access to my mind and that they were inserting thoughts that were primarily threatening and judgmental. The lack of privacy in the street was no better than the lack of privacy in my studio, so it was better to be under a roof. I began to feel as though I were physically evaporating, becoming just sensory input. My mouth was doing a linguistic battle with what I thought I heard around me while my eyes tried to explain the people I saw who I doubted were there. I ate little, which must have added to my feeling of not entirely existing. It was as if the aftermath of the dream I had at eleven when I felt I was no longer fully among the living was reaffirming itself.

I failed to show up at my job for many weeks when I was deeply psychotic. I began eating into my savings. Early in my crisis, Lucas had stopped by my studio and tried to see if I was alright. I wasn't there the first time he visited, but the second time I was. I told him I expected that I would lose my job.

Lucas replied, "I am afraid that's already happened. After you failed to show up for so long with no explanation, Amelia fired you. Did you get her letter?"

"I can't remember," I said honestly. I managed to "act normal" in front of Lucas, so my symptoms were less evident. My mother also had been able to act normal for short periods, even when she was psychotic. However, my performance didn't fool Lucas. He knew me well enough to realize I was terrified and not truthful about how I felt. Lucas offered to visit me regularly to see if I was OK, but I asked him not to do so. I thought I would erode our friendship in my current state.

At some point, however, I thought I could save my job and lost sight of my resolve to avoid Lucas. I turned up at the real estate agency one midday in a highly agitated state, asking what I could do that afternoon to reestablish myself there. The boss, Amelia, pushed me outside and said firmly, "If you come here again, I will call the police. You no longer work here."

Lucas saw what was going down, and he was upset with Amelia. He joined us outside and said to Amelia, "Can't you see Sarah is harmless? She's going through a protracted bad patch because two men mugged her a while back. Can you please go inside so I can talk to Sarah gently? If you call the police on her, I will resign."

The absurdity of Amelia's overreaction, which had shocked and frightened me, was washed away by Lucas taking my side. Lucas told Amelia that he would take me home and make me understand that I had lost my job. That is what he did. He told me to call him anytime I wanted a friend. Ultimately, I did not take him up on that offer as he was associated with the real estate agency. If I had to learn to avoid the agency, it was better not to trouble him. I told myself again that my friendship with Lucas would not survive what I was experiencing.

Lucy called me a few days after my appearance at the agency. She said, "I think Amelia overdid her rejection of you, but please don't repeat the mistake of turning up at work. You did make me feel uncomfortable before you stopped showing up here. We all understand that this discomfort was a prelude to something worse and that you are struggling. I am making it plain to Amelia that you were a fabulous coworker and that, like Lucas, I resent how she treated you. Maybe one day you will be able to work here again, but now is not the time. Let me know if I can help you in any way. Lucas will also help you if he can."

Although I resolved to leave Lucy and Lucas alone, their support in the face of Amelia's threat to call the police on me did help enormously. I could understand why I lost my job because I failed to turn up. All the same, putting me in the dangerous category was unfair, even given all I was experiencing.

I had remained in touch, mainly by phone, with my friend Enoch throughout the crisis. He suggested I consult a psychologist and gave me the name of one he knew. She was well-known, and I felt lucky to get an appointment. Unfortunately, she made me feel worse and not better. Her whole focus seemed to be Freudian, and she tried to link my problems to my sex life, or lack of it. I remained in a state of anosognosia. A second psychologist I consulted diagnosed me with depression combined with trauma from my parent's marriage. That I had post-traumatic reactions to my childhood was a correct assessment. My childhood dramas would strongly affect how my mental illness manifested itself during a relapse. However, I was never depressed. That's one of my problems when I get sick with schizophrenia: it's all go, go, go.

I hadn't attended the book club or the food bank for many weeks since my psychotic break began. One Saturday, I was feeling better and turned up at the book club. It was common for club members to miss meetings, especially as we met at the weekends when they were often busy with families. There was a core of about five members at every meeting, and one of them was Meredith, the book club organizer. She was in her fifties with soft grey hair and hazel eyes. She was a divorcée with a considerable hatred of men. I was greeted by Meredith, who said, "Where have you been? You've lost a lot of weight! Were you sick?"

I replied, "I am excellent, but, as you know, the world has completely changed since I last saw you. How are you coping?"

Everyone stared at me. Meredith asked, "What do you mean?"

I replied, "Oh, nothing. Let me look at the books you are reading. They should reflect any significant change in what you are experiencing."

The book club looked uncomfortable, but, as was their custom, they displayed the books they had read since the week before. What happened next was torturous. As they set out the books, I looked at the titles and thought every single one was a judgment of me. All the verdicts were adverse: I was unwanted, I was a liar, I had abused my parents, and we cannot wait until you die. In my mind, the book club agreed with these messages and decided to make them clear to me. In the middle of a discussion about one of the books, I said, "I see the pathway of the titles. I will not kill myself, no matter what you judge as my place on this earth."

Meredith asked me, "What is going on with you, Sarah? You sound crazy!"

I froze. I was suddenly afraid they would call the police because of Amelia's reaction when I turned up at the real estate agency. In retrospect, although this reaction of mine was pure terror, it perhaps saved me from making an even worse impression on the club. Throughout the rest of the meeting, I said nothing except goodbye after the last coffee.

A few days later, Meredith, who had my telephone number, called me. I answered. Meredith said, "I am afraid I have to ask you to stop attending the book club meetings. All the members agree. Your behavior at the last meeting was most alarming. Your comment about the world having changed frightened some members, as did the statement that you will not kill yourself. We cannot tolerate that situation. You are so skinny that I assume you have undergone a period of depression. Severe depression can lead to psychotic behavior, and no one feels safe in the face of that prospect. Please leave all of us alone." Having no choice, I agreed to quit the club and avoid its members.

I reflected on Meredith's phone call. She knew enough about mental illness to know that psychosis can occur at one end of the depression spectrum. I learned this fact from looking up depression after one of the psychologists I consulted suggested I was depressed. I had a poor understanding of what I read, as I had yet to understand I was psychotic. However, all those books Meredith had read over the years hadn't softened her attitude toward someone with a presumed mental illness. Of course, I didn't make this evaluation from the standpoint of someone who knew they were mentally ill, but her reaction still disappointed me. She had also cut me off from a simple social situation that, with a bit of kindness and effort, may have worked well for me as I navigated my fears and delusions.

The Sunday after Meredith had called, I turned up at the food bank in an angry mood. I felt the weight of rejection and judgment that I should commit suicide, and I was outright argumentative, over straightforward tasks, with some of the staff at the food bank. They told me to leave and not come back.

After these disasters, I began to isolate myself. I avoided even Enoch. I was careful to be polite to anyone I encountered, even though I felt victimized by everyone as my paranoia grew.

When you are drowning in paranoid schizophrenia and don't even have a correct diagnosis, as was my case at thirty-one, you debate with yourself about reality. What your mind tells you about your sensory input seems logical and proven. Yet, a small voice inside you knows something is wrong, which makes you terrified.

After months without my job, I realized I would soon have no savings. The only avenue to improve my finances was to apply for unemployment benefits. I went to the appropriate office to make such an application. I told them my previous employer, the only one I had had, fired me and that I had no references. The people working there were gentle with me, even though they could see I was agitated and scared and that I was coming out with comments that had nothing to do with applying for the benefits. Somehow, we made it through the application process, and soon afterward, my unemployment benefits started. It's been my experience that, sometimes, people who do not know me at all are better able to handle me in a period of crisis. This quality is especially true if they have experience coping with people in distress and are goal-oriented. They agree with you on a specific objective and help you make it there with kindness.

This psychotic break lasted about three years. Unaided by the medical profession and living on unemployment benefits, I was alone with symptoms that seemed real to me. What finally helped was the realization of the damage to my cognitive abilities. I couldn't focus on my interests except for listening to music. Watching TV or listening to the radio was impossible as I felt the shows were talking to me. They were also challenging for me to follow as everything was so chaotic. My pastimes needed a grasp of language and could not interact with the word salad inside my head. All sensory input was laced with paranoia too.

I decided to act by going under everyone's radar and focusing on improving my mind and body at home. I rested a great deal and ate more regularly. I tried each day to solve a small mathematics problem from my old high school textbooks, which I had bought after I returned the school copies. It was initially unbearable and discouraging, but I slowly built my cognitive confidence. I moved on to reading books. To gain an advantage, I focused on books I had read already.

Towards other people, I resolved that, no matter how unnatural it felt, I would be the most polite and reserved person alive. It was, at times, challenging, and I only coped by thinking of myself as an actor playing a part. If I kept my end up, maybe I would encourage a few friends to reestablish contact. One or two of my friends, like Enoch and Lucas, never deserted me in the long run.

18

Propaganda

I was raised in my mother's oral tradition, her version of the events in our lives, and her take on the family history. At thirty-eight, after confining herself and me for hours each day in our home in Newcastle, she became compulsive about handing down, during those hours, this knowledge to me. She was never tired of it. She took up most of my spare time and much of my energy.

However, despite this significant change in my mother, the content of her stories evolved subtly. In the meantime, she continued to be a superb mother in many ways. The house was always clean and neat. She ensured that I continued pursuing my cultural and intellectual interests at a level way ahead of my classes at school. Whenever I was ill, she would wait on me hand and foot, speaking to me gently and cooking my favorite meals to tempt me to eat. Later, in my mid-teens, Jodie handed me much of the household work and became less sensitive to my needs. Her paranoia was becoming increasingly possessive, depriving her of some of the mental space she had until then used to maintain her role as wife and mother.

From the time I was about thirteen, I began to seriously doubt the voracity of significant portions of my mother's indoctrination. She had always been a colorful storyteller, but I had learned enough about the world to see that her wildest claims were skating on impossibly thin ice.

My mother's constant compulsive conversations with me were an attempt to bend the truth of her history to match her changing perception of reality. She wanted me as a witness, like a mental scribe who would keep track. She created separate worlds for herself and me. She permitted no disagreement on my part, becoming upset if I attempted to question her story with an errant reaction in her eyes. As I grew older and drifted further apart from her, I kept my vision of the world a secret from her.

When we were back in Sydney, despite significant pieces of my mother's world faltering in Newcastle, Jodie got a job in a shop working for charity; I was about twelve. She had applied through an advertisement for the job in a newspaper. I was surprised that, after being so housebound, she would envisage going into the workforce. The move to Sydney landed us in a delightful suburb on the northern beaches. I believe that helped my mother, at least temporarily, to envisage joining the outside world. The occupation proved beneficial; she was often proud of how she'd handled her day and would tell me all about it. For example, she told me, "I have overhauled the window dressing and the organization of the shop's interior. Those steps attract more customers. They feel they can shop with us to benefit a worthy cause and, in doing so, buy a pretty dress in a pleasantly decorated store." In making these changes, she was not overbearing, as, by her reports, she got on well with the rest of the staff at the shop. I was so happy for my mother.

Most notably, in contrast to the wake of her crisis at thirty-eight, this job got her out of the house for most of the day. She seemed to have no difficulty. She had solved the problem of our dogs by locking them in the home while away and asked me to take them for long walks when at home. If I couldn't do that for any reason, my father was happy to take them for a walk before leaving for work or after returning home. He left later than my mother and got home earlier, as he traveled by car, whereas my mother went by bus. He loved the dogs. Even outside the house, we kept them on a leash. Thankfully, we didn't have dog-hating neighbors this time.

At about that time, I was often down with cold, flu, and tonsillitis. My mother was worried about leaving me alone on days I skipped school. I will never forget how sad I felt when she came into my bedroom to say gently, "I have resigned from my job, Sarah, because I want to be able to look after you when you are sick." There was no tone of resentment in her voice, though I knew how disappointed she must be. I felt guilty and begged her to change her decision, but she wouldn't. I often thought back on her leaving this job and wondered if keeping it may have changed the course of her paranoia. As an adult, when I became familiar with my relapses into psychosis, I realized that my mother's job may have ended badly. This possibility hasn't helped my guilt of being the catalyst for her giving it up.

After she gave up the job, she had more time to spend on her oral history. Her employment had not updated her script. She took up from where she had left off before her job, with me in the same role of mental scribe.

Jodie was highly critical of Dalaigh; his genuine flaws were evident to me. I had experienced his selfish reaction to my grandfather's will. I sensed he had a friend he kept secret from us, an institution grown-ups called an *affair*. He often reminded me that he doubted I was his daughter and that Robert was my biological father. When I was about ten, he upped the frequency of his threats to harm me physically and often criticized me for my rapidly maturing body. I was chronically underweight, but Dalaigh still accused me of being overweight by overeating.

He was disagreeable not only about my looks but about my mother's, whose appearance he often derided despite her beauty and pride at how she dressed, even around the house. I once heard him remark to her, "You look fine, in the distance, in a crowd!" My mother was initially hurt before we delegated the remark to a joke and often laughed about it. I would say, "It could have been worse! He could have said, 'You look fine, in the distance, in a crowd, with your back turned!'."

Even though we both agreed on the obvious and had lots of material to tarnish Dalaigh's image, Jodie found it necessary to reveal to me her imagination of much more profound depths to his nasty character than was fair. Even as a child, I forgave my father somewhat. I believed much of my father's bad behavior was beyond his control. With us, he was living in an unhappy and eroding situation.

One of Jodie's favorite topics was her father, Feivel. It is not uncommon for people living with schizophrenia to think they are much more important to society than they factually are. In my mother's case, she attached this delusion to her father. Feivel was a Zionist and often talked to his two daughters about it, as Beth and Jodie remembered. After Jodie's decline in mental health at thirty-eight, she elaborated on this memory. She subtly morphed it over several years into a conviction that Feivel was a vital member of a Zionist movement in Australia. The flip side of this story was that Jodie thought a secret network of fascists in Australia was out to persecute her as retribution for her father's political activities. She told me because Beth was a passionate Christian, the Church would protect her from the fascists.

She didn't give many details at first, but as the years passed, she considerably fleshed out this imaginary story and looked closely for evidence. She would tell me, "As soon as my father returned from his overseas tour when I was five, he made it plain that he had met many important people, including heads of state. Of the family, he confided only in me, as he didn't trust Beth and my mother. His work became particularly vital during and just after World War Two." These stories reminded me how important my mother's father was to her and how close she must have been to him. Despite my gradual realization that these stories about Feivel couldn't be true, he became my favorite deceased relative because of my mother's deep love.

These conversations were an example of retrospective paranoia. I also suffer from this type of delusion when I am deep into a relapse. It isn't only delusions about what is happening in real time that plague you. You also rethink many things from the past, and your mind twists the truth into something more suited to the present condition of your suffering mind.

Jodie now had an established delusion, Feivel's greatness as a Zionist, which fed her most damaging conclusion that she was a target of fascists. She convinced herself she was on the hit list of vicious anti-semites because of her father's spy work for Zionism.

Dalaigh's mother, being southern Irish, raised him Catholic. By the time I came along, he was solidly atheist due to his communist beliefs. Dalaigh was highly prejudiced against Jews, espousing the typical libel that they controlled too much money. Dalaigh's antisemitism didn't affect his attraction to Jodie, but they had many fights about it. In any case, his attitudes pushed Jodie further into her delusions about Feivel and fascists.

For my part, I vehemently reproached Dalaigh for his racism, which also extended to black people and other minorities. He shared with me that, despite being a Communist, he had read Hitler's *Mein Kampf* and condoned part of its racism. I was never sure whether he said these things to provoke me or whether that was, incredibly, what he honestly thought. I was disgusted in any event. One day, when I was about eleven, my father came into my room and said in a solemn voice. "Did you know your children will be Jewish? 'It' is passed down through the woman." I had no clue what the problem was with that! I did know that by Jewish law, if your mother was Jewish, then you were Jewish. My father talked about it as if being Jewish was some disease! When I argued with him about his antisemitism, he came out with the most amazing clichés about German Jews before

World War Two, no doubt gleaned from Mein Kampf. He'd say, "The Jews had the purse strings of Germany. The Jews were bad in Germany." I would argue with him about his racist views but to no avail.

In more modern times, it is frequent to pinpoint a severe fault in a person, reject them, punish them, and then delegate them to irremediably evil status. Such action is justified, in my view, for people like Josef Mengele and Adolf Eichmann. My mother raised me to think this way about war criminals and others who perpetrated human atrocities. However, to put my father into this category is inaccurate. As her marriage grew more challenging, my mother's attitude that my father belonged alongside the most evil of the leaders of the German SS in World War Two didn't help anyone. It arose in tandem with her belief that Feivel was an influential Zionist. Dalaigh, by contrast, must be in league with the worst of fascism, a delusion that thrived thanks to his views on Jews.

Dalaigh was physically and emotionally abusive to both my mother and me and harbored abhorrent racial views. However, he was not, in my mind, an evil man. The only way I have found to cure myself, at least partially, from the damage he did to me is to forgive him. I have every right to say that my father abused me mightily, and it is undoubtedly true that he damaged me as a result. However, I want to rise above it, even though at each relapse in my mental health, the post-traumatic stress disorder from Dalaigh's treatment kicks in and makes recovery much harder. I get well quicker, despite all Dalaigh's faults, due to my forgiving behavior. He was a complex person and not all bad.

As a child, on hearing some of my father's obnoxious views, my principal frustration was not knowing how to improve them. I gradually realized that they were a product of his upbringing, things he had been encouraged to accept by his mother and aunts. How far is it profitable to go to find the source warranting blame? The only helpful reaction was firmly stating my opposition to what my father got wrong and sticking to it. That I forgive him lessens the trauma of his bad side and frees me up to worry about my character and where it falls short.

19

Feivel

Jodie idolized her father, Feivel, and was less close to her mother, Edith, who was forty-three when she gave birth to her in 1927. Edith suffered from depression, worsened by the death of her infant, born in 1925. From what I can gather, no doctor treated the depression. Still, my grandmother's sad expression and pessimistic state of mind were evident to those close to her. For all that, Jodie confirmed that she was a gentle person who was a conscientious mother during Jodie's childhood. In their teens, Jodie and Beth took the responsibilities of housework and cooking. After Jodie left for Sydney to do ballet, all the duties fell on Beth. They would remain her responsibilities until her parents died in 1957. Beth was close to her mother and had a problematic relationship with her father. She was, nonetheless, an alternate source of information on Jodie's immediate family, which she shared with me.

Putting aside my mother's delusions about him, Feivel still had an unusual story. He was born in Ballarat, Victoria, Australia, to parents who had immigrated from Eastern Europe, along with Feivel's grandfather. The family was Jewish. The parents and grandfather first went to England to escape persecution and then to Australia on assisted immigration. Feivel was the eldest of three children, and his siblings were Herman and Irit. He was born in 1894.

When Feivel was eight years old, in 1902, he came home one day from school to find his parents missing. His grandfather was dead by then. He stayed alone with his siblings in their home for three days waiting for their mother and father to return. They didn't. The person to visit the house was a social worker who immediately put the children into the foster program. Feivel and his siblings were separated, without any means of communication to keep in touch. Feivel became the victim of some of the corruption in the system. His foster parents only wanted the money they received from the government for housing a child. They lived in a rural part of Victoria and had no children of their own. Feivel was not allowed into their house but had to live in the stable with the animals. He had to do many chores around the farm. He had no light in the stable except for candles lent to him by his foster parents. At that time, foster children had to attend school until fourteen. Feivel did well, despite having to do his homework by candlelight while sharing a stall with a horse. This part of Feivel's story matched what he had told Beth and Jodie.

Feivel's foster parents were abusive. They beat Feivel when he didn't measure up with his chores or became uppity. The only time Feivel's foster parents let him in the house was to amuse guests. He had the talent, even as a child, to make people laugh. It's one aspect of Feivel that my mother loved, but back then, the situation was not friendly.

Feivel's foster father was openly hostile toward him, a little Jewish boy who was losing his religious identity.

Surprisingly, Feivel's foster mother was Jewish. That's one of the reasons the system assigned Feivel to her. He remembered her as someone too timid to do anything else but bend to her husband's will, and she transmitted nothing of her Jewish background to him.

When Feivel was about ten, his future wife Edith, then twenty, started to visit Feivel's foster mother, who was her sister. She fell in love with Feivel and felt pity and shame for his treatment.

At fourteen, Feivel left his foster home. He went to Melbourne and, through attending synagogue, convinced someone to employ him. He took lodgings with Edith, who lived in Melbourne. He had reached out to her remembering her kindness when he was on the farm. He still lived there when he contracted pneumonia in his early twenties and almost died. Edith nursed him, and he fell in love with her. They married.

However, Feivel was never out of the woods of his childhood. He refused to see Edith's family ever again, which she accepted. Out of sight, though, was not out of mind. Both Jodie and Beth remembered him having fits of anger against his foster parents and his birth parents. "They left me to grow up like a potato," he would yell. Though committed, his marriage was not overly happy, especially after the infant's death in 1925.

When my mother was five years old, in 1932, Feivel went on a world tour, which was typical for Australians at that time if they had made a bit of money. Edith did not accompany him. In those days, many Australians felt that Britain was their true home and even referred to *going home* when they went there. Feivel was ambitious for his trip. He traveled worldwide with a flair, for example, staying at the Waldorf Astoria in New York. My mother boasted that he met Haile Selassie, but I always thought that sounded far-fetched. Feivel sent my mother postcards of every place he visited. She showed me, for example, Feivel's postcards of Yellowstone National Park. When he returned to Australia, my mother was totally in awe of him.

In his thirties, Feivel hired a private detective to track down his two siblings. He found his brother, Herman, in Adelaide, and his sister, Irit, in Wales. He went to Wales during his 1932 trip to visit his sister and got close to Herman.

Often delusions that blossom have a grain of truth. There was no doubt that Feivel was a compelling person with significant accomplishments, given where he started. For example, he learned literature, politics, economics, and other university-level topics. He passed on his education to his daughters as much as he could, just as my mother did to me. However, he was troubled. He was addicted to gambling and had a fondness for whisky that developed when his marriage cooled off.

Jodie was proud of being Jewish, even though her parents sent their daughters to schools with religious classes given by representatives of the Church of England. The hope was that by doing so, their girls would fit in better with their friends in the private schools they attended. Despite this precaution, Feivel talked much to Jodie about the Jewish faith he remembered from his childhood. He had forgotten most of it but, for example, remembered having matzot at Passover and bought some for the occasion each year. He didn't forget about the Sabbath candles and the challah bread.

Jodie's central delusion about Feivel being an influential Zionist, and the persecution she suffered as a result, once in place, never shifted. It only deepened. As well as being a fantasy to match her changing view of reality, it was also a way for Jodie to feel important as the daughter of a fascinating and influential man. The difficulties of her marriage, and the decline in her mental health, made her feel that the dreams of her youth were slipping away. She sought to replace them with something else that made her feel important. However, her choices were not arbitrary but rooted in facts she embellished. The evolution of the symptoms of her schizophrenia strongly influenced the way she built this inaccurate history.

20

Sarah: Thirty-five

I had just turned thirty-five, and it had been about a year since I felt more or less back to normal after my psychotic break at thirty-one. Of course, I didn't know it was paranoid schizophrenia as I had no correct diagnosis. I had been living on unemployment benefits in the small rented studio in Dee Why. My life was frugal, but money had always been scarce in our family, so I was used to that. I shopped on a strict weekly budget and forced myself to make the food I had bought feed me the whole week before the next shop. I had plenty of records to play that my mother had left me. I had no TV, but I did have a radio. After almost four years of living with at first full-blown, then waning psychosis, I convinced myself I could be happy with my simple life.

I still wanted to get employment now that I was on more solid ground mentally. I returned to the real estate agency that employed me before to see if they could hire me again at the same afternoon job.

Amelia had left the agency as she had moved with her family to the Northern Territory. Lucas had taken over as boss. He and Lucy were surprisingly welcoming despite my lousy record from losing the job at thirty-one. By pure chance, they had no one doing the job I did for them back then, and they seemed eager to employ me again. "You did your job well," they said when they decided to give me another chance at employment. "A warning, though, if the problems you had last time recur, we will have to let you go!"

By then, Lucas had married. I hadn't met his wife, Athena, but when I did so, she was extremely kind to me. She was beautiful with a figure like a top model, a fair complexion, and blonde hair like Lucas. She asked me to visit their home, and I did so a few times with no problems occurring. I had retained a few other understanding friends, like Enoch, but spent most of my time alone. I continued to write letters to Beth, who was still in Adelaide, that I read and re-read until I was satisfied they passed for normal.

Then, suddenly, my world became too rosy. Despite my isolation, I thought I had acquired many disciples who needed my input for critical political matters. Ironically, politics, for me, was about not taking sides. I was a swing voter. Paradoxically, the absurdity of the notion that I could have a leadership position in politics made my new identity more credible in my mind. It made for a huge ridiculous event I hadn't foreseen that abruptly appeared inevitable. I felt under a great deal of stress.

This euphoria didn't last long. Within a few weeks, I believed many people persecuted me for my political beliefs. Then, I lost the delusion about my stance in the political world, but I rapidly descended into total paranoia. I felt all the symptoms I had experienced at thirty-one, but they were much worse this time. I had, again, no idea what was happening to me as my changing world had no definition from the doctors I had consulted. I had bizarre visual experiences. When I looked at people's faces, I often had the impression they were melting before my eyes, as if made of wax and suddenly exposed to extreme heat. I wasn't able to read anything in black ink. I had to write and read in blue ink to manage. Black was dangerous, blue my safe color, and green ambiguous. Green could mean go ahead and trust your decisions, or it could mean you've got the go-ahead to kill yourself.

I felt my life was an open, published book and that everyone was judging every action I had ever performed in the harshest possible way. It was a global appraisal with no pockets of safety. Even if people behaved poorly towards me, somehow, that was also my fault. I would experience moments when I froze out of fear of where I would end up. Like at thirty-one, I was convinced there had been a global assessment of me and my situation, followed by a universal recommendation that I commit suicide. I wasn't suicidal, so I did not harm myself, but the verdict was terrifying. Everything pointed to it, everything.

I believed that I only needed to look at a person for them to know what I was thinking and that everywhere I went, people were inserting thoughts into my mind. I was engaged in a silent global debate where the verdict was my complete unworthiness. Everything I thought I had accomplished with my life was a cloud easily dispersed. My relatively humble circumstances, siding with my mother rather than pursuing a career, helped me. I wasn't boasting of much that would impress society, so the put-down was livable. What wasn't bearable was the push to get me to commit suicide.

During this relapse, everything was a coded message. I thought I saw people making obscene gestures. The feeling was so oppressive that my only relief was to swear to myself out loud. I didn't manage to confine such monologues to my studio. I got into trouble in some of my favorite places, like the extensive public library in the city, which banned me.

I failed to show up at work and, for the second time, lost the job with the real estate agency I had enjoyed and was, under normal circumstances, well within my abilities. This time, it was Lucas who had to fire me. It was difficult for him, but I didn't make a fuss as I was distracted by what was happening inside my head. I went back onto unemployment benefits. The administrators who helped me get these benefits again were kind. They understood how to put me at ease and calm me down enough to process my claim.

Soon afterward, Lucas and Athena moved to Perth in Western Australia. Athena was a photographer and got a job *with a geographic magazine based in Perth; Lucas found work with another real estate firm. They left their new address and phone number with me when they dropped by my studio to say goodbye. Luckily, I was calm when they visited, so it was rewarding for all three of us to say goodbye pleasantly.*

At some point, the police visited me. A neighbor in my building had complained that I was scaring them and mouthing obscenities. When the police entered my studio, I was sitting at the Jesse French piano I had been able to keep all these years. I returned to that seat and began to play. I was calm and collected. Like my mother, I was capable of pockets of sanity if I felt in danger. The police were kind and gave me the card of someone on their staff who dealt with mental health emergencies. They told me to call that person if I was in crisis. I never did, but I tried to be less noisy when talking to myself at home in deference to the neighbor who called the police. The slap on the wrist also helped me to cut down on the foul language.

Due to the rejections from the book club and the food bank when I was thirty-one, apart from Lucas and Athena, the only friend I had was Enoch. I was nervous about losing this last friend. I telephoned him and said, "Enoch, I am having the problems I had a few years ago again. I have decided to battle them alone. Please don't feel I am rejecting you if you don't hear from me for a while." Enoch replied, "I am always here, and you can call me if you need a friend. However, at this stage, you must consult a psychologist and psychiatrist. You need professional help."

Unfortunately, I did not consult a psychiatrist or psychologist as I had lost faith in the medical profession. Given the visit from the police and my extreme fear, I decided to go under everyone's radar as I had at thirty-one. Though it did not protect me from my symptoms, my home became my safe place, and I seldom left it. I would be extra careful not to arouse suspicion when I did go out. None of these actions helped me, but they made me less afraid I would be killed or locked up.

Due to the sheer weight of my sensory overload and mental interpretations, I couldn't do much. I couldn't listen to the radio since all the broadcasts seemed threatening. I often forgot to eat, but I always had canned food in my home so that when hungry, I could eat something that hadn't gone bad.

One refuge was music. I played many of the records my mother left me and found that, despite everything, I could play simple pieces on my piano. I bought recordings of Glenn Gould and listened to them a lot. He plays most verbally to his audience, and this was the only two-way conversation I had that made sense. I played the funny records I had and imitated the voices. I found it amusing, and that gave me a little relief.

My relapse affected every aspect of my interaction with the outside world. Everything hitting my senses was significant. It made seeing other people extremely difficult. That I chose to be a hermit until I had a different lifestyle idea seemed the only choice to make.

Despite the relative safety of my home, it could not protect me from all my symptoms. I began to hear loud knocking noises on my roof, synchronizing with what I was thinking and doing. I listened to these knockers laughing amongst themselves at my efforts to please. They were having conversations, commenting on what I was doing. They mostly tried to convince me that I was failing, that the people knocking would eventually take over my situation, and not to my liking. I wanted to appease them by putting into the garbage can anything I was looking at when the knocking was at its worst. I realized after a few days of discarding that I was losing some of my favorite items, so I stopped.

I couldn't read because the melting of people's faces was now happening to words. I could shop when needed and attend to any invoices that arrived. These pockets of "sanity" didn't last but were a crucial help.

I did a lot of compulsive talking aloud but softly because of the neighbor who complained. My mind heard everything I had listened to since I was three. On top of that were piles of thoughts I believed were inserted from the outside. I had to defend myself. I had to order those thoughts somehow.

Despite my terrible situation, I never cried and didn't feel sad. I felt like a soldier trying to save their life and sanity. The only emotion I felt was anger. It wasn't a vengeful feeling, just a reaction to all I had to do to stay in one place and not go completely under. It was acutely frustrating.

Everything was related, and there were no coincidences. My mind built up an intricate array of codes like it had done for colors. I had to interpret even certain gestures others made using my evolving code. Individual letters had more meaning than entire words. I started to guess acronyms hiding in the words I heard. I had learned some Hebrew, so some of the acronyms used letters of words from right to left.

I had always loved my pen and paper. I started to write profusely, even though I couldn't clearly see what I was doing. That was the second most helpful action I took after the most useful one of listening to music. It helped to cut down the talking to myself.

I didn't have a pet at that stage due to the building rules where I lived. It was a pity as I am sure a bird, cat, or dog in the house would have helped me. I have always loved and trusted pets.

In my case, the delusions I had were not something made by a mad brain but by me desperately trying to make sense of what my sensory input was telling me.

During my troubles when I was thirty-one, a doctor diagnosed me as suffering from PTSD (Post-Traumatic Stress Disorder) from childhood experiences. Subsequent doctors gave the same verdict. During this relapse, and the ones that would follow, I suffered vivid flashbacks to traumatic incidents from my childhood. However, at the time, I always congratulated *myself on how well I had dealt with a lot of what happened in my early years, so I was shocked that the more harmful incidents could nonetheless revisit me.*

These flashbacks were terrifying and reflected fears I had as a child. My physical fear of my father growing up came back during this relapse. As he had often threatened violence when I was working on my schoolwork, I couldn't sit at my writing desk now without extreme fear. This terror was brutal to manage as I lived in a studio with one room apart from a separate bathroom. I took to carrying out my writing activities in my bathroom for long periods to get away from these recollections. For my sessions with pen and ink, I used the toilet as a seat and a tray on my lap as a desk. Other bad memories that resurfaced included the feelings inside me of violation because of my father's cruel remarks about my body, especially when I reached puberty. I had terrible dreams about it as a pre-teen and young teen. These recollections resurfaced, even though my father wasn't living with me.

I gradually improved once I understood that I had to spend as much time at home as possible and strictly control my surroundings to foster encouragement and have as little contact with the outside world as possible.

21

Education

I have competed with myself to learn since my first memories. I was so keen to start school that, at age four, my mother bought me all the trimmings, like a briefcase, pencils, erasers, paper, and so on. These acquisitions responded to my worry that I wouldn't be ready for school at five without them. I remember my mother remarking to someone in the shop where we acquired these treasures, "She is so excited about starting school that she insists on a full dress rehearsal." My mother loved such theatrical terms. I recall this agitation quite clearly, including my intense thirst for knowledge. This passion came, no doubt, from my mother.

Jodie had started teaching me to read and write at three, so at four, I knew my alphabet and could read children's books for an age group a few years older. She trained me to run a cash register when I was very young. She even supplied me with a working cash register for my fourth birthday. She also taught me to total a column of numbers. "If you ever work in a shop, Sarah, you'll need a good head for figures! When you add a column of numbers by hand, always add down the column and then check your answer by adding from bottom to top." Jodie considered home education to be part of a mother's duty. Her parents, especially her father, had seen to it that Jodie and Beth considerably fleshed out their school education. The end game was cultivation for its own sake, not preparation for a career. They both left school at fifteen with the family assuming they would marry and raise children in place of a job. My mother harbored similar ambitions for me until much later, when she wanted me all to herself.

At that time, in the state of New South Wales, Australia, where we lived, the policy was not to advance precocious children to a class with children more than one year older than them. My kindergarten teachers immediately put me ahead one year, which meant I was often the youngest in the class, given that my birthday was in August. The Australian school year matches the civil year because the seasons are what they are in the Southern Hemisphere.

I was mildly happy to always be at the top of my class, but I knew it resulted from hard, systematic effort. Simply put, I outworked all the other students. What pleased me most was overtaking the goals I set for myself at home. I was exceedingly studious. I preferred to be alone rather than with other children, and I wanted to make a world independent of my parent's marriage. I had plenty of spare time until my mother began encroaching on it when I was eight. Even then, I adapted my study techniques to continue to do surprisingly well.

Despite her demands for my attention, my mother continued to enhance my education considerably until she became too sick with schizophrenia to focus on it. I remain eternally grateful for her academic enrichment. That part of her that could still function cognitively grew smaller as she aged. I believe she was happy to share with me what she could still enjoy intellectually.

High school is six years in Australia, usually from age twelve to eighteen. We had stopped moving, and I was able to have this part of my education mostly at the same school. That I attended the same high school for the last two years helped both my grades and my relationship with other students. In my day, it was common to leave high school after four years if you didn't aspire to a profession needing a university education. I did the full six years. Again, I worked hard on my studies. I was at, or near, the top of my class in every subject. I had a terrible problem with teasing by a group of popular students that lasted several years. For the last two years of high school, I began to aim for second or third position in specific classes to ease my nerd reputation. It helped! As if in admiration, some of the kids who had teased me shouted, "You aren't as smart as you think!"

My parents never worked with me on my schoolwork. It was all extra-curricular intervention. When I was eleven, my mother started suggesting university-level adult educational interests, as her father had done for her. She gave me classic books to read, including those by some famous Russian authors. She passed on what she had learned about poetry from her poet friend, Robert. She gave me books by Aristotle to start me off in philosophy. My father's considerable contribution was to buy me an at-home science experiment kit and to provide me with a biography of Einstein. When I was eleven, my mother introduced me to the biography of Marie Curie written by her daughter Eve Curie. She wanted to teach me that girls can be as smart as boys. I loved the book and found it inspiring, but I couldn't relate to Marie. I knew I was not that personally ambitious.

Jodie's role models were always female, and she identified with many successful women and some fictional women from famous movies or books. It was a harmless habit that often encouraged her when struggling because of her actual or imaginary situation. She tried to pass this aspect of her personality on to me but to no avail. When I was daydreaming about a role linked to fame, a relationship with a successful man almost always featured. As for Jodie's females, such men were both real and fictional characters. Mostly, I would dream about what I would say to them in a conversation, and this exercise had an encouraging effect on me.

It was tremendously helpful to me that this homeschooling continued to take place during some of the worst times in my parents' marriage, especially my pre-teen years. I could appreciate my mother and father as sources of knowledge and not only as a pair of adults in serious trouble.

For me to do optimally with my studies, I found I needed a lot of time to study alone. My mother understood my need for privacy, and never intruded on it to judge my progress. She would wait until I was ready to discuss my intellectual pursuits with her, and that was always a rewarding experience for me . They did not pass on a sense of personal ambition in society, and I grew up to care little for it. What mattered was how my mind felt, not how I could use it to advance myself in a socially recognized way.

Apart from his gift to educate me in science, my father didn't talk about intellectual matters except about politics. He became a communist after World War Two and never wavered in his views. He especially admired China. When we had some moments alone, he often espoused his political thoughts. This influence didn't take as I grew up undecided about my political affiliations, but it was still educational. It's a pity about his racial views. They made it hard, at times, for me to feel he deserved sympathy.

I consider myself religious, but it is a strictly personal matter that I don't share. My parents' left-wing views dictated that they omit religion in my home education. At school, a Church of England minister gave some religious classes that were quite good. I developed a thriving interest in beliefs in the Judeo-Christian tradition. As an adult, I augmented these topics to include some Eastern religions I encountered due to taking up meditation.

When I was about eight, my mother enrolled me in the Argonauts Club, a radio show for children that encouraged them to contribute essays and poems. The idea was that members identified with rowers of ships sailing in quest of the Golden Fleece. The radio, not the television, was our primary source of entertainment until I turned twelve.

From age eight to thirteen, I wrote a lot of poetry. That pastime angered my father as it made him think of Robert and strengthened his suspicions that I was Robert's child. My mother initially encouraged me but became so preoccupied with the difficulties of her life that she lost interest in my poems. At fourteen, I decided to burn all of them. My logic was that my work would, at best, be a child's work. Now that I was growing up, I needed to be more discerning.

22

Friends

My father's job in a chain of department stores required frequent shifting until my parents were in their forties. Some of them were promotions. My father rapidly climbed to the store manager level but with no hope of advancement beyond that. The moves didn't stop even then. They were all over New South Wales, Australia, and came out after every six months. The company did not move us that frequently, but the most time we spent in any one place was three years, which was rare. More typical was moving after eighteen months in one place. We had changed homes ten times by the time I was twelve. The moves helped to isolate my mother as she cut off friendships she had made and tried to make new ones. It added to the problems she started showing when I was about eight. When I was about twelve, my father changed his job that didn't require him to move.

The last tea party I remember my mother holding occurred in Mudgee, a rural town in New South Wales, when I was about seven. She went to a great deal of trouble. My mother told me to stay in the kitchen during the party. It was typical of the times; children could help in the kitchen but didn't sit in adult parties. I got into trouble for eating some of the cakes for the party that were stored in the kitchen. My mother rarely slapped me, but she did for that infraction. Again, it shows the times.

The party was a disappointment to my mother due to its conversation. My mother tried to talk about what interested her and found little common ground with her invitees. After the guests had left, my mother forgave my cake-eating. We laughed together at one of the guest's comments. "I was trying to talk about the white Russians I knew through the ballet," my mother said, and of course, she meant Russians who fled or whose ancestors fled the Russian revolution. One of the women retorted,

"Don't be silly, dear. They're all red!" By that, the guest referred to their complexion, not their politics. It became a saying between us. If someone said something naively stupid about a group of people, we'd chorus, once alone together, "Don't be silly, they're all red!"

My parents had some mutual friends for about the first ten years of their marriage. Usually, the friends were people my father had met at work, and they were mostly married. Still, my parents were friendly with some couples they met when my parents lived in Sydney when they got married. Two of those couples remained close even after my parents had difficulties entertaining them because of the ongoing misunderstandings between them and my mother due to her psychiatric problems. Eventually, however, the apparent preference these couples had for my father's point of view on his marriage translated into my mother becoming paranoid about these friends. She banned them from the house. By the time I was about seventeen, they had lost all their friends.

The history of my friendships is somewhat parallel to my parents'. For the first eight years of my life, though my peers often teased me at school, a few misfits who were in the same classes as I became friends. Before my mother's sharp downturn in mental health at thirty-eight, she was a pleasant hostess to the friends I brought home. However, as her paranoia rose and her marriage went downhill, she did not welcome my friends. The few I did invite home usually didn't visit again because my mother was weird. In addition, when my father was home, my parents were always fighting.

Despite the negative environment at home, at fourteen, I had a big romance. It was with a pianist, Chesterton, who everyone called Chester, at his request. I was back in Sydney and met him at some concerts at the Sydney Conservatorium of Music. It was a long commute for me from the suburb, Clareville, where we lived then, to the city center. Neither my mother nor I used our car, as my father needed it to commute to work. The bus ride was almost two hours each way. However, I often went to the city not only for concerts but for foreign films and, primarily, to study at the State Library of New South Wales. There were good libraries closer to where we lived. Still, none had the same ambiance and smell of books as the city's extensive library. My mother didn't want us to be apart by then, so she often accompanied me to these activities outside school.

Chester was twenty-one and beginning a solid career as a pianist. He was a cheerful, kind person and slim in a healthy way. I never saw him pass on a chance to eat. The seven years difference between our ages alarmed my mother. Would Chester be a gentleman with me? Chester's mother phoned my mother to ask if I would be a lady with him. I quickly informed Chester of my mother's no-sex-before-marriage rule and that I intended to follow it. He was not upset but pleased that I didn't draw back when he held my hand or kissed me on the cheek. He said, "We'll have to get married!" Like that, quickly, we became incredibly close and sworn fiancés.

At the beginning of our relationship, we spent little time in my parent's house, so we didn't have to deal with the tensions there. Chester began introducing me to his mostly older friends in the music world, and we mainly socialized with them. I thoroughly enjoyed these get-togethers. So much talent, so many hilarious anecdotes, and so accepting of me despite my age. I became more and more committed to the planned marriage with Chester. We aimed to get married when I was eighteen, as by then, I would have finished high school.

We had long conversations about our interests and what we would do after we got married. There was no talk of leaving Australia. Chester was happy and appreciated in Sydney. I was worried, however, about where my mother would fit in. By marrying Chester, I would have the double responsibility of his wife and caregiver to my mother. I told Chester, "My preferred choice of activity would be to work with animals. I want to be a poet if that doesn't work out. I want to do mathematics for fun and keep my mind sharp. I would also like to read the Bible from cover to cover each year. It's an important and influential book, even if you aren't religious, which I am." Then, I added, "In any case, don't forget my mother. She'll never agree to be separated from me, so we'll have to look for a house with a self-contained apartment for my parents."

Chester wasn't against that idea, which I thought was sweet, but I was still worried about how things would work out in practice. I didn't tell him how demanding my mother was on my time. This situation was at the core of my weakening hope of career prospects. Also, I lacked personal ambition. That was no one's fault. When I found the time, I loved to walk about in nature. Human excesses, including social success, seemed so petty in that context. By the time I reached sixteen and had to think about upcoming university studies, the problem of my mother needing constant care had worsened considerably.

I talked a lot to my mother about my love for Chester. I remember saying, "Any girl should be happy to marry someone as kind and loving as Chester." He was dating me in style, taking me to concerts, fancy dinners, the whole nine yards.

After our relationship seemed on solid ground, Chester began to spend more time in our home. He thought it important that my family got to know him. Then, my mother became jealous and solved the situation in her way. She could see how happy and secure I was in my love for Chester. My happiness posed the dual burden on my mother of highlighting the problems of her marriage and risking losing me as audience and caregiver. At first, she was genuinely happy for me. Still, little by little, she became palpably worried as to how this romance would affect her future.

Her solution to all the above was, when it seemed my marriage to him was a done deal, to seduce Chester openly when he was in our home. She did so in front of me and often with my father present. At first, she limited her conversations to gaining Chester's respect intellectually. I was deeply hurt when, on one date, Chester went on and on about how riveting my mother was in conversation. He added as an afterthought that he enjoyed our chats too.

My mother knew much about classical music, and we still had our piano. She knew the right balance between showing her erudition and flattering Chester. She understood a lot about the composer Chopin and would plead with Chester, "Please play Chopin Prelude such-

and-such." After Chester's performance, she would say, "That music is so emotionally important to me, and to have you play it brilliantly in my home is overwhelming." She would ask him to play other pieces of music that were all part of the standard repertoire of a good pianist. She loved Beethoven's Moonlight Sonata and would ask Chester to perform it. After him playing, my mother would be in raptures, again, about what the music meant to her.

This back and forth with Chester was not unlike the conversations I had with my mother when we first got the piano when I was eight. However, back then, my mother was modest and gentle in her dialogue about music. Now, she was like a Valkyrie on the loose. Her conversation was overdone, yet Chester fell for it.

The seduction became more pointed and less acceptable as time wore on. I could see my mother had impressed Chester, and I was a distant second. At fourteen, I didn't know how to compete with what my mother was doing. I also grew disgusted with Chester for letting my mother lead him into an obvious unsavory trap. My mother's behavior hurt my father too, and he became furious that she so openly courted Chester in his presence. He would say to me, "It's disgusting how your mother openly makes a play for Chester in front of us!"

Later, I would understand that about that time, when my mother was in her mid-forties, she began to need reassurance that she was still attractive to men. She was even beautiful then, but unkind remarks by my father about her appearance undermined her self-confidence. This quest worsened as she got older and whether she could attract a target man or not. She convinced herself by alluring him.

I broke off with Chester. My mother then went after him hell for leather. When their relationship reached the inevitable point where Chester asked my mother to sleep with him, she refused and broke off the relationship. She told me, "Chester put the hard word on me." She had achieved her goals with Chester in any case.

I was less upset about breaking up with Chester than my mother behaving in a way that was beneath her. Unfortunately, her need for reassurance that she was still attractive to men interfered with all my attempted romances in high school. Then, she became so sick with schizophrenia that I had no choice but to be a full-time caregiver and forget marriage. I could also no longer invite most friends home as my mother's behavior was too unstable and unpredictable. I retained a few friends later in life when I started working.

Many years later, I looked Chester up online and saw that he had married an opera singer. I couldn't help but smile. Most of the jokes at the parties Chester and I attended were about opera stars!

We were particularly close to a couple of Italian birth who were my godparents. Feivel had told my mother that, as Dalaigh was Catholic, it was best to baptize me so he would accept me. It was all in vain, of course. My godparents were getting brainwashed by my father about his unbearable marriage. The last time they visited us, there was a genuine, not imagined, fight between them, my mother, and me. My father and these friends launched a scathing criticism of our home. They targeted what my mother did to make a home for us and derided it. My father must have explained that he wanted to be out of his marriage, and they seemed only to visit to browbeat us into believing my mother and me were impossible. My mother was deeply hurt. This rejection fed into her paranoia. She invented some tall tales about my godparents that I am sure she believed at the time. I was annoyed enough with them to accept my mother's terms: we would never see them again. We didn't.

23

Sarah: Cacophony

As my mother's schizophrenia worsened, she became increasingly talkative about subject matters that were more and more troubling. My memories of our conversations until around my eighth birthday had been pleasurable. She told beautiful stories about her young life and those who inhabited it. After she turned thirty-eight, Dalaigh was angry about her father's will and started to take out his frustrations with girlfriends. Jodie locked herself in the house because of the complaints about our dogs. Her conversation turned to stories she wanted to be valid as her grip on reality faltered.

They were still remarkable tales that entertained. The most challenging part for me was not the increasingly deluded versions of her stories. She worked on these stories for hours, with a great deal of repetition, and I was the audience. It was *the consequent heavy brainwashing that was almost unbearable at times. When my father was at home, the continual arguments became disturbing. I was a witness because my mother demanded it or because I couldn't ignore the fights due to their loudness. I enjoyed being alone at home in an auditory environment I controlled, but that became more difficult as my parents' situation worsened.*

For schizophrenia, as I live it, those inescapable long hours of verbal menace were the most harmful part of my upbringing. I am susceptible to auditory input and derive amazing pleasure from natural sounds and music I enjoy. When I get sick, a great deal of the linguistic environment of my youth comes back unbidden. It is incredibly potent in its ability to worsen my symptoms.

24

Inappropriate

For reasons I did not understand then, over time, my mother's language became more undesirable. It was often downright obscene by the time I was midway through high school when she was in her early forties. Not all of her conversation was so afflicted, but the offensive part was distressing to me.

The swearing began when my father stopped hiding his affairs and left us several time to be with his girlfriends. He always returned as my mother threatened she would get him terminated. She also went to great lengths to embarrass him publicly. She would find out where he was hiding, I had no clue how, and throw a tantrum. Sometimes she would return home with bruises from my father trying to keep her out of his accommodation. Still, eventually, she would also return with my father. Believing that Dalaigh must have more girlfriends, she would get whipped up about them and began speculating about what they were getting up to in bed.

"They have a drunken orgy," she would say, "and are heavily into alternative sex. Your father forced me to have deviant sex with him when we were married before I cured him of it. I bet he has retaken to it like a duck to water." It was way over my head at the time. I was old enough to know that sexual desire was strong in both my parents. If I had missed that point, they told me often enough. However, lacking the curiosity of my classmates and without my parents explaining sex properly, I viewed these desires as some pit you can get stuck in forever. Moreover, some force would push you to talk about it non-stop. Indeed, my mother would repeat the whole speech about my father sinking into decadence again and again. As her paranoia deepened, she went over and over the same verbal ground to convince herself and me that we must know her interpretation of reality by heart. That would keep her world in focus as she grew increasingly terrified she was losing her grip on it.

That I fell in love with Chester at age fourteen certainly helped. We had some honest conversations about sex. He told me that if my father played around, my mother, with her jealous nature, may feel driven to think about nasty things. He didn't find it normal that I should be an audience to such an adult drama. It didn't stop him from falling in love with my mother.

Through my experiences with schizophrenia, I now know that a good deal of my mother's obscene talk may well have been a symptom. Her verbal thoughts were simply out of control, and with obscenity being part of the linguistic spectrum, she had no qualms about going there at times. What was shocking for me was the change in her. She had always been so cultivated and so careful with her speech.

The memory of all this repetitive diatribe had catastrophic delayed effects during my multiple relapses into the psychosis of paranoid schizophrenia. They became part of my linguistic makeup too. Sometimes, I resorted to obscenity to get my point across or because I was terrified. I learned to control this aspect of my schizophrenia, but not before offending many people I liked.

Dalaigh also declined linguistically, without the excuse of a mental illness. It was not my mother's ranting but barbs targeted at demoralizing my mother and me. He told my mother she was unattractive, though they were still sleeping together. He made highly crude remarks about changes in my body because of puberty. He made me feel that everything about my body was changing for the worse. I was in the wrong shape. I was flat-chested; I was plain. This head-on attack hurt me. I began to try to solve all these problems by eating better, exercising, and wearing less conservative clothes. Although harmful, my father's remarks pushed me into a healthier way of life, and, in the end, I did look much better and as if I cared about my appearance. The effect of his linguistic attacks on my mother was purely negative. She was hurt and depressed.

At some point, when I was about fifteen, they began arguing about the sex they were having. My parents would go to bed. Then I would hear some noises. Immediately afterward, my father would come into my room. He complained that my mother was trying to get him to do something naughty. The complaint didn't sound genuine, coming from my father. Then, my mother would join us with the same complaint. It was more credible coming from her. There would be a heated argument that mostly went over my head but that I presumed was R-rated. My parents, especially my mother, could make careful, insightful, and enjoyable conversations, but they lost control over holding back on profanity.

25.

Sarah: Disintegration

I am seventeen, and having a nightmare. I am seated with a book open on my lap. The book is in Hebrew. My grandfather, Feivel, stands behind my chair, looking down at the book. Suddenly and heavily, he puts down his hands on the book's text. The words disintegrate into individual letters that separate from the page and fly into my face. Feivel is trying to tell me that I will only grasp individual letters and will find it hard to organize them into words. He accuses me of being attracted to Hebrew because of its beautiful letters and for no better reason.

This nightmare foretells how schizophrenia will one day affect me. At my sickest, only letters will make immediate sense, and I will struggle to order them to make meaningful words.

26

Nature

The natural beauty that Australia has to offer is unique. The city of Sydney, where I spent much of my youth, has areas of untouched and protected parkland where you can enjoy the sights and sounds of this thrilling ecosystem. Even in suburbia, there is a lot of respect for indigenous nature. Many of the smaller cities in New South Wales where we lived are also beautiful. Even the modest circumstances in which I grew up exposed me to some of the best Australian scenery in New South Wales. The one thing my family never argued about was the importance of appreciating nature.

My mother, father, and I shared a profound love for the outdoors. Dalaigh was more into the flora, and Jodie and I the fauna. My father was a wizard with plants.

Everything he planted thrived, and no noxious interloper survived his weeding. He sometimes shared this activity with my mother while they both declared a temporary truce.

Several of the moves dictated to us by Dalaigh's first job landed us in locations surrounded by bushland. When I was around seven and eight, we lived in a country town called Mudgee, in the central west of New South Wales, so my father could manage a store there. It was an old-fashioned place. The day we moved in, the local band came and gave a concert in front of our house. Despite this warm welcome, I was teased at school for a few months after we arrived, but I soldiered on and eventually made some friends.

My primary recreation then was walking alone in the bushland around Mudgee. My interest in animals inspired me to collect many skulls and bones of indigenous fauna. I also brought home the skulls and bones of domestic animals that had wandered from their farms into the bushland to die. I covered my bedroom floor with my finds and arranged them according to a classification that only made sense to me. In those days, at least in my family and among my school friends, no one thought it dangerous for a seven-year-old to wander far from home for most of the day. By that age, my mother thought I was too old to need constant supervision, although she did care for all my needs and provided a lot of love. Indeed, nothing terrible happened to me. I nonetheless don't recommend letting your seven- and eight-year-old children do what I did. I was lucky.

When we moved from Mudgee, movers refused to transport my skull and bone collection. "No way we are touching that," they said. That particular move took place on my birthday, and these same men ate my birthday cake without sharing it with me. I was most out of sorts.

After my father left his first job when I was twelve and started with a different company in Sydney, we had some control over where we lived. My mother insisted on living in Sydney's northern beach area. She was familiar with it from family holidays when she was a child. We rented a house for a few years in Avalon Beach, and for the rest of my years in high school, we were in nearby Clareville.

The northern Sydney beaches, like Avalon, lie on a peninsula, the same side as the Pacific Ocean. Avalon is about 25 miles from Sydney's city center. Public transport by bus was relatively slow but afforded some incredible scenery on the way, especially during the northern part of the trip. On the other side of the peninsula is a bay called the Pittwater. The beaches attracted the surfers, and the Pittwater the sailors. In Clareville, we were within walking distance of Avalon Beach and Pittwater. We could even see some of the Pittwater from the house my parents bought.

The house in Clareville was my parents' first experience owning a home rather than renting. Living in the first home they owned in such gorgeous surroundings wasn't lost on them, but their demons had no appetite for a rest. They took out a mortgage, and my father's job paid well enough to meet the payments, even though the arguments about money continued. It was a crying shame that our time in gorgeous Clareville was one of the worst periods of my parent's marriage.

I appreciated my mother's effort in finding a house to buy in a beautiful area of Sydney. I often told her, "Thanks so much for bringing us to such a scenic place! I'll always be grateful for it."

My mother's mental health problems did not improve, despite the happiness she felt from living in such a pretty place. They would have been far worse, however, without the natural beauty.

I found pockets of time to go alone into the untouched bushland near our Clareville home to experience both Pittwater and Avalon Beach. No matter what happened with my parents, I could exit outside for an instant emotional uplift.

In Clareville, my outdoor experience was profoundly sensual. None of our previous homes had put us this close to nature. Our house was on a block of land where only the local plants, birds, and animals were permitted, except for our two labradors. The whole family of wild parrots would greet us each morning with loud, rhythmic, and melodic songs until we served them breakfast. When they finished our meal, they would go to a neighboring house and repeat their performance for food. The kookaburras started and ended their day laughing. They have vocals like a laugh. I looked forward to it, and their concert never failed to cheer me up. There were also the whipbirds with a call like a whip but a kind one and the melodic currawongs.

In the trees around our house, we had many koalas. Their babies made a noise not unlike that of a human baby. I loved listening to them. Such delicate animals as they survive on only specific eucalyptus leaves. What soothing trees, whose leaves hung from their branches. A feast for all senses was everywhere.

Then, there were beaches on both sides of the peninsula. I adored the rhythm of the sea on the surf side and the ability to take long walks along the shoreline of the bay side.

These experiences were all folded together in a profound ecstasy felt by all my senses that moved me deeply.

27

Sarah: Words

Imagine waking up one morning to find yourself drowning in words and going deeper with the letters comprising those words. You had been doing so well, too well. It had felt odd, disproportionate. Then, something in your brain flips the switch. It's not that you're going upwards, but going downwards. The linguistic filter that helps make sense of the meaning of words has disappeared. Time ordering is absent. You hear conversations from your childhood taking equal rank with something said yesterday. You remember every word you ever heard, read, or thought, all turning up at once to demand your attention.

My paranoid schizophrenia exhibits symptoms of this brain disorder that are relatively well-known: paranoia, visual and auditory hallucinations, and feeling judged, to name a few.

These are terrifying to experience and can be scary for others to witness. Behavioral therapy and medication can significantly attenuate them. A stressless and kind environment also helps.

In my case, the most potent symptoms are a loss of time ordering and the emergence of a verbal brain soup. These symptoms are always there, even in healthier times, but they are front and center when I am ill. The syndrome feels as if it originates both from within my head and via thought insertion by others. To look at someone, even across a room, is to hear the words you believe they insert in your ears. These voices can be silent as well as loud. Their content draws on the experiences of your whole life as your memories have lost their proper place in time. Such temporal and linguistic afflictions can be overwhelming. Trying to make sense of them is immensely tiring, especially as words and even individual letters can be significant in a way they don't objectively merit.

The manner in which my mother and I manifested the mental anguish caused by words had a common crucial factor. We both, as we aged, lost control of our verbal communication at pivotal moments when vital ingredients in our fate hung in the balance. The result was a relegation to the "too mad to tolerate" category by some people we knew. My mother had already passed when this problem plagued me. In her late forties, she began to fight a losing struggle I witnessed in controlling her tongue and writing. It caused distress for her and torment for me as the captive audience to her repetitive, at times R-rated, far-fetched oral mythology. The sea of words in her head and mouth overflowed onto paper, and sometimes she could not resist the temptation to share her written thoughts with the worst choice of a person at the time. A similar disaster beset me in my late thirties, resulting at times in a stream of talk and letter correspondence that I couldn't control. The familiarity with my mother's struggles did not help me manage mine. Amid my anguish, there was only room for what was happening to me.

A kind of verbal PTSD (Post-Traumatic Stress Disorder) did not help me. When afflicted by word salad, the long hours spent listening to my mother filled my brain with her conversations when she was out of control. I would typically never have condoned having such dialogues in public. The R-rated part of my mother's uncontrolled conversation infected my brain with sentences highly uncharacteristic of the communication others expected from me. My paranoia convinced me that everybody else was talking in this way and that my degeneration into the obnoxious, and at times obscene, was a response to a new linguistic currency I believed had overtaken the world. What others were saying was far worse than my defensive response. Mixed in with the bad was a lot of well-expressed and perfectly acceptable oral and written behavior on my part. Unfortunately, most people who had contact with me during these dreadful phases did not consider that.

The above problems were made considerably worse by time boundaries and ordering disappearing during my psychosis. My brain registered time as a vast corridor full of randomly selected yet complete memories of everything I had experienced since I could remember. Once a doctor diagnosed me correctly and helped me find suitable medication, I learned to control these symptoms to the point where they did not spill over into my communication with others. Jodie was not so lucky as she refused to work with a doctor. She died, still reporting on her disarrayed thoughts.

We will speak of such matters again. Their importance merits their repetition.

28

Violence

By my mid-teens, I constantly felt under threat, and so did my parents.

It was not all unpleasant. I believe that, despite everything, my parent's relationship initiated in love, and neither of them was happy about the challenge the years brought. Yes, my father did not want marriage and children, but when they first met, he did want a loving relationship with my mother. My mother reciprocated these feelings, though her goals for their union weren't the same as my father's. Even after some of their worst fights and some of my father's attempts to leave us, I sensed both were reluctant to entirely give up hope on their love. In my teens, I read Oscar Wilde's poem, *The*

Ballad of Reading Gaol, and it reminded me of my parents, especially its famous passage:

> *Yet each man kills the thing he loves*
> *By each let this be heard.*
> *Some do it with a bitter look,*
> *Some with a flattering word.*
> *The coward does it with a kiss,*
> *The brave man with a sword!*

What was so constantly subtle about our situation was that we all loved each other after a fashion and found ways to express it even during the worst times. First, there was our shared joy from nature. We had a television in Clareville and shared our enjoyment of our favorite shows. Later in her life, when she didn't go out much, my mother watched as many classic movies with me as we could. We loved them, identified with some of the characters, and would be them for part of the day, which amused us both.

As a teen, it was hard to understand why a moment of affection could turn so quickly into antagonism. I had no idea how to control the changing winds. I was always frightened. My father could see his life ebbing away and felt threatened by time. My mother felt threatened by my father and the slipping of her reality into something terrifying.

During all this time, my father had secret friendships outside the home. My mother suspected it and was extremely jealous and hurt, but it did help my father feel less alone and marooned in a marriage going downward.

During the last two of my high school years, Dalaigh's threatening behavior towards my mother and me, which downgraded to physical violence more frequently than before, became harrowing.

I had my bedroom, which housed my study, right next to my parent's bedroom. They spent most of the day my father wasn't at work arguing viciously with each other. He wanted to end the relationship and was making it plain with total savagery in his language, physical threats, and occasional blows. He gave me an even bigger dose than he gave Jodie. Every time I tried to do my school work, he would come into my study with his hand raised over me and my desk, blaming me yet again for existing. Without my birth, my mother would never have returned from Adelaide. I had grown up to be a strong defender of my mother, though I tried to give Dalaigh some affection when we were alone. Being alone with Dalaigh at this point gave no room for niceties. He was frightening, and he repeatedly and convincingly threatened to kill me. This situation lasted for about two years, the second year being the most traumatic. It was my last year of high school.

Fortunately, my situation at school improved. During the last two years, the teasing stopped. Many students became more studious as they wanted good grades to qualify for university. With my elephant memory and years of overwork, I was an ideal source of answers to tricky homework questions. I had also learned to be less of a nerd. I tried to meet the other students halfway, and it was working. I had a few close friends who knew my situation at home, even though I could no longer entertain them there. I at least had someone to talk to about my problems. My schoolwork didn't suffer too much because of the domestic situation. I was well ahead of the curriculum and still managed to escape from home occasionally and use the closest public library, the big one in the city being too far away for someone in a rush.

The school gave me a lot. The beauty of Shakespeare's plays, the novel *How Green Was My Valley*, whose memory and re-reading prompted me to take up Welsh at sixty. It's a beautiful language. Then, there were the mathematics and science classes in which I excelled, especially in mathematics. Mathematics is something I could study while my parents were asleep, and I would know the correct answer to a mathematical problem keeps that status forever, in contrast to applied science where even the most ingenious model aimed at explaining reality can be toppled by a new experimental result. Mathematics made a world of common sense for me that didn't change. I still dabble in amateur mathematics, solving problems for my pleasure. Without school and the new small circle of friends I had made, life would have been even worse. At home, I was miserable and scared almost out of my wits. What wits remained were given over to learning.

29

Police

My father began bruising my mother, not only from blows in their bedroom. On some occasions, he tried to move her out into the street and lock the door with the same anger and frustration with which he threw me across a room when I was three. Ironically, the person suffering the least from our situation was Dalaigh. My mother was mentally ill, though we didn't have a correct diagnosis. I was Dalaigh's other target while trying to continue to be my mother's caregiver.

However, that analysis forgets feelings. We cannot help our emotions, and Dalaigh felt the worst of us three. He was getting older. He wanted some life away from my mother and me. I had teamed up with my mother, something Dalaigh could not forgive.

After a particularly violent and alarming attack on Jodie by Dalaigh, my mother begged me to call the police. I hesitated, but then, seeing how frightened she was, I complied. I called the police and told them my father was beating my mother. They turned up reasonably rapidly, but their visit was a disappointment. They told me that they didn't usually interfere with domestic arguments. At least, that was the policy back then. They advised me to get a boyfriend and move out, which had no relevance to anything I was able or willing to do. Then, they left.

My father felt that not even the police would help us and became more violent and menacing. I called the police a second time. This time they arrested my father.

My mother and I turned up for the hearing in court the next day. The judge told my father he would let him off this time with no punishment, but he had to learn to keep his hands to himself.

On the way home with Dalaigh, my mother and I had to laugh at what he said to us, despite everything. The first thing out of his mouth wasn't an apology or an accusation that we had been unfair to him. Instead, he complained, "All they gave me for supper was a sandwich!" He then said, "The night in jail means I can never be a taxi driver or a politician," and he repeated that about five times. These were two careers he had no desire to pursue!

The effect on Dalaigh of appearing before the judge was to stop hurting my mother but to step up the brutal campaign against me when my mother wasn't within earshot. He seemed to understand that I wouldn't call the police again, as they would do nothing to solve the situation satisfactorily. The threats of violence, especially when I was in my bedroom, became incessant, and he also terrified me in the kitchen. I was the only person preparing meals at that stage.

This violent chapter of our lives subjected my mother to severe stress and rejection. It accelerated the progress of her mental health problems as parts of her inward paranoia were relatively well-matched with her reality.

30

Sarah: Knife

It had become too much. The nightmares of my pre-teen years were coming true now I was seventeen. My mother demanded and got my total allegiance. It took an enormous amount of effort and time to help her with her struggling mental health and to try to protect her from my father. I was showing signs of cracking up, from loss of appetite to excruciating back pain. I badly wanted to graduate from my final year of high school. I began working through the night while my parents were asleep.

It had become too much for Dalaigh, also. He genuinely wanted me out of the way so he could dispense with my mother in one way or another without me supporting her. He had talked about having her admitted to a mental hospital, leaving her and changing his name, or simply taking her somewhere far away and dumping her on the roadside to give him time to pack and leave.

A few years before, he had called the police on my mother while I wasn't there, and they sent her to a mental hospital. No doctor in that mental facility gave the correct diagnosis of paranoid schizophrenia for my mother's mental health problems. She never went through a formal committal process. She was put under observation and was out in two weeks. When they sent her home, I looked after her. Ironically, the police had no qualms about starting possible committal for my mother but only, after two calls, confined my father in jail for a night.

After the jail episode, Dalaigh stepped up his repeated campaign of telling me he never wanted me and that I was someone else's daughter. He began harassing me even more frequently with his raised hand and repeated threats of murder. He petrified me. Sometimes he would hit me, and I never knew when to expect it, as so much of his bullying was threats. The threats did more harm than the hits. I came to believe that his control was weakening fast. I sensed, and correctly so, that I was in dire danger.

One day, I was in the kitchen carving some cooked roast beef. My father entered the room with an ashen face and seething with anger. Even given all that had gone before, I barely recognized him. He was on the other side of the kitchen table from me. He told me, "This time, I mean it. I am going to kill you." He started to move around the table with his arms outstretched. I presumed he wanted to strangle me. I blacked out for a second. When I could see him again, he was closer. Instinctively, I threw the carving knife I held in my right hand at his feet in a move to scare him but not hurt him. I misfired but succeeded in getting him to back off. The knife had landed in a fleshy part of one of his lower legs.

To hurt him more than intended upset me, but I was grateful to see that the wound looked pretty harmless. I was relieved that my action had the desired effect of making him think twice about killing me right then.

My father was not angry. He was pleased he had broken down my control, that I had done something over which he could shame me. Instead, he looked victorious that he had finally impressed upon me that our situation was life and death.

Death was the perfect solution in his mind for my mother and me.

He went to a doctor, who told him the wound I inflicted was minor, would soon heal, and would leave no permanent damage, not even much of a scar. I was relieved, which irked my father as he wanted me to be more shaken.

After the knife incident, Dalaigh didn't hit either my mother or me again, and there were no more threats of violence. There were, however, terrible fights between my parents. Dalaigh was determined this time to leave for good. He was depriving my mother of all hope of reconciliation.

31

Divorce

In 1974, the year I turned seventeen, Dalaigh left my mother and me and, with surprising swiftness, sued for divorce. My mother didn't contest. They divided their modest possessions equally. My father never sent any alimony, and after the divorce went through, we never saw him again.

My mother did act on her threat to cause him to lose his job. She rang the department store where he worked at the time and told them my father had been having an affair with one of the female staff. She heard back from the store that they fired him. This action by my mother seemed neither fair nor justified to me. I understood the why, but somehow I remained disappointed in my mother.

I decided then and there never to try to find my father again. He could always look up my telephone number if he wanted to see me. I did not attempt to disguise either myself or my whereabouts. Though he didn't have a mental illness, my father had become deranged due to years of a life that brought no reliable happiness, despite some periods when our relationships worked better.

It was not only the build-up to the knife incident that spelled danger. A few weeks before, I was alone in the house and received an obscene phone call. I picked up the phone to hear a man's voice, "I am going to come over to your house and force you to have sex with me to show you what you're missing!" The voice repeated the threat about three times before I put down the phone. I was afraid and felt sick to my stomach. My instinct was to go out, locking the house behind me, and find a place where there were plenty of people. While trying to calm down by drinking some sweet tea in a crowded cafe, I realized the voice on the phone was my father's. I knew something about the call was creepy, over and above its threat! The realization made me even more concerned for my father's sanity and any future for my mother and me with him.

Sometimes you have to close the door on a relationship, even if it is one in the immediate family. I would make sure I was easy to find, so my door was ajar, but I suspect my father took steps to lock his door firmly by making it a headache to track him down. I wasn't upset at the loss of Dalaigh. It was a question of mutual survival.

The following year I turned eighteen. It was an eventful year for everyone in Australia due to the so-called 1975 *Australian constitutional crisis*. My mother supported the center-left-wing Australian Labor Party and, after a continuous period of twenty-three years under conservative rule, was excited to see, in 1972, the Labor Party, with the charismatic Edward Gough Whitlam at its head, finally win an election. However, on the eleventh of November 1975, the party and Prime Minister Whitlam were dismissed from office by Governor-General Sir John Kerr. In Australia, the Governor-General is the representative of the British

Queen or King and has certain constitutional powers. After dismissing the Australian Labor Party, Kerr commissioned the Leader of the Opposition, Malcolm Fraser of the Liberal Party, as Prime Minister. Despite its name, the Australian Liberal Party is a center-right-wing party. Depending on how you voted, many people viewed the parties they didn't vote for as either far-left or far-right. The reasons for the dismissal were complex. In the end, the chain of events ended in an election with a landslide victory for the Liberal-Country Party under Fraser. The Country Party (now called The National Party of Australia) was more to the right than the Liberals.

Historians debate the 1975 Australian Constitutional Crisis to this day. It's a huge topic. The reason given was that the Governor-General sacked Whitlam for refusing to resign or to advise an election after failing to obtain Supply, also known as an Appropriation Bill, that authorizes certain expenditures by the government. Most people, especially Labor voters, were shocked, as the dismissal happened so quickly and was unlike anything

Australians had seen before. For many, it ended an exciting period under Whitlam redressing some of the balance after twenty-three years of conservative rule.

I was proud of how my mother handled this crisis. She didn't go overboard or try to see herself as part of what happened. She was reeling from the divorce and had been so happy that Labor was in power, yet she managed these setbacks well. She would never have admitted it, but she felt relieved to have Dalaigh out of the home and viewed the constitutional crisis as something much more important than her problems. Jodie, the dancer, was making an appearance, even if only for a limited time.

32

Bedridden

My mother suffered, and I suffer, from epileptic absence seizures, usually caused by stress. However, there are other triggers, like lack of air. We both took the same medication for it. Nothing in our shared epileptic condition called for extensive bed rest. However, after the divorce from my father, my mother, on most days, stayed in bed. She justified this change by convincing herself that her epilepsy was worsening rapidly. If someone had exchanged the word epilepsy for schizophrenia, that would have been helpful. However, despite talking about my mother to several psychologists, none helped me with advice as to how to convince my mother to let go of her convenient fantasy about epilepsy. They put her suffering down to a lousy marriage, probably with depression. They did not suggest any medication over and above what she already took for seizures.

My mother's daydreams from her youth were in danger of fading into nothing. She was, in any case, losing her grip on reality. She needed to work extra hard on fabricating a personal world more sympathetic to her. She needed me to follow her verbal explanations so that they had an existence also outside of her. Her bed was a safe zone where she only had me to contend with and where she could hide her myriad of internal problems under the blanket of her epilepsy.

During this time, my mother and I shared our love of classic movies, watching them on TV rather than venturing out to the cinema. Before my mother took to her bed, she insisted I accompany her to cinemas in Sydney showing foreign movies. I sat through many movies by the Swedish film director Ingmar Bergman. There was no way my father would join us to watch what he deemed pretentious art. I did enjoy the movies and have watched them many times since. I was the only student taking advanced French in the last two years of high school. My teacher recommended French movies playing in cinemas so I could hear the language I was learning. That meant a lot of films by François Truffaut. Movies would be a significant resource for me during my relapses. The ability to escape and live in a movie to good effect was common when I struggled.

One of Bergman's films that helped me understand my parents was his 1973 *Scenes from a Marriage*, about the dissolution of a seemingly ideal relationship between a husband and wife. Bergman's films pull no punches, and I saw behavior that compared closely to some of my parents'. The scene "The Illiterates (Analfabeterna)" from the movie is especially chilling, as it shows two outwardly-cultivated parties descending into physical violence. It struck me how alike this portrayal was to some of my parents' arguments, which suddenly went from a discussion to blows. His 1957 film *The Seventh Seal*, set in the Middle Ages during the Plague, is about a knight playing chess with an ambassador of death. It invoked, when I saw it in my middle teens, the bad dream I had at eleven about the face of death. The movie made me feel less alone with this nightmare. I felt that its characters would understand how I felt.

Soon after my father left us, I went to see, alone, the 1976 film *The Tenant* by Roman Polanski. It concerns a timid schizophrenic living in a studio in Paris who loses his identity and adopts one from the previous tenant, a young woman who committed suicide. My mother's schizophrenia, as it was then, didn't match the film well, so I failed to link Polanski's hero and my mother. Yet, it's chilling how close some scenes in the movie match symptoms I would have many years later.

Despite the state of the union at home, I did exceptionally well in my final year of high school. I was the *Dux of the Year*, the best student in my graduating year. I was among the top fifty students in New South Wales in the standardized physics exam. My teachers assumed I would go on to university. I applied to the University of Sydney for the science program there, and they accepted me.

However, I couldn't ignore the time and effort I needed to help my mother. No doctor with whom I had discussed her mental health had been able to tell me what was wrong with her. At seventeen, my age at the end of the final year of high school, I didn't know. I thought my mother's problems were unique and rooted in some traumas from her childhood. I knew she was a rare individual and loved many parts of her uniqueness, but the years ahead would not be pretty. The teachers I talked to the most about my situation at home told me, "To become a successful professional, you need to ditch your mother." These teachers knew my mother was unstable and consuming most of my time.

I knew they were right, and I loved my studies. However, morally, as my mother had no one else, I felt the correct choice for me was to forget university and remain her caregiver. What other path was there? I couldn't just leave my mother on the side of the road, as my father had dreamed about doing. I loved her too much to do such a thing. It was, in any case, a wicked thing to do to anyone. As Beth had told me by then in her letters, "Follow your conscience."

One of my favorite assigned novels at school was *How Green Was My Valley* by Richard Llewellyn. As a young teenager, Huw, the main character, has to choose between being a scholar and going down the colliery like his brothers and father. His father wants him to use his sharp intellect to go "in the law or doctoring or something good." Huw says, "I will go down the colliery with you... No examination and no doctoring and no law." He selects the colliery to remain close to his family and to do what his parents raised him to view as honest work in which to take pride. I identified with Huw, which helped me decide to ditch university for my mother.

There is no reason that someone living with paranoid schizophrenia, with the appropriate education, an excellent medical team, and a supportive family behind them, shouldn't go to university. They could make a brilliant professional career if their schizophrenia stays manageable and they get the same breaks every person needs to succeed. However, that doesn't mention the differences in the situation, personality, philosophy, and degree of ill health of the person with this brain disorder. It also doesn't allow for someone who is a caregiver for a mentally ill person, without any support at home, and has begun to show symptoms of their own.

By the time my mother was bedridden, it was clear that there was something different about me, just as there had been about my mother for many years. I failed to recognize, until many years later, the similarity of our mental illnesses. That was in part due to the failure of doctors to diagnose both my mother and me correctly until my mother's last years and until I was about forty. It also measured how different two people with paranoid schizophrenia can be. A correct diagnosis can be the beginning of a journey to better health if it is accepted and taken seriously. However, it cannot predict every aspect of the evolution of different individuals with that diagnosis. There were never two people more unlike each other than my mother and me.

33

Job

As we had no alimony from Dalaigh, just a small nest egg from Jodie's half of the divorce settlement, I had to work. My overriding problem was finding a job that would allow me to be a decent caregiver for my mother. I told her that the government benefits due to her divorce with no alimony were insufficient to rent a small apartment and feed us. She had to accept being alone for some part of every weekday while I went to work.

Jodie and Dalaigh split the money equally from selling the house they owned in Clareville. Jodie and I wanted to keep some of our share of the money unspent for emergencies. Over time, most of that money went to my mother's needs. I was glad we had saved it for what turned out to be many rainy days. So, we needed a place we could rent cheaply. We found a pleasant studio for the two of us at Dee Why, a suburb of Sydney. The studio's building offered larger apartments also, but we couldn't afford them. We were fortunate to find this studio as it was within walking distance to Dee Why beach. My mother and I loved the water, so the open spaces of the nearby beach and its clifftops overlooking the ocean more than counterbalanced the tiny proportions of our studio.

I decided the best option for earning a salary was a part-time job that would reduce Jodie's hours alone. The logical avenue was to find a job my excellent high school grades merited. Still, I wanted a position that occupied a small mental space. I had not only my mother's problems to contend with but also a growing confusion in my abstract thoughts. I did consult doctors, but they put my problems down to my parents' stormy marriage and didn't recommend medication for my nascent issues.

I found a job as a part-time assistant for a real estate agency in Dee Why, close to our studio. The job was mainly filing, window dressing, coffee brewing, and so on. I self-taught myself accounting, so I was able to help with their financial records. I worked from 12:00 pm to 4:00 pm, Monday through Friday. I could get my mother's day off to a good start, leave her to go to work, and still have time to see, with her, the beach before sunset. The job paid more than we needed when combined with my mother's government assistance. It was enough to keep our heads above water. It turned out that I was well suited to this employment, and I enjoyed it.

Neither my mother nor I owned a car. My mother had learned to drive, and my parents had a car for most of their marriage. My father took the car when he left for good, and we didn't fight to get it back or get half of it, whatever that would have meant. I never learned to drive. Sydney's public transport system was enough for me, and it was inexpensive. Now that we were near a beach, we had a place to relax within walking distance.

34

Sarah: Thirty-Eight

At thirty-eight, I was still living in the small studio in Sydney that I had rented with my mother in the suburb Dee Why. I survived on unemployment benefits. I applied for jobs but was unsuccessful due to my lousy record with my only previous employer. Having lost the same job twice, I had no valuable references. Also, even without a correct diagnosis, I knew something was wrong with me. Although I was still primarily intelligent, I had periods with poor cognitive and executive skills and difficulties perceiving people. I had found that I had enough money to live frugally. The lifestyle suited me. I could navigate my problems in relative privacy and be content with a simple life.

I lived in the shadow of the relapse that began when I was thirty-five. However, my symptoms had been manageable for a *good part of the previous year. I still wrote to Beth and Lucas. I had remained friends with Enoch. We were even going together to concerts and museums again. Enoch shared his partners with me on these outings but never seemed to keep his boyfriends for long. That baffled me, as he was such a kind, sweet, and exciting person.*

Despite the alarming mental health of my thirties, I managed a few sexual partners. My mother had been the main obstacle to my friendships when we lived together. Now, my mental health issues were the main problem. When I was deep into a relapse, I avoided having sexual relationships. Those I did have belonged to the periods between relapses when I was reasonably stable. They only lasted a few months as I did not want to get too close to anybody. The periods of bad mental health made me afraid of long-term intimacy, as I was sure my boyfriend would dump me as soon as I was in trouble. Emotionally, I wasn't geared up for a long relationship anyway.

I developed casual friendships, aside from Enoch, during the past year when my symptoms were manageable. I volunteered at a nearby pet rescue center. Being around animals aided me a great deal emotionally. The team there was happy to have someone extra to help. There were six volunteers. I sometimes ate out with some rescue center people and enjoyed the experience. I joined a bible study group. It was non-denominational, and we covered the Old and New Testaments. There were about twenty in the group. Again, I would sometimes go to a restaurant with some of the members.

And then, suddenly, I had the worst relapse and psychotic break of my lifetime at thirty-eight. It eradicated my equilibrium. Preceding the regression, I had been deeply upset by the spread of large wildfires in New South Wales, the state where I lived, and their effect on wildlife. Like many others, I was beside myself with worry, and perhaps the strain of the long period for which the fires burned was too much stress.

I still did not know I had paranoid schizophrenia. The doctors I consulted most recently said that my complex family experiences had given rise to permanent trauma and that I was consequently depressed. Severe depression can lead to psychosis. Although the diagnosis of PTSD (Post-Traumatic Stress Disorder) from childhood experiences was valid and weighed heavily on my mental health, I was never depressed.

One of these doctors prescribed an antidepressant and a tranquilizer. I had a bad experience with both. Viewing the tranquilizer as the least essential drug, I went cold turkey, only to find the withdrawal devastating. It was like having horrible flu. I kept taking the antidepressant. I found it interfered with my appetite and began losing weight, something I could not afford at the time. I also found it interfered with my sexual reactions. I worried that this side effect might be permanent and that the drug would snuff out this natural part of my life. When I asked my doctor for help with this problem, he replied, "There's nothing I can do about that." Soon after he made this remark, I dropped the antidepressant as well. It wasn't helping my symptoms and only seemed to introduce new ones.

The persistent failure of the medical profession to find the source of my mental health problems and, when pressed, to opt for depression was partly due to their lack of competence. At the same time, part of the problem was my attitude. Despite the extensive exposure to paranoid schizophrenia through my mother, who eventually received the correct diagnosis, I persisted in anosognosia, not recognizing that I had related problems. When I met with doctors, I tended to want to perform *well, as, deep down, I felt no one would understand what I was going through. I thought I might be confined to a mental institution if I confided too much, even though I was confident I could continue to look after myself at home. I put on a good show, which didn't help my doctors or me find the truth. Another factor preventing me from understanding my mental illness was that, in its early stages, I experienced it differently from my mother. I tried to internalize most of it. In contrast, my mother had always been vocal to everyone who would listen about precisely what she was experiencing.*

Some of my composure now broke down. My linguistic control was considerably weaker this time compared to the period of the former relapses. I finally began to say to people precisely what I was thinking. At times, there was no meaning to what I was saying, and at others, I was downright offensive or scary. I know that's how others perceived me, as they told me. My paranoia developed into a blanket that covered everyone. I asked no one for help, not even Enoch or Beth.

I resigned as a volunteer at the pet rescue center, convinced I wasn't wanted and would only get into trouble there. It was a great pity as I missed the animals. I also left the bible study group for similar reasons. I did not want a repeat of the rejection I had suffered from Amelia of the real estate agency and Meredith of the book club when I was thirty-one.

One of my worst recurrent symptoms this time around was retrospective paranoia. I seemed to suffer at a much deeper level than my mother and I had during my previous relapses. It's a dreadful process, your mind returning to its earliest memories and rethinking everything you thought was valid. Meanwhile, you battle presumed thought insertion by those who want you dead or mad and confined. The fact that many people react to severe mental illness with repulsion doesn't help. Do they know they could push someone to suicide that way, someone way more fragile than me? There is an elevated risk of suicide among people who live with schizophrenia.

I felt that my head was turned inside out by my mental illness. My thoughts became exposed along with all my history. I was terrified to see that my nightmares, especially the one I had at eleven about the vast face of death, were being played out in public. Every time I saw a stop sign on the road, I thought it was that face, and I looked left, seeking hope, as I did in that nightmare. It's fortunate that I never owned a car and that I kept enough wits about me to obey the traffic lights for pedestrians. The word "car" means "because" in French, a language I had learned in high school. When I saw a car on the road, I often associated it with the word "because," and usually a negative connotation, like "you are in this mess 'because' you are not welcome on Earth." Experiences like this problem with cars led me to seek solitude and go outside my studio only as necessary.

When I feel pushed toward death by everyone's judgment, I go back to my dream about death at eleven. I face death down. I may not be able to move from having it straight in front of me, but I can, with a lot of effort, not move any closer to it.

As the linguistic and time boundaries evaporated, I descended into a global paranoia that not only affected my present, but also my interpretation of my past. The doctors were correct that part of the process was PTSD from my childhood. The episode where I threw a knife at my father at seventeen came back to haunt me, as did his constant bullying of me in my bedroom office. Although I didn't feel driven to leave my studio, I was terrified there and couldn't even touch a knife when I needed one to eat. I feared the knife would leave my hand and stab me in revenge on behalf of Dalaigh.

I felt like I was suffering total recall of all conversations I had overheard since I was three. Indeed, I must have forgotten many, but the feeling was that I couldn't forget anything, and it was terrifying. It was as if the long fight I had waged against my parents' problems had been a useless effort. The world was reducing me to nothing, with all my achievements going out the window. There were no "better times" that I could look back on to gain confidence. What I thought were positive periods of my life were simply part of a chronic failure everyone recognized.

I suffered all the sensory problems of the previous relapses. People's faces would change shape or melt as I looked at them. I again heard people talking about me at home, primarily via my ceiling. This phenomenon was incredibly eerie as my studio had no attic and was not on the top floor. Yet, the conversations seemed to come from an attic that didn't exist. This roof or attic had sound effects that commented on my thoughts, pushing me toward some surrender. I knew by now that leaving my home didn't help, so I lay as low as possible and tried to work on not saying what I honestly thought when I was in contact with others.

Being stuck within the symptoms is like having a tremendous amount to do but being bored nonetheless. The sheer onslaught of sensory and cognitive delusions means you fight all day to stay in some place of relative peace but often fail to do so. The same paranoid thoughts turn over and over again in your mind for days, even weeks. There is a great deal of repetition in your experiences. I needed to repeatedly use the small arsenal of escape tools, like listening to music, usually favoring a small collection of the things I like best. Though that gives considerable relief and, in my case, is powerful, it's not a cure. My illness would be much worse without music, humor, classic films, walking, and other interests. On their own, they are not enough to stop the symptoms.

Not every thought during this time was delusional. Some of the time, what I thought was quite reasonable, except that I experienced too many choices of possible reality going forward, making decisions extremely difficult. When I tried to put together some way forward, I chose a hodge-podge of pieces of *harmless facts that nonetheless usually ultimately failed to be valuable and desirable.*

In relapse, it's not like happy versus sad. It's more meaningful versus nonsense. I did a lot of laughing, or more like giggling, at abstract thoughts I found funny but worrisome. On looking back, they were maybe alarming, but not funny at all. My disordered linguistic thoughts often gave rise to such personal comedy. Or, it could be a song that suddenly acquired a dissociated meaning. Some more severe worries usually underwrote the inappropriate behavior. For example, I may see something about the energy measurement TWH (TeraWatt-Hours). Then if I, shortly after, see someone wearing TWH=The White Hat and find the coincidence of the two acronyms significant, I nervously giggle. The person wearing a white hat has no idea why I am laughing. Yet, in my mind, I suspect the coincidence is part of the drive to eradicate me, and the best weapon I could bring to bear against it is humor. That would not occur to me if I weren't sick. As another example, I may run the chilling, frightening, fascist song "Tomorrow belongs to me" through my head. It's from the 1972 film "Cabaret," set in pre-WWII Germany. I may giggle with this song as a backdrop each time I think of someone who has rejected me with force due to my problems, as this reaction seems fascist to me at the time. Of course, the label "fascist" is too strong, not for the song, but someone, "ignorant," or "confused," being more appropriate.

Sometimes, the underlying "melody" in my head was a memory I was pleased to recall during these relapses where it was impossible to forget anything. One time, I suddenly remembered the melody of the music box for jewels that my father gave to my mother early in their marriage. That would cement my assumption that not everything that passed between my parents downgraded to war. Much of it could have upgraded to peace had they understood each other better. Such improvements may not have saved their marriage, but they would have made them both feel that they achieved more in their lives than they seemed to judge. In any case, I could do my bit to reflect for them on the better parts of their relationship.

Implementing any strategy to fight my symptoms was made much more difficult by my inability to focus. I was incredibly distracted by paranoia, thought insertion, sensory perturbations, and trying to do the minimum to keep out of trouble. There was time only for surviving from day to day. The simplicity of my life helped tremendously. I shopped weekly, paid bills, and avoided all social situations. I talked aloud a great deal at home, often having heated conversations with myself. One-sided discussions were going on in my head, so reserving the right to respond helped me to feel as if I could eventually win over them. I was careful to keep the dialogue low in volume to avoid eviction from my studio.

The overriding emotion I felt was anger, not directed at an individual, but at the impression of rejection and the global wish, or so I thought, that I should eliminate myself. It reminded me of the poem "Do not go gentle into that good night" by Dylan Thomas, particularly the line "Rage, rage against the dying of the light." Just the fact that he wrote that line was a help to me. It expressed my will to live despite the evidence that I was the only one desiring that outcome.

Even though what I was going through was horrific, I didn't shed a tear. It would have been difficult for anyone to identify my emotions because this time around, apart from anger, I didn't seem to be able to express any. I experienced a vast array of latent emotions but couldn't unlock them to express myself.

How people reacted to my descent into madness did matter. I had tried to shelter myself from that reaction by leaving the animal rescue center and the bible study. Unfortunately, I did repeat the error I made at thirty-one of forgetting why I left these groups. I turned up at the animal shelter one day and told them outrightly some of the thoughts I was having. I said, "Rumors about me chasing after men who have no interest in me are totally false, as are expectations I will kill myself." I must have made a lot of other inappropriate comments as well since one of the volunteers told me to stop using offensive language. The volunteers at the center treated me kindly, despite the alarm I must have raised. They took me into the kitchen, made me hot, sweet tea, and gave me biscuits. They brought a few furry friends for me to hold. I started to calm down. "I'm sorry," I said and kept repeating the apology. "You don't need to be sorry," they kept reassuring me. One of the volunteers, Amanda, a woman about fifty years old with a generous figure and sympathetic face, tried to reason with me, "You've done nothing harmful," she explained, "but you are *clearly not in your right mind. We cannot have you coming here right now. Have you seen a shrink? Do you have a relative we could contact?"* I remember saying, *"That's a 'no' on both counts and is likely to stay a 'no'! I am not killing myself!"* Amanda then asked her co-volunteers, *"Do you think we should call the police, or an ambulance?"* I thought to myself, not the police! *"I will be OK. I am leaving,"* I said. Amanda offered, *"This is my phone number, and you have the phone number of the shelter. Please, as soon as you get home, call me, so we know you are OK."* I left and went straight home. I called Amanda, *"Thank you, Amanda, for helping me to calm down. I feel better now I am back home. Please don't worry about me."* Amanda replied, *"You can always call me if you need to talk. Please don't show up at the shelter until you are doing considerably better." "I won't,"* I promised. I looked back on what had just happened at the shelter, and the kindness shown did make an impact. It reinforced what I knew. I had to dig my way out of the misunderstandings caused by my current verbal communication, or I would be in conflict even with such lovely people as those at the shelter. I did not return to the bible study *group, which prevented a similar situation with them. I had the bible at home, and I didn't want to upset more people.*

Amid this fatiguing confusion of my senses and the prospect of total rejection by everyone, I decided that the most crucial goal was improving my home environment. Your home is your sanctuary. To make it more so, I had to cut myself off from others, except for necessary shopping, communications for paying bills, bringing in my mail, and the like. When you relapse, your executive skills are poor. Still, I always managed to do the bare necessities, which were not many in my simple life. I rested a good deal. Sleep often escaped me, but putting my feet up and letting my favorite music wash over me was beneficial. It helped me feel less afraid and diverted my thought processes to something beautiful. As I began to feel a little better, I watched movies and read books. I gradually strengthened my cognitive skills, so beaten about by the onslaught of this downturn in my health.

Ever since I was a child, I have experienced the feeling of "evaporating" from within and a different personality filling the vacant space inside me. The new person was usually a fictional character who interested me at the moment. It may be a role from a film or a novel I read. I was never curious about the private lives of successful artists, but the ability to act as part of the fiction they created was something that became a tool when the real me was in trouble. If I had to leave my home to go to the bank, for example, I often became someone else from within who could cope with the task at hand. Sometimes, these fake personalities became overwhelming, which was a signal to stay home until more of me returned. As a child, I used to amuse my family with impersonations of various well-known people. My parents didn't realize this was not playing but rather getting someone out of my system.

People living with schizophrenia have to deal with delusions, but how this dissociation from reality occurs can be subtle. In my case, a good part of the wrong ideas I harbor during a relapse comes from losing the ability to filter reality. I go into sensory and mental overload, and the attempt to sort out this overdose of honest truths competing for my attention can cause me to reason falsely. In other words, too much reality can make me delusional.

Losing your delusions can be distressing when your path finally begins to lead to better mental health. After all, your disordered delusions are your new reality when you experience a psychotic break. Once I am able, the response is to try to behave as well as I can toward others, despite what I am thinking. Not all delusions are disagreeable, although those don't last long for me. These thoughts with "news that's too good to be true" have a walk-on part, but they can be temporarily comforting. After all, the bad news is that you shouldn't have existed in the first place. Indeed, suppose you are trying to help someone struggling with schizophrenia. In that case, an aggressive, head-on attack on their false reality can be damaging. What they need more than anything is kindness, comfort, and, if possible, a hands-off reaction to whatever they may say that appears weird to you. Your "weird" is their temporary "sane," and they may view you as the one needing mental health support. Only trained and competent psychologists and psychiatrists can safely help the person with schizophrenia find a way to better mental health. The best help an untrained person can provide is a stress-free peaceful environment in which better mental health can grow without fear and rejection. Some mental health support groups offer a social setting with suitably trained people who can immensely support someone struggling with mental health. Sometimes they also provide support groups for caregivers.

35

Remissions

The evolution of my mother's psychiatric problems was fairly unremitting. However, throughout her life, there were remissions of one day, several days, or even a few months when she seemed happy and functioned well. At those times, the mother of my childhood was back with all her intelligence, sensitivity, and humor. She was affectionate with me, and we shared our love of music, films, books, and walking in nature. She never let go of her delusions and idolization of her father. However, they were in the background, resting, while she enjoyed being herself at her best. These remissions kept us both going, giving us some relief from her psychosis.

She insisted on being the dominant personality, which had nothing to do with her schizophrenia but was just part of her character. Her father had dominated her, and I guess she liked that parental image. I had a high opinion of my mother that never faltered because I knew how kind, generous, clever, and cultivated she could be. She was, at the base, a decent person who loved me with deep conviction. My mother didn't consciously engage in one-upmanship. She loved simple people and made fun of any pretension. I did feel second best to her, but I admired her so much this qualified as a worthy self-judgment.

We didn't have a car once Dalaigh left, so during these better times, we would rent a car on a few occasions, and my mother would drive. She drove well, and I couldn't take over as I had never learned to drive. The activity that most pleased us during these remissions was exploring the natural beauty of the coast of New South Wales and its national parks.

Our favorite one-day trip was visiting Ku-ring-gai Chase. It's a national park about 15 miles from the city center of Sydney. Its most notable feature is the view from the West Head outlook, with spectacular coastal vistas. You can see Broken Bay, Pittwater and Barrenjoey Headland, and Lighthouse. There is a walking path with Aboriginal rock art and carvings. You can also enjoy incredible sights across the Hawkesbury River to Lion Island, which, predictably, is a small island that looks like a lion.

In my thirties, I discovered recordings of aboriginal music recorded at their ceremonies, some of which are called corroborees, which may be ritual or social. Their famous instrument, the didgeridoo, is incredibly flexible in how it sounds and what it conveys to the senses. The aboriginal people believe they are part of the land they live in, and their primal passion for Australia comes across in their music. It sends shivers down the spine at times. It makes me feel guilty about what the British colonials enthusiastically did to try to snuff out the aboriginal culture.

Like my mother, I have always loved large bodies of water, like rivers and oceans. The tryst between the sky and the sea means the views constantly change. One day, a glistening blue almost hurts the eyes, another a dark blue seems home to all humanity's sympathy. The land was magnificent in its different ways. Eucalyptus trees were everywhere when you turned away from the water. When you turned back, there was a wonderful land versus water montage.

My mother loved the aboriginal art that sometimes graced these walks in nature. Australia was brutally racist back then; the aboriginal population had suffered genocide and disrespect throughout Australia's history. My mother made me ashamed of this history as a white person living in Australia . That's how I felt. For example, the anti-aboriginal feeling was strong in Mudgee, where we lived for a while. One day I invited a boy from school to tea at our home. He turned up but refused to come inside. My mother went to the door to see why he was so shy. He was a good-looking boy and trying to encourage him, my mother said, "That's a gorgeous suntan you have," The boy replied," I've always had this suntan. My mother is aboriginal." My mother reassured him that we welcomed him. He came inside, and my mother gave him a fabulous tea party as only she could have given him; she was so wise and sensitive back when I was seven.

My mother lit up outdoors during the breaks from her symptoms. She often said, "I can't imagine anyone born in Australia who could bear to leave its natural beauty." My answers varied depending on my mother's mood. "Well, we are lucky. Despite being relatively poor, we can still find the time and money to visit these beautiful spots, and what's more, they are within reach. Not every person in Australia is so blessed." "That's true," she often replied," also, there are cultural limitations here compared with what Europe and America have to offer." I would reassure her: "Australia will catch up in its way. There's no point in reproducing other countries' cultural scenes in our gorgeously unique nation."

Our biggest holiday adventure was a trip to a rented vacation home in Pearl Beach, where we stayed for a week. Pearl Beach is about 60 miles from Sydney. You can see Lion Island from there, also. We lived near Dee Why beach, but a trip to another beautiful beach seemed like the best vacation, so much we loved that setting.

At Pearl Beach, my mother rapidly got involved with a man next door called Peter. Peter was most pushy, introducing himself within five minutes of our arrival and flattering my mother. He was about fifty, as was my mother. Dalaigh was out of the picture, and my mother was always receptive to kind comments about her looks. Though we were in Pearl Beach only for a week, that was long enough for a romance to form between Peter and Jodie and long enough for them to argue ferociously during the subsequent break-up.

Each day, once we'd finished enjoying the beach, we'd return home to make dinner. Peter would usually turn up at our door about an hour and a half after dinner when we were ready to choose a movie to watch on the TV in the rented accommodation. The first few days, we invited him inside, and my mother entertained him within my earshot, though I was watching TV with the volume low in another room and couldn't see them. "I just can't get over what a lovely couple you make," said

Peter. "There you are, mother and daughter, both slim and attractive, striving to make each other happy. I'd love a piece of that. Not Sarah; she's too young, but you're dynamite and about my age." My mother was reckless enough to appear flattered and drawn to Peter. After a few days, he began asking my mother to come to his place at what seemed like a late hour that may extend into a whole night. My mother loved leading men on to reassure herself that she was still attractive, but she hadn't lost her moral code, which dictated no one, or even several, night stands. That's how the arguments started. "What do you expect?" our neighbor asked. "I expect that you respect me," retorted my mother. "The sex is out as we've just met, and we're leaving soon, but we can still communicate intellectually." Peter was furious. "You've been leading me on," he shouted, "it's humiliating! We should get on with having sex, and the intellectual stuff, as you call it, is rubbish." I was in another room, where I was rooting for my mother. Let her give the guy a bloody nose for thinking of women as only something to bed. "Who do you think you are anyway," Peter yelled. "Get out," yelled my mother, "and don't come back. Adieu!" I was thinking, "That's telling the racist, male chauvinist pig where to go! I love you, Jodie, the dancer!"

Despite this backdrop, we enjoyed our vacation in Pearl Beach. It was almost as if the human drama was some play to amuse us when we were not at the beach. My mother was a match, always in danger of lighting! I have a fond memory of this holiday. It's all to do with sand and water and nothing to do with human conflict.

Since before Dalaigh left, my mother had turned the housework over to me. She knew how to run a house, despite the constraints during her marriage due to Dalaigh controlling the money. When I took over the housework, I followed my mother's home management techniques. Growing up, I appreciated that Jodie was immaculate. She washed the bath and shower daily. She kept the floors in the bathroom and kitchen spotless. We changed our sheets weekly and washed our towels every three days. We emptied the fridge and freezer once a fortnight and thoroughly scrubbed them. We cleaned our windows once a month. We discarded any food past its date of sale.

There were rarely leftovers. Growing up, if I did not finish my plate, my mother served me these remains at the next mealtime, and so on, until that plate was clean. My mother drummed into me that many children in the world were starving and that I could do my part by not putting undue pressure on the food supply. Closer to home, it was a way to convince my father we were trying to save money.

After Dalaigh left, and if we had a lean spell with money, I sometimes missed a meal to help our budget, but without my mother knowing it. I became good at this deception. I may have grown a little thinner during such a period, but I was healthy as I, all the same, had enough to eat.

During her remissions, Jodie often participated in the chores, usually taking on the jobs I didn't have time to do regularly. She would put on suntan lotion and a sun hat and enthusiastically neaten our modest garden on our studio porch. We decorated the patio with small cacti and succulents. They didn't need much care, but everything looked so neat and fresh after my mother gave them the once over. We never had alcohol in the house, except for the beer she bought to wash the leaves of some of our larger indoor plants.

When we arrived at our accommodation in Pearl Beach, after getting past Peter, the first thing my mother did was clean the entire house from top to toe. In earlier years, whenever we moved into a new home, she gave it the same treatment before she would let the moving men put anything inside.

Except at the very end of her life, my mother was strict about personal hygiene, which applied even when she wasn't in remission. I am similar. I can be drowned in paranoia and nonetheless register that I must shower daily and wash my hair once a week. My mother was more ambitious about her appearance when she was in remission. She went to hair salons, fussed about her clothes, put on makeup, and worried about keeping her figure.

In her mid-fifties, my mother suddenly lost confidence in her looks, a worry especially evident on her healthier days. By then, she had no one except me to reassure her that she was beautiful and trim. Many women who go into ballet emerge from it sensitive about their shapes. That was part of my mother's problem. However, the rest was a need for comfort, with only one person prepared to offer it, me. I remember us sitting on Dee Why beach when my mother was this age. She started to cry. When I asked her what was wrong, she replied, "Some women have trouble accepting the changes in their bodies as they grow old. I think I am going to be one of those women." "You'll always be beautiful," I would say. It's what I felt, and it seemed to cheer her up a bit. My mother's solitude, apart from me, was by then virtually total. The dreams of her youth were now only in her imagination and mine.

36

Acquaintances

My mother and I had difficulties maintaining friendships due to our mental health problems and my desire for solitude.

After I broke up with Chester, I didn't fall in love again with a view to marriage. I had several boyfriends in my twenties, some of which were sexual relationships that I enjoyed, and each lasted a few months. I had to keep them secret from Jodie; otherwise, she would have become jealous. I didn't want a repeat of what happened with Chester. Maintaining a relationship between my job and looking after my mother was challenging. I met the boyfriends I did have via Lucas and Enoch. They both acted as matchmakers by inviting the candidate to join us when I was on a date with them. It took resolve for me to have my first sexual encounter because of the deep-seated indoctrination from my mother that sex before marriage was a sin. I came to view my sexual encounters as a way of escaping some of my mother's grip on me, and I was correct. However, given the clandestine nature of the dates I had with these boyfriends and my refusal to confront my mother with news of them, the relationships were short-lived.

For all these difficulties, I was not unhappy about sex being relatively rare in my life. I enjoyed abstinence and found it easy to fight sexual frustration. It was sufficient for me to distract myself with one of my interests, and the need evaporated.

One legacy of my parent's story was that I never wanted to live in the same home as a partner. I knew living with someone else could bring deep love and a supportive companion, but if Jodie pre-deceased me, all I wanted was to live alone. Being a caregiver for my mother had been an all-enveloping experience, and I wanted to taste independence at home from everybody, even those I liked. I confided this decision in a letter to

Beth; she said she lived alone quite happily. She encouraged me to follow my instincts.

While my mother was alive, keeping any friends, even the most casual, required some skill. My mother tried to isolate me, and my bent for solitude made her job more manageable. Fortunately, I managed to keep my friendships with Lucas and Enoch. Lucas and I mainly saw each other immediately after work. After a date with Lucas, I told my mother I stayed behind to work with a friend for a few extra hours. That went well. Enoch found an answer which included my mother. When we went out together, Enoch would stop by our home before and after the date and spend some time talking to my mother about art. She loved these conversations and seemed to be comfortable around Enoch. It was so decent of him to visit her on both sides of our outings.

The other people I frequented before Jodie died were more acquaintances than friends, people my mother or I had met, for example, our neighbors, and who could deal kindly with my mother. These acquaintances were mainly women. Some of them were friends from the days

Jodie was in the ballet. In her fifties, my mother tracked them down. They renewed contact with her and accepted her state of mental health exceptionally well. They would visit from time to time and talk with Jodie about the topics that interested her and that she could still discuss coherently. The coherence would go near the end of my mother's life, as would the civility that made her pleasant to visit. These friends would telephone me for news of my mother but stopped visiting her. I would ensure they also talked to Jodie for a little while each time they called.

Less sympathetic were several relatively famous males my mother contacted starting in her fifties. She figured they would protect her from harm if she could reestablish a friendship with them. It was not so much "too big to fail" as "famous enough to give shelter." All these people knew Jodie, as they had all been part of that artistic circle she and Dalaigh frequented before their marriage and for a short time afterward. As they knew her, my mother usually succeeded in making an appointment to see them. The meetings were a disaster as she talked about her persecution by fascists and her importance as Feivel's daughter. These famous people were too busy and unsympathetic to want to see my mother a second time. After returning home from such an encounter, she would tell me that the person she had visited was part of the plot to kill her.

I tried to infuse her bad experience with something funny to ease her disappointment. I would ask, "What do they look like after all these years? They must have been in their twenties when you first met them." My mother went a lot by physical appearance, a leftover from her ballet days. "They've grown fat! They are balding!" was the most usual response. "Did they look happy?" I asked. "No!" she replied. "I think you are the more successful person," I would say to encourage her. "You still have a gorgeous figure and all your hair!" This statement aimed to reassure her that she still looked attractive. Then, with that boost, she started to find things that amused her about her failed encounter. "You should see the pretentious office where we met, with its expensive but bad modern art." Well," I'd say," if someone doesn't even know how to decorate their office tastefully, they won't have the intelligence to help you feel more protected by their friendship. I think we can do without them." Peter Sellers often came to the rescue at this point. His *Balham - Gateway to the South!* recording is a study of a clueless American commenting on an English town. After playing it, which always brought laughter no matter how many times we heard it, I said, "I assume the ex-friend you visited was just as clueless about what matters to you." "Absolutely," my mother would say. Then, I would propose the ultimate remedy, "Let's have a sweet cup of tea and forget about them." Given the memory of grudges that my mother entertained, it's remarkable that these one-time visits to old male friends did not upset her for long. As a youngster, I remember how comforting it was to have my mother waiting at home for me on days other students teased me at school. Now, I had reversed the roles. So, some guy who thinks he's a big shot just upset my mother. That's something to battle with a hot cup of sweet tea and then forget!

The underlying aim of most of my mother's attempts to attach herself to someone she viewed as solid and successful was to be "adopted" by them. If she could live in their house with me, that would provide comfort and financial security for both of us in return for what my mother considered our good company. It was, of course, a plan destined for failure. My mother not only frightened other people on her bad days, but she also frightened herself. My goals during my worst relapses were different. I responded to these fears by wanting to be as alone as possible. My mother overdid her plan, and I overdid mine, but mine was easier for society to bear. Part of my mother's wish to be adopted was, I am sure, nostalgia for her young childhood. She wanted to feel like a child again, brilliant, lucid, and attractive with successful parents, and to have these parents care for her and protect her from what she perceived as her growing number of enemies.

After Jodie's death, I specialized in acquaintances rather than friends. My desire to be alone had never been so strong. I was unknowingly headed for my first psychotic break as I sank into schizophrenia.

37

Diagnosis

My mother's psychological and psychiatric symptoms in her fifties inherited all she had before Dalaigh left when she was in her late forties. Her central delusion about being persecuted by fascists remained unchanged, but the army of people she accused of joining the cause increased. She did cease analyzing Dalaigh. She told anyone who asked about him that he was dead. She insisted I narrate the same lie. Somehow it helped her move on from the divorce, though it had little effect on us and, I imagine, none on Dalaigh.

The main developments in her symptoms were an increasing paranoia about people with whom she would interact when outside and fragmentation of her storytelling so that, for long periods, her carefully crafted revisionism degenerated into a rant that only I could more or less follow.

Her state of mind moved me. She was terrified for large portions of her day and found no one, except me, who would put up with what gradually became tiresome and incoherent verbal symptoms. She never hurt anyone, but she was at times vehement in her denunciation of imagined enemies.

When Jodie was fifty-eight, and I was twenty-eight, I finally found a doctor who diagnosed paranoid schizophrenia as my mother's psychiatric problem. I had made an appointment with him without my mother as she, by then, mistrusted all doctors as being part of a fascist conspiracy to kill her.

I knew my mother would never accept that she had psychiatric problems. She was unaware that her increasingly restricted life and expanding far-fetched terrors were anything but apt.

I described to the doctor aspects of my mother's weird behavior. I pointed out that some of it became normal for me as I repeatedly allowed my mother to run with it, with me as her only companion. For example, in her early fifties, her central delusion that her life was in danger due to fascists began to make her afraid to go out. When we walked outside together, she insisted, "We must take a complicated path to our destination. That's the only way to confuse the people trying to follow us and kill me." Indeed, she developed several ways to go to the local shops she believed were safe, even though I had to go with her for extra protection. "I feel so much safer going this way," she would comment, and, as usual, I did nothing but comply. Over time, this avoidance technique gradually seemed natural to me.

The doctor formed his conclusions from my description of her behavior. However, he told me that no one had the right to medicate my mother by force, for example, by committing her to a mental institution. As long as she wasn't harming herself or someone else, the only choice I had was to convince her to seek treatment. I knew that was impossible, but it did help me to understand that her problem had a name.

Unfortunately, partly because I was so convinced of my mother's uniqueness, I did not educate myself on paranoid schizophrenia. That wasn't helpful for my mother. It wasn't helpful for me when I began to have symptoms of the same disorder without being able to perceive the similarity with my mother's. My correct diagnosis had to wait until much later.

Another reason I wasn't at the time more curious about researching paranoid schizophrenia has its roots in the tremendous amount of time I had spent with my mother over the previous twenty years. I felt no amount of explanation of her disorder could bring me knowledge about my mother that I didn't already have. Also, I despaired from applying anything I may learn from a book about mental illness, as my mother would never admit she had a psychiatric problem.

The doctor who diagnosed Jodie agreed to see me a few more times. During those few visits, he went into a lot of detail about paranoid schizophrenia and how it can affect someone. He told me always to strive to keep Jodie as calm as possible and to do all I could to prevent her from alarming other people with her delusions. His advice partly made up for my ongoing ignorance about mental health matters but was still insufficient for me to recognize my schizophrenia when it surfaced.

The stigma surrounding severe mental illness means people often greet paranoid schizophrenia as the end of all hope for the afflicted. They assume the consumer of mental health has no worthy Overlife past the discovery they live with this brain disorder. While it's true that paranoid schizophrenia can bring great mental torment and social catastrophes, it's better to have the correct diagnosis as early as possible and treatment immediately afterward to ensure the best possible outcome for the patient.

38

Cancer

By the time my mother was in her fifties, she no longer trusted the medical profession. She neglected to have a yearly physical and was especially terrified by the prospect of a check-up by a gynecologist, so she stopped seeing one.

I visited my family doctor as needed and at least twice a year. Not only did I want reassurance about my physical health, but I also wanted to talk about my mother. We both consulted the same doctor, one who diagnosed my mother with epilepsy in her thirties. As my mother aged, her exception to the rejection of doctors was to use my family practitioner to write her a prescription for an anti-seizure drug. She took the medication as her epilepsy was her excuse for tailoring her day to what she could manage. In my twenties, I was diagnosed by my family doctor with the same type of epilepsy as my mother. This doctor prescribed me the medication my mother took. Our seizures were not severe, and my doctor called them absence seizures. Petit mal is a synonym for that type of seizure. In our case, that wasn't entirely accurate, as the loss of consciousness during our seizures lasted longer than the typical petit mal. However, on the severity level, we experienced nothing graver than it.

Between the ages of twelve and sixteen, I was often ill. I seemed to pick up cold and influenza regularly, and they would completely overtake me, resulting in often missing out on school. My grades didn't suffer, but my mother's state of mind did. She was gentle and caring when I was ill, but she worried about the root cause of my lapses in good health.

During this period, my tonsils were giving me problems. When I was sixteen, we consulted a doctor about the matter. My mother argued with him and was most upset by it. In my mother's defense, this doctor devoted a lot of time to discussing tonsillectomies that had ended badly, encouraging us to ride out my problems until I miraculously outgrew them. In seeking a second opinion, we found a doctor prepared to remove my tonsils. I was underweight by then, and my mass plummeted further downhill after the tonsillectomy. I never dieted, yet I resembled an anorexic in my late teens. I am sure the war between my parents contributed. I have always lost weight during periods of stress. My physical health improved after the tonsillectomy, but the stress level caused by my parents worsened.

My mother was forty-six by the time my wretched tonsils were no more, and I am sure that my ordeal added to her growing paranoia about doctors. Her central delusion still cast her father as an important spy for Israel and herself as persecuted by fascists who wanted revenge on her father. By fifty, she believed all the doctors she consulted were part of a fascist plot to kill her. Her prudishness added extra pessimism about gynecologists. After several check-ups from them in her late forties, she felt raped. The upshot was that by fifty, she avoided doctors altogether. After that, I acted as the middle figure between medical practitioners and my mother, relaying the messages to and fro. This approach added little to help my mother concretely.

The major player to everyone seemed to be my mother's deteriorating mental health, and they sidelined her physical health. It was impossible to commit her to a psychiatric hospital as no one could prove she was dangerous to others or herself. She always looked rather slim and fit and had carried into middle age the healthy diet she started in her twenties. Physically, she looked good.

In her fifties, my mother's mental state alternated between periods of extreme paranoia, when she did virtually nothing out of fear, and relative paranoia. During the latter, she trusted no one but still ventured out, mostly with me, and found pleasure in the outdoors and such pastimes as listening to music. However, my mother was, by then, at all times, psychiatrically sick.

One day, a few months before my mother turned sixty, I came home after shopping and found my mother passed out and covered in blood. She had harmed herself. She had for some time abused the drugs she took for epilepsy on the false pretext that her epilepsy was more severe than her fascist doctors had diagnosed. Perhaps that was the cause of her accident. I saw a chance to have her hospitalized for her good. She was admitted to the hospital and sent to a psychiatric ward. The doctors there confirmed the diagnosis of paranoid schizophrenia.

She had been admitted to the hospital at an average weight but did not manage to maintain it and lost weight dramatically. Again, the doctors and I thought her fragility was due to her eating little through unhappiness at being locked up.

Just after my mother turned sixty, an astute doctor at her hospital, alarmed by some physical symptoms, like bloating and feeling full after eating just a little, ran some tests for ovarian cancer on my mother. He diagnosed her with late-stage ovarian cancer. Ovarian cancer can be tough to diagnose before it reaches a critical stage. Even if my mother had trusted the medical profession, there is no saying a doctor would have recognized her ovarian cancer in its early stages.

The doctors at her hospital then made a tough decision. They decided not to treat her cancer except to aid my mother in dying in as little pain as possible. Due to her fragility, they said she might not even make it through the extensive operation to remove her cancer, and even if she did, her mental state by now was appalling. The doctors did not think she would survive more than a few months after an operation, and she would not benefit from this extra time due to her madness. Behind this opinion was the stigma that her life was not worth living in any case, as she had advanced paranoid schizophrenia. I do recognize her physical prognosis was dim, so there may indeed have been only a few months difference in when she died had she been treated for cancer.

Except for never leaving my mother's side, other than work, holding her hand, and talking to her, I was useless. I was frozen. I could not speak most of the time, except to my mother, and could not answer many of the critical questions the doctors asked me. The doctors were sympathetic and even debated putting me on psychiatric medication. They decided not to do so.

I let Beth know that Jodie was dying, but she elected not to visit her. Beth knew that Jodie did not trust her. She was well aware of my mother's mental state from my letters and feared a visit from her would only distress Jodie by possibly adding to her paranoia.

39

Death

My mother passed away within a month of being diagnosed with ovarian cancer. Although I did nothing but stay beside her as much as I could, in those final weeks, she trusted me. I am so grateful she did not die alone and that my love for her shone through her dark thoughts. She had no idea she was dying and persisted in elaborating on her far-fetched stories, with their villains and heroes. I knew how to respond through years of experience. One day, we shared a meal. I ate mine after I had fed her. She seemed to enjoy it. She talked, I listened, and I contributed what I thought would please her. We held hands. She died in the early morning of the next day.

I was the only person who attended my mother's funeral. I was devastated by her death and was convinced no one but I would care enough to attend her funeral. No one, but I, visited my mother in her final months. It was a silly move, as Enoch at least would have been there, as would some of the friends who had abandoned visiting my mother but kept in touch with me to have news of her. I eventually contacted these people to inform them of Jodie's death a few months after the funeral. I, of course, phoned Beth to tell her of my mother's death as soon as she passed. We had a loving conversation, but Beth preferred not to attend the funeral. I felt I should inform Dalaigh of Jodie's passing, but I wasn't sure he'd welcome me contacting him even to convey that news. So, I didn't search for him.

40

Confidant

A few weeks after my mother's death, I received a phone call. "Am I speaking to Sarah?" the caller asked. "Yes, I'm Sarah," I replied. The caller resumed, "You don't know me. My name is Sasha, and I live in Adelaide. I met your mother when she was about sixteen. I was twenty-six then. We were both involved in the same ballet studio in Adelaide, run by our mutual friend Wally who was about my age. Did Jodie ever mention it?" "Mention it!" I exclaimed, "On most days, she talked to me about Wally and ballet. She often mentioned your name and called you Wally's special friend. She was in love with Wally, you know, and told me that, while Wally was kind and generous in instructing her, he loved you more! For all that, she praised you for being one of the many brilliant artistic people attracted to Wally."

"Jodie didn't tell you the full story," Sasha said, "I learned of your mother's final illness and death from her sister Beth. You have my condolences." I was intrigued, "Did you and Beth stay in touch after Beth left ballet?" Sasha rejoined, "Not only did Beth and I stay in touch, but your mother and I also stayed in touch. I have known them for over forty years. I am seventy now. I became your mother's confidant when she realized Wally had died. At that time, she was in Adelaide at her parent's house. It was 1957. Your mother was suicidal with grief over Wally's death. I had never left Adelaide, and your mother reached out to me as someone who would understand how she felt. We met for lunch, and your mother shared her unhappiness about her marriage to your father. She thought that she belonged with Wally and was contemplating joining him. I succeeded in calming her down somewhat. I tried to make her understand that her feelings were normal and not so far from mine. I lost my closest friend when Wally died, and he was irreplaceable. Despite my attempts to support your mother, I feared she would kill herself."

Sasha continued, "While I was working on how to save your mother, she learned she was pregnant with you. Everything changed as she wasn't going to kill a fetus by committing suicide. Jodie began to improve and asked me to keep in touch to help her struggle through her grief for Wally and her questionable decision to return to live with Dalaigh and save her marriage. We decided on a phone friendship once she returned to Sydney. Jodie always called me collect. That way, she could hide our friendship from Dalaigh and you, as there wouldn't be a fuss about her telephone bill. I meet Beth for coffee and a chat a few times a year. That also started in 1957. It's a delight to talk to Beth about ballet, as she is so erudite. At the same time, we are much less close than I was with your mother."

I was dumbfounded! My mother's paranoia typically led her to recount everything she knew or thought she knew about significant events in her life. She coped with her mental confusion by having me as an audience who kept track of her evolving stories. For example, she told me that she was suicidal in 1957. That she would have remained silent on such an essential ingredient as a continuous life-long acquaintance with Sasha did not fit. Moreover, Beth had also been quiet about keeping in touch with Sasha. I hoped that Sasha could shed some light on what transpired.

I asked, "Why are you contacting me now, apart from offering condolences?" Sasha replied, "I promised your mother I would contact you should anything happen to her. She was worried about you, as you were such a loner, and concerned you may lose sight of the history she so painstakingly implanted in your mind. Jodie knew you were in touch with Beth but didn't trust her sister. She asked me to offer to be your friend by telephone and, as you hadn't much money, to always let you call me collect. In some sense, she was leaving me to you in her will."

"There is an important matter before we go into other details," Sasha continued. "I have your grandfather Feivel's watch he gave to your mother in 1957, and she handed on to you." I was aghast! "I always thought my father took that watch and sold it! My mother led me to believe as much, though my father denied it. It was like my mother to lose touch with reality, but not to tell outright lies." "Let me try to explain," Sasha responded, "your mother lied about the watch because she was sure your father would end up selling it if he knew where it was. She didn't think her nine-year-old daughter, who looked at the watch every day and loved it, would necessarily be able to refrain from sharing it with her father. Dalaigh had used for himself some money Feivel left you. That incident convinced your mother to hide the timepiece with me. As time passed, even after Dalaigh divorced Jodie, your mother decided the watch was safer with me while she was alive. She was afraid Dalaigh would find a way to get it from her even then. Please give me your postal address so I can mail your grandfather's watch. That's what your mother wanted me to do after her death." I gave him my coordinates. I was delighted the watch would soon be on its way to me! I wasn't angry with my mother for lying, given how Sasha explained the reason. She was leaving me the watch and her confidant in her will.

Sasha took over the conversation. "First, I want to return to when I first met your mother at Wally's ballet studio. Indeed, Wally and I were by then deeply in love. However, we were Catholic, and religion remained part of our makeup. We felt guilty about our passion. A graver problem is that I don't like anyone to touch me, a phobia that surfaced when I was about fifteen. I believe this problem is called haphephobia. I was a fragile and effeminate young boy, making me a target of some of the school bullies who repeatedly beat me up and made me do disgusting things, like eat dirt and worse. No one stood up for me, not my teachers, parents, or friends. Everyone seemed to believe I needed to "man up" and solve the problem myself. I began to have trouble with physical contact, even with my parents. When I met Wally in my late teens, I feared touching him. Even now, I live with this phobia. I had learned ballet from quite a young age, but when I began to avoid physical contact, I had to give up on dancing. That's why I wasn't a dancer in Wally's ballet but was involved in choreography, music, costumes, and stage sets. It helped Wally tremendously to have someone organizing such ingredients for a ballet performance. That way, he could focus on the dancers. Wally was a brilliant dancer, though his battle with lung cancer near the end of his life reduced him to a bystander."

Sasha continued. "The problem, in light of what I just told you, was what to do about our love. We consulted a priest who said that, from his viewpoint, for us to be in love, but celibate was not a sin. The passage to homosexual physical acts would be, however. I explained to the priest that we had considered the celibate option, especially as my attraction to Wally was primarily intellectual and emotional. I found Wally's looks beautiful, but I had no wish to touch him due to my phobias. The priest seemed satisfied that physical homosexual acts would not be part of our future."

"Wally and I agreed to leave touch out of our love. Wally's readiness to accept this situation convinced me that he had problems with the idea of physical homosexual acts, something that went beyond religion. Unlike me, Wally was physically demonstrative, but there was always something asexual, though forcefully attractive, in his physical contact with others. The priest didn't know that Wally was more flamboyant than me as long as he was in the company of people who would understand him. I believe he never slept with another man, but he expressed his homosexuality openly in other ways. Some ballets contain comic parts for male dancers dressed as women, and Wally loved to dress up for them. He even put on women's clothes and makeup at home. It was not unusual for me to see Wally dressed as a woman when I visited him. I am sure the priest would have been horrified." I wanted Sasha to know I was following him, so I said, "My mother and father recognized that Wally liked to dress as a woman, especially as he turned up once at their apartment in full drag."

Before Sasha continued, he asked, "How do you feel about homosexuality?" I tried to be honest, "I am conservative in my sex life and a religious person, though I rarely discuss these aspects of myself with others. I view them as private matters. I am not shocked by homosexuality, especially the love itself. I don't devote any time trying to figure out how homosexuals express their love physically. So, even if I love some religions that reject homosexual acts, in my heart, I don't have a problem with gay people. I should try to love everyone and refrain from judging what they do, especially if it doesn't affect me."

I felt I had the perfect rejoinder by asking Sasha, "How do you feel about mental illness? My mother lived with severe psychiatric problems. At the end of her life, she was in the hospital due to self-harm. The doctors there said she had paranoid schizophrenia." Sasha replied, "I didn't know your mother had an official diagnosis of schizophrenia. Still, it was clear from our conversations that she was struggling with her marriage and losing touch with reality. By the time Jodie was in her fifties, the conversations with her were often challenging, but we managed, all the same, to make them worthwhile for us both." "I am so happy to hear that," I interjected.

Sasha continued, "I'm afraid I find the word "schizophrenia" scary, as I do other words associated with psychiatric problems. Your mother was often disturbed in her conversations. I was glad that our relationship was by phone, that I lived in Adelaide, in South Australia, and that she lived in another state entirely. My relationship with your mother has caused a lot of prejudice towards the mentally ill in me, and I am ashamed to admit it. However, there was much more to your mother than her mental health problems, as I am sure you know full well, and that's why I stayed her confidant. It was only in the final months of her life, shortly before she was hospitalized that we ceased communicating. I then turned to Beth for news of your mother. With Beth, a casual friendship formed when she was in Wally's ballet that continued after Beth left. She knew I was in touch with your mother but seemed disinterested in what we discussed. I gather that Beth and your mother did not get on well. She seemed to use Jodie's problems to blame her for things that went wrong in their family. However, I could tell that Beth was most upset when your mother was hospitalized and then diagnosed with ovarian cancer. She was also clearly shaken by Jodie's death."

Sasha tried reassuring me, "I want to be your friend. I want to learn more about you. You can talk to me about your mother, so I can better understand what she endured. I hope familiarity with my prejudices breeds my contempt for them. I went through grief over my identification as gay, and I have haphephobia, so I should have more sympathy for those battling the stigma surrounding mental illness."

I asked, "Why did you agree to stay in touch with my mother even though you preferred a relationship with her by telephone, as it made you feel safe? Why did my mother keep it from me? Why did Beth? My mother was no fool and must have sensed that you wanted to keep your physical distance from her, that distance being considerable indeed, as it turned out."

Sasha tried to explain, "The key to my relationship with your mother is two words, 'Wally' and 'ballet,' whereas that with Beth, one word, 'ballet.' Beth is a fanatic, and she stayed acutely interested in the evolution of ballet. That topic is what we share during our coffee chats, and we enjoy it. I genuinely looked forward to my conversations with your mother too. Often, when she called me, she was upset about her marriage and afraid that there was a plot by unknown people to bring her down. That opening brought my reflex to bless the large physical distance between us. However, after her initial remarks, she always said she needed to talk about anything but that. We would reminisce about Wally and talk ballet. Unlike Beth, your mother had not kept track of what happened to ballet in Australia after she left it. We talked about the classical ballet and the performances we organized with Wally. Your mother was brilliant and shared with me her interests in other pursuits, like literature and movies."

I wasn't sure I should ask, but I did, "Can you describe Wally? What was the big fuss?" Sasha joked, "Well, often in gay relationships, the fuss is what it's all about!" He continued, "Wally was dashing in appearance, tall, blue-eyed, with black curly hair. He was slim but muscular, except during his final struggle with lung cancer when he faded away. His face was beautiful and incredibly photogenic. He did not like people taking his photo, though. He always said people should not immortalize themselves, that everything was in the current moment, especially dance. He was a fantastic dancer, both technically and expressively. He was a patient and devoted ballet teacher. To know him was to feel his magnetism. The key to it was his open invitation to everyone to partake of those aspects of his gifts they needed. He only asked people to recognize his explicit boundaries. One such limitation was his refusal to sleep with girls. As I have said already, I suspect he didn't sleep with boys either. He loved to seduce, but he shied away from consummation. It was obvious to everyone at the ballet studio that your mother was in love with Wally, but it seemed a natural emotion of a naive young woman towards her charismatic mentor."

Sasha continued, "What kept my role as your mother's confidant going was all she had to share that had nothing to do with insanity. I believe she made an extreme effort to keep our friendship interesting to avoid losing it. Jodie told me that you were her at-home confidant, and I was her confidant at large, out there beyond the confines of her house. She lacked any relationship like that. Even when she was fielding the demons of her delusions, she managed to maintain something that meant a lot to us. As a frail gay man who doesn't want to be touched and who has lost the love of his life, I needed a confidant, too, someone who also knew the old ballet days. Your mother fully appreciated why I had loved Wally. Jodie filled a void in my life just as I helped support her. I couldn't strike such a rapport with Beth, who loved the ballet but had lost interest in the people involved in it when she was dancing. What she looked for from me was an entertaining cup of coffee."

"I believe the key reason Jodie kept her phone friendship with me hidden from you was she wanted a relationship outside her home and, therefore, independent of you. She loved you greatly and told me without your support at home, she would never have survived her marriage ."

I volunteered, "My mother was afraid of losing her youthful dreams, and, as her friends deserted her due to her mental health problems, she felt her life was losing significance." Sasha replied, "That fits well with how I view your mother's friendship with me. She wanted a relationship based on her promise as a youth, and I was the only person she knew who could understand what that meant. I was also a ballet enthusiast full of bright ideas when I was young. I was afraid of losing that identity. We kept each other's memories alive. What we shared above all was Wally. I was happy to talk to someone who appreciated Wally's genius."

I took up with Sasha the relationship he and Jodie had planned. I called him collect every fortnight. Like my mother, I didn't want to lose this friendship as it was a link to my mother's promise as a young adult and a way of keeping alive some of what she forfeited to insanity. As my mental health deteriorated, I made the same mammoth effort Jodie had. During my phone calls with

Sasha, if I was struggling, I concentrated extremely hard on playing a part. I pretended to be an actress in one of my favorite movies and tried to keep the conversation interesting. Sasha probably guessed when I had psychiatric problems, but he never used it as an excuse to dump me. Sasha had been a jewel in Jodie's crown, and he became a jewel in mine.

41

Sarah: Symbolism

A feature running through all my periods of psychosis was an emergence of a vast array of mental symbols associated with what my senses encountered. For example, specific colors involved an associated mental reaction independent of their context. This phenomenon gave rise to some difficulties I have briefly mentioned before. I had a tremendous problem with black, to the point where I couldn't read or write anything in black ink as the words seemed hostile and danced around with their letters flying apart. I don't know the cause of my problem with this color. I learned that blue was a safe color. I could read and write better if the text was in blue ink. I was always happy to see blue. The ocean's proximity to my studio was a tremendous support as I could walk down to the seaside and see a vast expanse of this friendly color. That encounter would calm me for a while, and I would try to engage in the parts of my day devoted to looking after myself directly after seeing the sea.

I had an acute and paranoid problem with gestures. A former colleague from work had a nervous habit that plagued me. She would put her hands together in front of her and fidget with them whenever she spoke. Suddenly she was everywhere. Someone would only have to put their hands together for a moment, and they would convince me that this person was watching me. Luckily she was never aware of the unique role she played. Concurrently with a loss of linguistic control, I experienced the problem that certain gestures seemed obscene to me. People who knew me during such periods were shocked by some things I said. They didn't understand that I was far more deeply shocked by what I perceived as a proliferation of obscene gestures alongside a global degeneration into verbal profanity.

Moreover, the people who were most repulsed by my lapses in polite behavior were often those I thought were propagating the worst vulgarity themselves. My ability to control myself was, for a period, weakened by me comparing myself with the widely accepted humor I enjoyed, and that involved sexual innuendo. My most shocking behavior didn't seem all that bad in this context, and I was correct in this conclusion. However, it was uncharacteristic of me, which alarmed some people.

The above examples are just that, a few problems typical of a whole basket of colors and gestures that acquired a meaning and made seeing other people sheer torture. My reflex to crave solitude kept me out of what could have been even more serious trouble.

The word soup in my head gave rise to an immense amount of symbolism as I tried to make sense of it. Certain words or letters would be symbols for threads of thought that I associated with them. However, these symbols generally kept their meaning for only a few hours, giving rise to a tiresome updating of associations that took up much of my day. The linguistic confusion was worse because I knew several languages. I studied French and German at an advanced level in high school, even benefiting from free private tutoring by an enthusiastic teacher. I learned the rudiments of Hebrew because of my interest in religion and Feivel. The verbal soup drew its ingredients from all these sources.

I was happy to say goodbye to most of the symbolism whenever my health improved, but part of it had formed a kind of support during my psychosis, especially the symbolism associated with words. As I began to do better, the harmless symbolism also lost meaning. For example, during my struggles, I often succeeded in making a "word bridge" from a useless thought to a more productive one via puns and word games like playing with acronyms. Here, knowing several languages was a plus, as there were more possibilities for word bridges. My passage to better health involved blowing up these bridges, and there was nothing to take their place. That left me groping toward reality by other means, mostly comparisons with a target behavior I knew was characteristic of my more socially accepted past self. All politeness involves lying, and I was not too fond of that part of it.

The mechanism that causes me to distrust friends due to paranoia can also, on much rarer occasions, lead me to trust people who are not my friends or who may not even know me or me know them. For example, I always have good associations with animals, as long as they are not an immediate, genuine physical threat to me. I don't know if anyone else living with paranoid schizophrenia has had the experience of thought insertion by animals, but on rare occasions, I did so. The thoughts were always kind to me. I believe the author Virginia Woolf, who many think suffered from bipolar disorder with psychosis, once said she heard the birds singing in Greek. One delusion I have had is that, to encourage me, "friends" place animals at strategic points along my path when I venture outside. These "friends" did not need to be people I had met. This phenomenon was helpful and supportive at the time, but it was another example of a lack of judgment under psychosis. As I came out the other side to better health, I missed these animal symbols.

42

Poet

About two months after my mother died, I decided to contact Robert. I was thirty years old, and it was November 1987. Robert was 75 years old, going by his birthdate on the published books of his poems. Of all the well-known people my mother asked for help, she never at any stage tried to contact this friend from the early years of her marriage. Finding Robert was not difficult. He was a successful poet in Australia. My mother, referring to the young Robert, had told me he was given to spend significant periods in the outback and didn't seem to have a fixed address. Undaunted, I managed to track down a number for Robert by calling telephone information. I called the number, and he picked up the phone at once.

"Hello, are you Robert?" I asked. "Yes," he replied. I went on, "My name is Sarah, and you knew my parents, Jodie and Dalaigh, from the early 1950s. I want to talk to you about my parents if you don't mind." "How are they?" he asked. I told him, "Jodie died about two months ago of ovarian cancer, and Dalaigh rode off into the sunset in 1974. I haven't seen him since."

There was a long pause at the other end of the phone, followed by "Poor Jodie! She was always so full of life!" "Well," I countered, "I presume you stopped seeing her when I was about three, so you're referring to the Jodie of a long time ago. She was a powerhouse of ideas and activity but struggled with psychiatric issues for much of her life."

"Well, Jodie always had psychological problems, even way back then. Why do you want to contact me?" he asked. I hesitated. Mainly, I was curious to see, or at least talk to, on the phone with, this person who strongly impacted both my parents, especially my mother. I also wanted to ask Robert about my father's claim that I was his daughter. I offered a related question instead, "Why did you stop seeing my parents? I believe that was around 1960. My mother idolized you and spoke to me constantly about you in glowing terms. I always found it strange that she didn't seem interested in pursuing the friendship further."

"It's a long story," said Robert.

I decided to take the plunge! "My father, Dalaigh, often claimed I was your daughter. I was born in August 1957. Jodie was trying to separate from Dalaigh when she found out she was pregnant with me. The pregnancy prompted her to return to Dalaigh to give her marriage another try."

I was frightened that Robert would think I was some crazy woman trying to lay claim to him. Instead, he was surprisingly calm. "It's possible," he said. He immediately reminded me of the 1957 classic film "*12 Angry Men.*" In the movie, Henry Fonda, part of a jury for a murder case, uses the words "it's possible" to try to convince the other jurors there was reasonable doubt. My mind is like that. A similarity in dialogue or written word can send me off on extended comparisons of different contexts where I have encountered those exact words. That softened the bombshell Robert had just dropped, which meant, if he was telling the truth, my mother must have slept with him while she was married to Dalaigh. Otherwise, why was Robert "possibly" my father? Then, an alternate scenario occurred to me. "Do you say: 'it's possible' because you had an affair with my mother or because you cannot remember whether or not you had an affair with her?" I realized Robert might not want to talk to someone he had never met about such personal matters.

I was right because his next question was, "Can we meet? Where are you?" I replied, "I live in Dee Why, Sydney." "That's convenient," he countered, "I am in Sydney for some poetry readings." I did not want to meet him at a public performance, so I said, "Please don't take offense, I love your poems, but can we meet somewhere more private? Say, for coffee? We could have coffee and cake in the restaurant at David Jones." David Jones was a department store in central Sydney with a fabulous restaurant on one of the upper floors. I used to go there with Jodie, and it was the only place I frequented when I ate out. "Sounds great!" he said. "How about 11:00 am tomorrow?" "That suits me," I said, "I know what you look like from photos in the paper. I will be wearing a fedora, and I am thirty. Blue eyes, brown hair, on the thin side." We exchanged a few pleasantries. I thanked him for being so open and generous in agreeing to meet with me.

At the appointed time the next day, I was sitting nervously at one of the café's tables at David Jones. I was partial to cheesecake and seemed to be able to eat vast quantities of it without my circumference increasing. David Jones served a delicious New York cheesecake. I held off on ordering as I knew it wasn't polite to start my coffee and cake before Robert arrived if he arrived. The thought that he may never show up plagued me and had kept me up the night before. Around 11:30 am, Robert, a tall man with wild white hair and piercing blue eyes, entered the cafe and followed my fedora to my table. Considering his age, he looked amazingly fit and agile. He had a large frame but had stayed slim and muscular.

I could imagine him still able to take long hikes in the backcountry, as he had with my parents all those years ago. "You must be Sarah," he said. We shook hands, and he sat down. "You look a lot like Jodie!" he remarked. "I don't think so," I said. "She was so dark in complexion with features much more striking than mine." He smiled, "I remember her well! What I mean is that you have the same look around the eyes. Yours are blue, but apart from that, they are Jodie's eyes. From what I can see of your physique, it's not so dissimilar from what I remember of Dalaigh's, so you could pass for the daughter of Jodie and Dalaigh."

We ordered coffee and cakes.

His flippancy was making me nervous. Would he tell me the truth or soothe me in some way so I wouldn't bother him again? As an Australian, I knew how to come crudely to the point. "Did you ever sleep with my mother, Jodie? Would you remember even if you had?" He respected my direct attack. "Yes, I slept with your mother. It was impossible to forget, not just because of the great sex but also because your mother idolized me, so it was an ego trip and an enjoyable time. The affair started in 1955 and carried on into 1957."

This answer was one I had entertained, but it shocked me. "I find what you tell me so hard to believe of my mother," I countered. "She was incredibly puritanical, and her morals were pretty Victorian. She didn't even believe in sex before marriage. I can't imagine her having an affair. Did Dalaigh know about it, or was he guessing? He certainly suspected something and, when in a rage, would often tell me I was your daughter. I want to get at the truth, not to ask you to give me something, but to try to make sense of part of my parent's full-scale war."

"Your mother was as you describe her," he replied. "At the time our affair started, Dalaigh was seeing a woman he had met who was a customer in the store he managed. He was never subtle about his extra-curricula activities. I had been close to your parents around the time they married. Then, Dalaigh realized that, to your mother, I was an intellectual hero. We were also physically attracted to each other, so that strained the friendship with him. By 1955, your mother had lost her first baby, as you probably know, and was extremely depressed about her marriage due to Dalaigh's neglecting attitude. In her mind, it was almost as if she was already divorced. I came on pretty strong as I was keen to start something sexual. By the way, your mother was extremely intelligent and receptive to new ideas, which was part of the bond between us. However, I was never monogamous, and your mother knew it. I also don't know exactly what happened between Dalaigh and your mother during this time, which is why I say it's possible you are my daughter. It's also possible you are Dalaigh's."

Dalaigh, for all his faults, did the distance, putting food on our table in an environment where he was grossly under-appreciated, especially by my mother. I replied, "It may surprise you that I am disinterested in applying to you the label of a father. Dalaigh is my father because he raised me. I care little for knowledge of my genetics. Like my mother, I respect you as a poet. As a former friend of my parents, you may be able to connect some dots. That's the most important output I wish from our meeting."

He seemed happy to continue talking on these terms. He visibly relaxed a little when he perceived I was only interested in information, not in some reckoning between us. "In 1957, your mother went to her parents in Adelaide, as you probably know. She was obsessed with a dancer called Wally and wrote to me to tell me Wally had died. Then, some weeks later, she wrote to me again to say she was pregnant and that our affair had to end. Your mother wanted the stability of marriage for her new baby. She knew I was the opposite of stable, always roaming to a new place and often to a new woman simultaneously. I asked her to please keep in touch. I suspected her baby was also mine, and I wanted to make sure she could settle matters adequately with Dalaigh. There were a lot of unknowns. Would Dalaigh let her come back to live with him, for example?"

"Well, I don't know much about the first three years of my life. My first memories were of Jodie and Dalaigh as a unit. I guess the idea to entrap Dalaigh within the existing marriage worked," I added," Dalaigh was far from happy, though, and blamed me for the fact that the marriage continued in 1957. By 1960, he was at times violent with me and deeply resentful of my existence."

"I know about some of that bad situation," Robert confessed. "Your mother did keep in touch, and the news was worrying. You mention 1960. It was at about that time when I made your mother a proposal. I told her I would support her in a break with Dalaigh and help her establish herself as a single mother. She understood that I was not willing to play the role of husband and father. I was too wild and too unfaithful in my relationships. She chose to stay with Dalaigh and strive for a better marriage. She asked me to please leave her alone. Her focus was her marriage now, even though it was in trouble. It had the potential to provide her with the stability she craved in a moral context she recognized."

"It went badly," I said. "Why did you stop staying in touch despite what Jodie said? You could have been a real support to my mother." "She didn't want it," he replied. "As a successful poet, I wasn't that hard to find, as you can imagine. She wanted to close the door on an affair she was ashamed of and on the ambiguity of your birth. From what you say, Dalaigh did not reciprocate, but he did stick it out for a long time. I am happy you want to be Dalaigh's daughter but proud of you as a possible child of mine."

I decided to quit while I was ahead. Robert seemed to understand me, and I now knew much more than I had before meeting him that day. I thanked him. "Let's swap postal addresses," I proposed. "That way, if I write to you, you'll eventually receive my letter. I won't make myself a nuisance. I so much appreciate that you met with me today."

"I would like to know more about you," Robert admitted. "If you are mine, you are not my only love child, but you're the only one I never saw past infancy until now." "Well," I pointed out, "we can do that in letters."

I wanted to respect my mother's wish to think of Dalaigh as my father but acknowledge the pride my mother had felt in knowing someone as gifted as Robert.

Putting him in the pen pal box seemed the ideal compromise.

I surprised myself by the matter-of-fact way this meeting had unfolded. I hadn't felt any strong emotions on meeting Robert nor on learning the likelihood that Dalaigh may have been right about my birth father. The drama of my parent's marriage eclipsed what went on between Jodie and Robert. Would my mother have been happier as a single mother with Robert's friendship and without Dalaigh? In my heart, I doubted it. She would have tried to get from Robert what he couldn't provide emotionally, just as she had with Dalaigh. It was better for Jodie to harbor Robert as a fond memory with a secret inside it than for the friendship to decline over time. A lousy ending would have spoiled it.

Robert and I said our goodbyes after exchanging mailing addresses. I felt the same as when Dalaigh would tell me I was Robert's child: if I must be illegitimate, I could do worse for a birth father.

I did keep in touch with Robert. We wrote to each other a few times a year. I never mentioned my parents to him again and avoided the topic of who my father was. I did not share with him my mental health struggles. Some inner resource gave me the control to only write to him, even when I was sick with schizophrenia, about poetry and other topics that interested him, like the plight of the Aborigines of Australia. Even when I was less unwell, I feared losing his friendship. If I felt too confused cognitively to write to him well on these topics, I delayed my letter for a better day in my health struggles. To my joy, Robert responded to me. He kept the topics to his poetry work and his concerns about the Aboriginal people, including examples of how he planned his poems, what motivated them, and all the intense work that went into them.

43

Beth

Despite the rather unpleasant trip she made to see us when I turned eight, I continued to correspond regularly with Beth by letter. She had been one of my pen pals since I was six, and I saw nothing in her visit when I was eight that justified stopping our correspondence. After that visit, she returned to her house in Adelaide, and I wrote to her about twice a month. She always replied. These were the days of handwritten letters.

Aunt Beth had discovered and loved Christianity through her private schooling. The classes on religion at her schools were in the context of the Church of England. Beth was awkward about her Jewish identity, unlike my mother, who was proud of it. It may have had something to do with Beth's complex relationship with her parents, or it may have been the intensity of her commitment to Christianity. She maintained a loving relationship with Herman, her father's brother, and his wife and children. He had married a Christian and raised his children in the Church of England. Herman knew he was Jewish but was so young when his parents disappeared that he didn't recall much about that religion. He knew enough about Christianity to let Beth express herself about religion and understand what she meant to convey.

Beth knew about my parent's left-wing views and mostly omitted religion from her letters to me. At age eight, I was highly interested in beliefs, and I wouldn't have minded her take on such matters. Still, Beth didn't want me to tell my parents her letters espoused Christianity. We did correspond a lot about our view of the world, which was more in the category of philosophy. When I was about eleven, my mother introduced me to philosophy, putting much meat on the bones of my letters to Beth.

Without any explicit references to a major religion, Beth taught me in her replies to my letters that, in moral affairs, the essential ingredient was your conscience. When, as an adult, I think of those exchanges, I recall Robert Bolt's play made into the 1966 movie *A Man for all Seasons*. It is about Sir Thomas More and his opposition to Henry VIII making himself head of the church and marrying Anne Boleyn. More only recognized Henry's first wife, Catherine of Aragon, and was obstinately Catholic. More says to men trying to get him to change his mind for fellowship, "And when we die, and you are sent to heaven for doing your conscience, and I am sent to hell for not doing mine, will you come with me, for fellowship?" Many of the dilemmas I would face regarding my mother's welfare and my place in it came down to matters of conscience. Should I put my ambitions first? Should I tailor them to fit a situation where I remained my mother's caregiver, given I was the only person who could fill that role?

Beth understood my internal debate. She wrote to me when I was about twelve in reply to a letter in which I expressed worry that I could have a life worth living with the problems at home. She said, "I felt 'called' to remain in my parent's house. I felt 'called' to carefully reexamine how their lives and mine intertwined. I want to understand them better. I want to liberate myself from my harsh judgments of them and my accompanying resentments. My love for you and Herman helps me be grateful for the family my parents left behind and, therefore, for my parents. Without them, by the way, I wouldn't exist. If you feel you are 'called' to continue to look after your mother, I would advise you to follow that 'calling' without resentment. No good alternative for your mother is available. You're extremely clever, so, even in that context, you can still achieve a great deal." Of course, she did not know that my schizophrenia would add to my difficulties. However, to Beth, in her words, "Success has little to do with how the society around you views your achievements or lack of them. Success can only come from within, from the study of your conscience and its relation to what you end up doing. Betray your conscience too often, and no amount of societal success will make you happy."

Some may perceive letters like Beth's written to a twelve-year-old as a bad influence. Parents ambitious for their children to succeed in society to their full potential may feel that's precisely the age at which life goals should be sky-high. However, neither of my parents cared about my eventual professional success, and Beth knew it. Handicapped by my mother's needs, I was limited in what I could hope to achieve. Beth was aware of all these ingredients, and she got to know me via our letters. The advice she gave me was what I needed as an encouragement to live the best life I could.

I expressed interest in knowing more about Beth's parents and encouraged her to reconsider them in a kinder context. A few years into our pen-pal relationship Beth started to give me many details of her family as she remembered it. Some of the less outlandish stories coincided with my mother's. Beth would recount, with much detail , the stories from her life. I gradually gained from her a much richer picture of her parents. Like my mother, Feivel especially fascinated me, even though, for Beth, telling me about Feivel was often painful. From what I gather, Beth took her mother's side and blamed Feivel for a lot of the grief when her parent's marriage began to decline. Over the years, I could sense in her letters a softening in Beth's attitude to her father, and I was so happy to think I may have helped bring this improvement about. Beth supplied me with many old photos of her family. Always fascinated by such material, I spent a long time looking at them and trying to imagine what my dead relatives were really like.

From Beth's letters, and from some of the stories my mother told me, I suspect there was some mental illness in every member of my mother's immediate family. My grandmother Edith fell into a depression after the baby born before Jodie, and after Beth, died. Even beforehand, she coped badly with change, for example, the family's moves as Feivel built up his businesses selling cars. During World War Two, Feivel farmed an orchard, considering it a better contribution to the war effort than selling cars. That involved a move and another project that kept Feivel busy while Edith was at home. She had little to do, given that her children were almost adults working on the orchard. My mother was twelve when the war began, and Beth was sixteen.

Near the end of his life, Beth and Jodie remarked on the change in Feivel. He had become paranoid about Beth, believing she was driving a wedge between him and Edith. After Edith died, Feivel only survived her by three days, during which he constantly accused Beth of poisoning him. My mother told me that her parent's neighbors answered a knock on their door to find Feivel on their porch, saying Beth was trying to kill him. My mother and Beth told me that Feivel was prone to fits of rage provoked by memories of his parents leaving him. Beth was eccentric and intensely passionate about religion and everything she took on. She did not enjoy company unless it was that of a relative she knew well, and most of her adult life was pretty isolated.

To what extent were my mother's and my schizophrenia problems inherited? It may be impossible to judge, given the environment is also a factor. However, some of my mother's and my anosognosia may be because weird was normal in our family. The attitude of

Dalaigh didn't help as it was so unsupportive. My mother and I needed to appear more robust than we were to cope with him.

As I grew older, the most beautiful aspect of my relationship with Beth was that she was always ready to hear from me. She didn't pass judgment on my cycle of relapses and partial recoveries. When my letters "got strange," she would reply with an example from her life. She would describe a situation that challenged her psychologically. She encouraged me to stick to the basics of looking after myself and trying to lay low. She never ran for cover, and I knew she was always there, even though I never turned up to see her while I was sick. I wanted, in some sense, to go easy on this relationship which meant so much to me.

44

Herman

Another person who exchanged letters with me since childhood was Herman, Feivel's brother. My mother told me about Herman's early history. "He was, like my father, a foster child after his parents disappeared in about 1902. The three siblings, Herman, Feivel, and Irit, were separated and given no means to stay in contact. When Feivel was in his thirties, he tracked down his siblings Herman and Irit, using the services of a private detective. Herman lived in Adelaide, in the state of South Australia. Iris was living in Wales, United Kingdom, with her foster family. Unlike Feivel and Herman, she had been happy in her foster home."

My mother possessed reunion photos of Feivel and Herman taken by a professional photographer; both were in their thirties. She gave them to me when I was about five. I looked at them many times as they gave me a sense of family, something solid and joyous in our history. Feivel was good-looking, with laughter lines bordering his eyes. Herman was a little sadder in expression but still a fine-looking man. For all that Feivel's foster family had been bad news, Herman had the added trauma of being fostered by several families, none of which made him happy. Beth provided me with photos of Irit in Wales in my teens. "I want you to have these photos," said Beth, "to complete the picture of your grandfather's siblings." My mother told me, "Feivel said that Irit had been happy throughout her childhood and settled in Wales to be near her foster family who came from there."

The pen-pal relationship with Herman began when I was eight, at precisely the time when my mother's mental health deteriorated, and she began shutting us up in our house. I did not relate any difficulties to Herman but spoke about my interests and ideas. Herman was paternal in his replies, sensing that I needed some parental guidance, perhaps because he was in touch with

Beth, who may have been frank about our family dynamics.

At that age, I began writing poetry, which didn't help my relationship with my father due to his conjecture about Robert being my father. I submitted one of my poems to The Argonauts radio club for children on ABC (Australian Broadcasting Corporation). They broadcast my poem on the radio in a show devoted to poetry. I asked Herman to please listen to that show and hear my poem. He did so. I was delighted with the broadcast that added background music to my poem. It was all about cats in a gang and their adventures. Herman called me straight after the show, "Your poem was the best one and so well presented. Congratulations! Did Jodie listen as well?" "Yes," I replied. She had always been supportive of my writing. My father refused to listen, but I knew why. It was because of Robert. Sometimes my father seemed "crazier" than my mother.

At age eight, my first ambition was to work with animals. Yet, I didn't know how to earn a salary that way without getting a degree at college that involved cutting up innocent specimens.

My next ambition was to be a writer. That choice would enable me to be home a lot. I began writing many poems and short stories. My mother was worried, "It's tough to make a career in writing," she opined, "Even Robert, a gifted and famous poet, had lean times financially. The competition is cruel, with the criteria for good writing continuously shifting. You'd be better off focusing on your talent in science and mathematics. Lots of professions need such qualifications." I did find mathematics and science easy at school, so I paid more attention to the associated classes just in case Jodie was correct.

At this stage, I had no idea that my mother would require so much of my attention that holding any job would be a challenge. I did not look ahead that much. My parent's marriage and my mother's needs occupied a lot of mental space. However, given the ease I found in topping every subject at school, I was still envisaging holding an exciting job as an adult and remaining my mother's caregiver.

Herman and Beth had a narrower perspective. They rated family duties highly and professional fulfillment for female adults lowly. As the problems with my mother grew, I adopted their viewpoint as a manageable alternative to personal ambition, the latter never being a quest that drove me to success as it did some other women. Mainly, I wanted the space to pursue what I found interesting. It had everything to do with accommodating my mother's increasing demands, together with keeping my own identity, and nothing to do with the search for social success.

I ultimately viewed the values of Herman and Beth as helpful. As encouraging as it was to have your poem broadcast on the radio, the care that my mother needed was, in every way, the higher calling to the three of us. I was extremely clever but no genius, and I thought then, at eight and as I aged into my teens, that my mother deserved the time and care more, especially as there was no one else to fulfill that role.

45

Sarah: Self-diagnosis

Amid the severe crisis I had at thirty-eight, I finally recognized similarities between some of my significant symptoms and those of my mother, even though there were notable differences. Several doctors had told me my mother lived with paranoid schizophrenia, so I decided to do what I should have done as soon as they made this suggestion. I bought several books on the topic and read them from cover to cover. Reading was challenging during a relapse, so the going was slow.

The similarity between what I was experiencing and the symptoms of paranoid schizophrenia portrayed in these books struck me immediately. I had many extra problems, and it occurred to me that the diagnosis of PTSD from childhood experiences may explain many of them. I wasn't upset by my suspicion that I suffered from paranoid schizophrenia. The information was reassuring. If that was indeed the verdict, then I could attack the problem. I knew what it cost my mother never to know, through ignorance, non-compliance, and inaccuracy of some of the doctors I consulted on her behalf, how to confront her illness.

I needed some decent doctors who would treat me for what was ailing me. However, I felt I had to put that off because I was in incredible trouble with myself. I wanted some semblance of order in my brain before finding such doctors. I was afraid they would commit me to a mental institution. In hindsight, that may have been a useful idea and helpful to me, but I was terrified at the prospect.

I began to write down what I was experiencing. It helped me, as it was a way to express myself, and I hoped it would explain my symptoms to the new doctor I was yet to choose.

46

Psychologist

At thirty-nine years of age, I finally found a psychologist, Dr. Paige Hamilton, with whom I hoped I could work well. I first saw her name in the newspaper, The Sydney Morning Herald. She had written an opinion piece I liked on schools' lack of sufficient mental health resources. I searched for other articles she had written and found them original and informative. I was favorably impressed.

I called her practice, expecting the receptionist to say Dr. Paige wasn't receiving any more new patients, but fortunately, she found a free slot for me a week away. Her consulting room was about half an hour by bus from where I lived, so most convenient.

I didn't yet want to see a psychiatrist, as I wanted first to improve my communication about my problems with a psychologist. My main concern was that after confiding with a psychiatrist, I needed the medication to target the correct diagnosis. There are no laboratory tests for gauging psychiatric issues; my verbal input would be the only information a psychiatrist could use. I knew I needed to be much more frank and explicit about my worries, psychological issues, and psychiatric symptoms with Dr. Paige than the previous shrinks I had consulted. Even if Dr. Paige were an ideal match for me, she would not be able to work effectively if I held back as much as I had in earlier encounters with psychologists.

Unfortunately, a feature of the acute phases of my relapses is that I am paranoid about everyone, including doctors. It took resolve to turn up at my first appointment with Dr. Paige, ready to work with her.

Her approach was quite different from the other psychologists I had consulted. The previous ones had a lot to say about what they thought was wrong with me. They all underestimated how much I was suffering and how far the remedies they suggested were from my capabilities and desires. They would tell me what my life lacked and encourage me to fix it as if turning myself into a cliché would be an easy way to renormalize my situation.

At the first appointment, I brought along a selection of my recent notes on my symptoms and told Dr. Paige that I believed I had paranoid schizophrenia, like my mother. She told me I must see a psychiatrist if that were the case to get appropriate medication. I told her I would not take that step until I could be more precise about what I was experiencing, an insight I hoped to gain through sessions with her. I was also reticent about taking medication because of some of the side effects I had experienced with other drugs, the "tranquilizers" and those targeting "depression."

Dr. Paige backed off from insisting on a psychiatrist. She didn't want to frighten me away. I gave her my notes, and she promised to read them before my next weekly session.

Then, she acted preciously. She let me talk while she listened. I admitted up front my most challenging truth. I told her that I was currently extremely paranoid, including about her. I told her, "I hope we can work on that first so I can be more open."

"You can trust me," she offered, "these sessions are my job, and I am most professional. I will always be on your side. That's why we're talking. If I feel you are acting in error, I will, of course, tell you. If you are in a paranoid state now, then it's natural you will have difficulties with me initially."

Unlike the other psychologists I had consulted, Dr. Paige didn't try to impress upon me that she immediately understood all I was saying. She erred on the other side, repeatedly prompting me for more information about what I was trying to convey and then giving me a chance to explain in my terms.

By the end of the first session, I was outpouring a torrent of what was going through my mind, combined with some information on my family history. I mentioned the diagnosis of PTSD from childhood experiences made by other doctors I had seen, but I viewed the likely diagnosis of schizophrenia as more serious. I talked extremely fast, but Dr. Paige didn't ask me to slow down. In the first session, her significant achievement was to get me to the point where I talked about what was genuinely upsetting me. I felt I had done nothing wrong during the appointment, even though, in retrospect, I must have been next to impossible to understand.

For the second session, Dr. Paige had read my notes and made some sympathetic and insightful comments about them. That immediately washed off some of the paranoia associated with her, and the process of her gradually earning my trust was underway. I was no less verbose in this second session and many to come. I had pent up inside myself so much of my mother's history and mine. I thought, correctly, that I had finally found a shrink who could take it.

Dr. Paige asked, "Why did you take so long to link your mother's diagnosis of paranoid schizophrenia and your problems?"

I responded, "It's difficult for me to explain. My mother never consulted a psychiatrist, and her initial correct diagnosis was a guess by some doctors I consulted alone. At the end of her life, she was in the hospital and officially diagnosed. I knew my mother inside out, and I assumed no book about mental illness could add to what I already knew about her. It was a stupid move. When my psychiatric problems began to surface, I failed for a long time to see their similarity with a number of my mother's issues, that conclusion occurring to me only recently. There were two main reasons. First, my periods of bad mental health are dissimilar to my mother's in many ways, despite some commonalities. I thought I knew paranoid schizophrenia through living so long with her and failed to link that brain disorder to my sufferings. Second, unlike my mother, I did consult some doctors over the years. A valid diagnosis of PTSD from childhood experiences stood out, but for the psychotic symptoms, the guess was depression. I even took anti-depressants for a while before ditching them as they made me feel worse, not better. No doctor offered paranoid schizophrenia as a possibility for me."

Dr. Paige's gift of accepting my self-expression without prejudice didn't mean she let obvious fallacies pass. She commented early on in our collaboration, "Do you realize that you talk vividly about some people, and it doesn't seem to occur to you that, before you mentioned them, I had never heard of them before?" She gave me an example. The man she cited was someone I knew slightly but who assumed vital significance in my paranoia.

I confided, "I am convinced people are spreading false rumors about me trying to become close friends with that person against their will. When I met him, that man frightened me a little, and I found him mean. He was one of the clients I briefly had contact with at the real estate firm where I used to work. I haven't seen him for years, but he plays a vicious role in my delusions. Because of this anomaly, I have a plan in case I see him by chance. I resolve to avoid him, even if it means crossing the street. My resolve will help me escape trouble, but the existence of the libel I am chasing after him is no less entrenched in my mind. As I assume, due to my paranoia, this libel is common knowledge, I thought you must know about it, and, in particular, you must have heard of the man at the center of it."

She kept saying, "I didn't know who that person was before you told me about him here in my office." We ended up devoting a whole session to this person I barely knew, and her insistence she didn't know him before I mentioned him still didn't have traction. It would only be about a month later that I would fully accept that my shrink wasn't lying. She didn't know of this man before I mentioned him. Of course, in the interim, we discussed many other matters. Approximately a year after that, I searched for this person on the internet to find that he was deceased. By that time, I was over the obsession and felt nothing. It's incredible to think that, within a year or so, I could go from terrified obsession to casual observation in this instance.

Dr. Paige's method included never telling me, "You shouldn't feel like that!" Her attitude was, "If you are undergoing some mental struggle, its precise nature needs my acknowledgment, and from that standpoint, we can work out how best to manage it." She often discussed my daily activities and asked simple but relevant questions, "Who would I see? What did I have to do? What was my immediate worry, if any?" Dr. Paige understood from our discussions and my notes that I could have difficulty getting through a simple day. She helped me enormously by saying, "You should not force yourself to try to feel what you are not feeling."

I told her, "To cope with people, I often pretend to be someone else for a while. Acting a part can help me accomplish a chore, like shopping, that involves other people."

Rather than raising red flags, she told me, "Everyone pretends in this way. It's called politeness. You may have to put in more effort when you are sick to act in a socially acceptable manner, but hiding for a little while to get there is no sin."

Like many people with paranoid schizophrenia, I carried a lot of guilt, especially over my mother. I felt I should have done more to help her with her mental health struggles. Dr. Paige was influential in getting me to understand that guilt is a wasted emotion if held for too long. It's often a good lesson, so we don't repeat an action we regret, but it's an unhealthy master.

We both agreed that our principal aim should be to get me onto some plateau where I had sufficient control over my symptoms to lead a life I enjoyed without alarming other people. I knew, and so did she, that there was no cure for schizophrenia, so this goal needed to be permanent, even if I went on to get appropriate medication from a psychiatrist. I told her of my conviction that the lifestyle I thought I would lead before my psychiatric problems set in would never eventuate and that I aimed to go on to live on my plateau as a different person.

I told her, "Part of the old me remains in this different person, all the same. I am finding, for psychological reasons to do with the PTSD, that returning to some aspects of the person I was before the traumatic dreams started at age eleven is helping me. This period preceded the onset of my schizophrenia, and that also helps me aim for the plateau."

Hoping Dr. Paige was not too modern for such an admission, I confided, "I have gone back to reading the Bible, both the Old and the New Testament, because I loved my religion classes at school. I had let my interest in the Bible lapse for many years, and rediscovering it is helping me. My goal is to work through the entire Bible every year. The intellectuals may laugh at me, but I find concrete advice on how to act and speak in the Bible, often summed up in small paragraphs that are easy to digest and remember. I try to take them on board to improve my behavior."

I went on, "I have increased my interest in animals, focusing on rhinos as they were always my favorite, and they are in danger of extinction, so they need all the support they can get. I watch classical movies, a hobby that started when I was a child. I have taken up knitting as it is a simple task, if you have helpful instructions, that I enjoy. I did a lot of knitting when I was young. My mother taught me."

I hoped she would understand the following, "The most important ingredient in my daily life is recorded music, although I enjoy playing some simple pieces on an old piano I have had since I was eight. The love of music never left me, but I am exploring more deeply the recordings of some artists I particularly appreciate, like Glenn Gould and Blandine Verlet."

I concluded. "By contrast, one activity firmly related to the present is compiling notes on my mother's mental illnesses and mine also. Writing the notes is helping me. I hope the notes help you too."

Dr. Paige exclaimed, "They do!"

"That's a lot of activity!" she replied to my list of deliberately nostalgic activities.

I elaborated, "Yes, but you must remember it's time-flexible. I may go a week doing absolutely nothing. Some weeks I manage several days where only about half of these activities are manageable. About twice a month, I can pay a visit to them all."

Dr. Paige replied, "You are unemployed and aren't running a race. While it's fabulous to have concrete goals to brighten your life, getting you stabilized on a plateau where you have the confidence to look forward as far as you can see is our most critical task. I talk of a plateau because it's clear stress triggers schizophrenic relapses in your case. Plateaux can be as beautiful as the high country. You must carefully define how much you can cope with at any given time, staying on level ground. You mustn't seek to climb any mountain that could induce a relapse. You will, at some point, need a psychiatrist and medication, but for now, we will do our best without one. Taking the step of committing to medication is huge, and it doesn't go well for everyone. I am optimistic about your case as you have so much courage and are stubborn. You're not the type to give up. I don't think it's useful for you to contemplate a stay in a mental hospital if we can keep you on the plateau." I agreed, except that labeling me as courageous but stubborn was perhaps her attempt to encourage me. It did.

Dr. Paige asked me about six weeks into our relationship whether I had any friends. I explained, "I have a good friend, Enoch, who understands I don't want to see him in person right now while I work through my problems to a better place. We do exchange phone calls. He was always adamant that I needed a shrink and a psychiatrist, so he is happy I am consulting you. I have a phone relationship with a couple, Lucas and Athena, who live in Perth. I am taking a break from that friendship while I work with you. I have a friend, Sasha, in Adelaide, who I call every fortnight. He knew my mother and knows I have inherited some of her psychiatric problems. That doesn't prevent us from talking. He is the most resilient. I have an aunt, Beth, to whom I write about twice a month. I am cautious with that correspondence and only write to her when I am doing better. She always replies. I have let everyone else slide. I have to fight now in relative solitude with your help and, ultimately, a psychiatrist's. If I improve, I can then worry about my social life. I was always a loner and am not missing people right now. When I leave my studio for errands, it's a huge effort to cope with the people I see by chance."

During one session about two months into our relationship, Dr. Paige remarked, "There is something about you that I find confusing. You can describe what it is like to be amid a relapse of paranoid schizophrenia and claim to still be in that same state. How does this objectivity arise? I would have thought that to be totally out of touch with reality would prevent you from being able to describe what that means."

I replied, "I believe this faculty has misled many people, especially the other shrinks I briefly consulted. If you must know, the observation you make distresses me, as I fear you do not believe my description of my symptoms."

Dr. Paige reassured me, "No, that's not what I am saying. I believe you, but I don't understand how you can describe your symptoms when sick."

I tried to explain, "At the nadir of a severe relapse, even writing is a challenge. The letters dance around in front of my eyes. I am distressed by words in black ink and can only get to the first base with blue ink, which makes it difficult even to pay bills. These linguistic problems at least partly explain why I have sometimes lost control over my speech and writing. I am grabbing onto words with a confused meaning, with a life of their own. You have read about other symptoms in my notes.

My schizophrenia is like an ocean with waves that are enormous and unpredictable. All I can do at the low point of a wave is cope with existing. At the high point, I am looking back at the low point I just endured and looking forward to the low point I know is coming. For that brief moment, I manage to be rather objective. I can write about the low point for a little while. The notes and observations about mental illness I am sharing are the product of a lifetime, first sailing my mother's rough ocean and then taking on mine. I go to the blank page and write when I have the high points of temporary relief. This relief may only last a few minutes when I am most ill. When I am making some progress to better health, they last longer, but it's always an effort to record symptoms that are so real to me and, if I am paranoid, that I am so convinced are general knowledge that I feel they shouldn't need explaining."

Dr. Paige confessed, "I haven't had many patients who approach their mental illness the same way you do, and not many who are independent adults. Most of my experience with schizophrenia includes working with worried parents consulting me along with a young daughter or son coping with the first onset of a psychotic break. It's usually the parent who is most in need, as they cannot understand why their brilliant child is oblivious to the reality with which they once had such a firm rapport. Schizophrenia can shatter the dreams parents have for their children. Usually, the child is not as concerned about that aspect. I notice the same phenomenon with you. You don't seem unduly upset about what your mother and your mental illness have cost you."

I explained, "I believe my relative indifference to excelling in society has nothing to do with my mental health struggles. It is a consequence of my personality, upbringing, and the fact that I loved my mother, and she was often a joy. I have little personal ambition. I want to have enough money so that poverty is not a concern, and

I want to lead a simple life enriched by my interests. I am quite happy to enjoy my life relatively alone. My mother was an incredible person, fascinating and intelligent, who, during my childhood years, raised me well. I loved her deeply, something the years of her torment, and hence mine did not lessen. Both my father and mother, and from what I can gather, my mother's father laughed at social climbing and taught me that exploiting your gifts was not as important as enjoying them. Do you know the song *Little Boxes* by Malvina Reynolds from the early sixties?"

"No," Dr. Paige replied.

"Well, it sums up what my father thought of middle-class social climbers. He may have been abusive, but he nonetheless passed on to me some of his values."

Little Boxes was not the only media I discussed with Dr. Paige. During one session, I hoped not to scare her by confessing that Polanski's movie, *The Tenant*, from 1976, was close to much of what I had experienced in crisis. She watched it herself before the next session and told me it was a brilliant portrayal of someone struggling with paranoia. She made me feel comfortable with my confession about the film.

I explained to her, "I navigate a lot of my bad times with the help of media I admire. For example, the 1963 movie *The Servant*, starring Dirk Bogarde, helped me understand my father." Dr. Paige watched that movie, too, but found it much harder to understand. "My father wasn't easy to understand either," I ventured.

Having a doctor prepared to devote extra time to my attempts to explain myself through media, especially movies and songs, was a first for me. I didn't want to overdo it, so I told Dr. Paige, "You needn't feel obliged to experience in its entirety every media I mention."

She said, "Well, that's not necessary. You can describe during our appointments what it is about songs and films that help you understand yourself and your parents. I don't necessarily have to prepare by exposing myself to the same media." I often saw Dr. Paige writing down the title of a song or movie that interested me. That may have been a cue to trust her. In any case, it did help.

Dr. Paige and I agreed that our second to most important work would be attacking the PTSD from my childhood that still plagued me. However, our first goal was to stabilize me on the plateau so that I could navigate my life and my inevitable sessions with a psychiatrist.

Three months into my consultations with Dr. Paige, she told me that I must find a psychiatrist to help with the symptoms of my schizophrenia from a medical standpoint. She advised, "I hope that by now you trust me enough for our appointments to continue to be constructive. However, I am not qualified, nor am I allowed, to prescribe anti-psychotic medication. My impression of you is that, despite your sterling efforts to self-correct what you understand to be untenable symptoms, you won't be able to rest easy on the plateau without medication."

47

Psychiatrist

A few weeks after Dr. Paige insisted I find a psychiatrist, I began to look for one. I wanted a female psychiatrist, so that further narrowed the field. Now that I was ready for this step, I aimed high, going for a psychiatrist who practiced on the prestigious location for doctors , Macquarie Street in Sydney. I went to my psychologist with my shortlist, and she helped me choose one doctor who her other patients had benefited from. The doctor was Dr. Pearl Reed.

The first time I consulted Dr. Pearl, I began the conversation by discussing the emergence into the current space-time coordinates of my nightmares as a pre-teen and teen. Although I suspected this tormenting symptom was PTSD and not paranoid schizophrenia, I had never discussed it with anyone except my shrink.

The dream I had at eleven about confronting the face of death was constantly appearing in the daytime, something especially true during the worst of my relapses. That dream had actual spatial coordinates for all the players, and I often imagined I saw people outside my home standing in the corresponding poses. Sometimes the gestures people made added to my certainty that my dream was everywhere. It was as if my brain was inside out.

I had written by then about forty pages of notes about my psychiatric profile that I sent to Dr. Pearl before my first appointment. She had read them. Dr. Pearl told me, "What you describe about your dream is undoubtedly due to childhood trauma, and it will be important to discuss it at some point. Your psychologist will also be able to help you with that kind of problem. Instead, I want to focus on the psychiatric aspects of the notes you sent me." She took a few seconds and then said firmly, "It is my opinion that your symptoms are consistent with severe paranoid schizophrenia. I am delighted you have a great psychologist. My first task is to find adequate medication for you. I must monitor your progress closely while we find the best drug and dosage to combat your symptoms."

Rather than the official diagnosis that I lived with paranoid schizophrenia being a cause for devastation, at this stage in my life, I was relieved to have a diagnosis in which I believed and two doctors with whom I could work to make a better existence for myself. Only by fully facing the diagnosis could I hope for an Overlife beyond it where I could gain stability and happiness. Part of my relatively upbeat attitude was my age and the fact that I had experienced so much schizophrenia through my mother. It's different being told at about forty that schizophrenia will always be a part of your life than receiving the same news when you are eighteen. My ambitions were curtailed first by my mother's illness and then by mine, and I had been working for a long time towards fashioning a life for myself within strict constraints that didn't make me unhappy. For many young people, the diagnosis of paranoid schizophrenia threatens their dreams for a successful life towards which they and their parents have worked for years. Even if they embrace medication and therapy, they often must adapt their expectations to this mental illness. They need lots of encouragement, kindness, and help to accept they may have to revise their life goals. There is always hope, but it can be hard to muster up that sentiment as you watch your loved one go through the torment of schizophrenia, especially if they are experiencing psychosis for the first time.

One of the many aspects of Dr. Pearl that earned my trust in her was that she never questioned my description of what I was experiencing during my episodes of lousy mental health. Additionally, she sounded matter-of-fact in her replies to what I described, impressing me that we would approach my symptoms practically.

Concerning medication, Dr. Pearl repeated, "Our first step is to find you an antipsychotic, along with the correct dose, that you tolerate and that is effective. I am so happy you've indicated you will cooperate fully with this quest and won't cheat by not taking your medication as prescribed. Part of this process may be unpleasant as patients exhibit disparate reactions to the same drug."

I will not name drugs, as everyone's journey with medication is unique, and I am not qualified to recommend even the medicines I take. A discussion about medication is for you and a psychiatrist you trust. I never discuss the medication I take with someone outside the medical profession. These are not recreational drugs. Despite annoying side effects, they are drugs that may tremendously attenuate various unwelcome symptoms. They may save a life if they relieve the patient of the word "suicide" popping up in their head unbidden. If you are battling schizophrenia and refuse any drugs for it, that is your story, and I sincerely wish you well with it. Let me say again everyone's experience with anti-psychotic medication is unique.

I believe my story with anti-psychotic drugs went well and continues to go well. The drugs may have some long-term side effects, but the benefit they provide offsets that danger for me. I had to try several of them during the first two years I worked with Dr. Pearl, but we finally hit on a relatively new one that helped me manage my symptoms and work with Dr. Paige for that plateau.

Forewarned is forearmed, and Dr. Paige and Dr. Pearl helped me recognize the danger signs of an impending relapse. The medication aimed at allowing me to objectively pull back from a descent into a total dislocation from reality. If it didn't, we adjusted the dose. After some caution, Dr. Pearl had no choice but to recommend a high dosage of my chosen medicine to combat my paranoia at its worst. The psychotherapy with Dr. Paige was essential to my work with Dr. Pearl.

In the long run, the medication did not turn out to be a cure-all for my symptoms. Indeed, even while taking prescribed drugs, I went on to have other psychotic episodes. My then-current psychiatrist approached those disappointments by adjusting the dose of a medication I tolerated well. We worked together to hit on an amount that mollified the psychotic symptoms, especially the paranoia, to enable me to be more objective about my state of mind. My psychiatrist and psychologist would work with me intensively to restore stability. Once I was doing much better, my doctor often decreased the dosage to raise it again if I hit another rough patch. Even with these modifications, my psychiatrist told me that my dosage was always high relative to most of their other patients with schizophrenia.

One of the most common side effects of anti-psychotic drugs is weight gain. None of the drugs increased my weight, and I still struggled against being too skinny. However, they used to make my mouth dry, which led to some dental problems that I worked through with my dentist. Another member of my support group was a family doctor, Dr. Penny Richards, recommended by Dr. Paige. Just because you live with schizophrenia doesn't mean you can't get sick in other ways. The new family doctor prescribed medication for my absence epilepsy. I told her in detail about my schizophrenia, and she said I should call her practice in an emergency if I couldn't get hold of Dr. Paige or Dr. Pearl. I should contact the nearest hospital emergency room if that doesn't work. There was a hospital a few blocks away from my studio.

At each appointment with Dr. Pearl, we discussed the medical side of my treatment. We also devoted time to my descriptions of how the memories of my childhood, and the problems I had accrued as an adult with a mental illness, were faring in my attempts to reach Dr. Paige's plateau. Dr. Pearl had embraced the idea of a plateau and remarked, "If you can stabilize yourself on this plateau, you will be able to see forever!"

After about a year of working with Dr. Paige and Dr. Pearl, I recognized that if I had sought help sooner, my prognosis would have been much better. Every relapse of a severe mental illness brings with it a cost you cannot repay in full. Both doctors recommended not to take on anything I didn't feel was easily within my grasp. I already had my at-home activities, which gave me pleasure.

For socializing, Dr. Paige was adamant that I only seek encounters I was confident would go well. Dr. Pearl shared this opinion. For them, the most precious aspect of their work was that I should be able to happily go about my simple daily life without conflict with anyone.

They did not view my solitude as a problem, even though self-isolating is often a side effect of schizophrenia. Dr. Pearl remarked, "You seem to have friends and relatives you communicate with by phone or letter, like Enoch and your Aunt Beth. I advise you to focus on friendship at a distance for a while until you are fully confident about taking the step of something closer." Dr. Pearl added, "I doubt you will ever be able to work again. Your schizophrenia is too severe. Since you've succeeded in getting unemployment benefits and can manage on them, I wouldn't seek employment." In my heart, I agreed with Dr. Pearl. Dr Pearl added, "I will help you apply for disability benefits. Schizophrenia is one of the conditions that qualifies for them and these benefits can be permanent."

After several years of work with Dr. Paige and Dr. Pearl, I was on the plateau that had proven so elusive for me. We had mapped out a plan for the eventuality that I began to get sick again, which made me feel even more confident. The idea was not to let a molehill become a mountain. As soon as I felt my equilibrium was failing, I contacted them and honestly talked about it. We all agreed that the overall feasibility of the plan was a significant victory. I finally felt something from my age-eleven dream that had often eluded me - Hope!

48

Trust

I trusted my doctors. There is another meaning of the word trust. It is a set-up in which one party, the trustor, or grantor, gives another party, the trustee, the right to hold title to property or assets for the benefit of a third party, the beneficiary. In 2000, when I was forty-two going on forty-three, I became the beneficiary of a trust. The grantor was none other than my grandfather, Feivel. The trustee was a lawyer in the same firm as my grandfather's lawyers before he died. Feivel must have realized that the AUD 600 he left me when I was eight wouldn't stay long out of my father's grasp. What was weird about the trust was it had to wait until I was forty-two. Maybe the new millennium signified something for my grandfather. Had I died in the interim, that money would have gone to Beth. Beth's parents left her their house, and she had a steady job in a bank for years, so she had no money worries. However, my grandfather couldn't have known that my circumstances at forty-two would be so financially slim. There was a mystery here, but for the moment, I was overwhelmed by my sudden fortune.

Receiving the irrevocable trust came at the best possible time. I existed on disability benefits with no nest egg for extra expenses, including those I may need for medical bills. The trust consisted of a studio in a modest suburb of Melbourne, Australia, protected from developers because it was of historical interest. My grandfather had seen the studio before making the trust. He had made some arrangements for a replacement in case the studio disappeared. That precaution was unnecessary as it happened. The small living quarters would ensure this new home was inexpensive to maintain. I was also left AUD 500,000 in cash, which helped me as I had few cash reserves for emergencies. Then, there was a stock portfolio worth about AUD

100,000. So instead of the AUD 600 that Dalaigh took over when I was eight, I suddenly received about AUD 600,000.

I was still too weighed down by schizophrenia to work. I remained eligible for disability benefits, though these would decrease in light of my new assets. I felt sure I could manage the new assets myself. Still, my psychiatrist suggested I hire an accountant to help me with the details of investing my assets. I did so and wasn't sorry. I was nervous about leaving the studio I rented in Sydney for the studio I would own in Melbourne, primarily because it would distance me from my doctors. Both my psychologist and psychiatrist offered to continue phone appointments. They also recommended their counterparts in Melbourne should I need in-person help. They urged me to contact those doctors, which I did, and I agreed to meet with them once I was in Melbourne.

My good fortune raised many questions, as had the meeting with Robert. Robert gave supporting evidence to my father's suspicions that I was illegitimate. Feivel's trust supported my mother's suspicions that her father hid money before he died. Shortly after receiving news of the trust, my grandfather's lawyers sent me a letter from him. It answered most of my questions about the trust. Here is that letter:

"Dear Sarah,

If you are reading this letter, you know I left assets in trust for you before I died. I decided to make the trust once I learned your mother, Jodie, was pregnant with you. I didn't inform Beth or your grandmother, Edith. I am writing this letter a few weeks after your birth in August 1957. Neither your grandmother nor I are in good health, so you may never know us. However, you and I have met. I flew to Sydney to see you in the hospital where you were born, something neither Jodie nor I shared with your father, Dalaigh. You were a beautiful baby in excellent health. You gave me hope for my legacy.

I love Edith and Beth, but the last five years or so have not been happy. Edith is depressed and never goes out. Beth looks after her but seems to blame me for her mother's condition. They lead a life apart from me, sharing secrets and hours from which they entirely exclude me.

Your mother, Jodie, has always been a worry. Relatively young, she exhibited extreme behavior, demanding a great deal of attention. With Beth so occupied with Edith, and Edith depressed, it fell on me to give her the love she craved. Edith was a good mother for all of Jodie's basic needs, like food, clothes, and kindness, but she didn't have the energy to respond adequately to Jodie's personality. Jodie was a pretty child, always smiling and extremely intelligent. I was never that keen on Beth and Jodie going into ballet, but they loved it so much I didn't object. I was worried that ballet would lead Jodie to go to Sydney to join a ballet group, which is what happened. We lived in Adelaide at the time. Jodie had been showing signs of inventing fantasies, and I was concerned about her managing alone. In Adelaide, she was in love with Wally, another dancer, who visited Sydney from time to time and had encouraged Jodie to move there. Wally was strictly a man's man, as I tried to explain to Jodie, but she wouldn't accept it.

Then, Jodie married your father, Dalaigh. I hired a private detective to look into Dalaigh. He found that, among Dalaigh's frequentations, were many petty criminals, as well as the artistic crowd where your mother met him. I was sick with worry, especially as Dalaigh refused to make the trip to Adelaide to meet us. Meanwhile, Beth had grown more and more hostile to me. I worried more for Beth's mental welfare than for Jodie's.

I decided to put my hope into the youngest of my clan, you! I figured that whatever I gave you would be claimed by someone else. It was best to let the trust wait until you were forty-two going on forty-three—the middle-aged need much more support than the young, yet can defend themselves better. Also, it would be the new millennium, the year 2000, which had a significance in my mind born of a love for numbers that began when I was in school.

The studio I have left you is in Melbourne because that's where I started my life after releasing myself from my foster parents. Melbourne was good to me, and it's sheer nostalgia on my part to situate my granddaughter in that city. I hope you will not sell the studio. That would disappoint me. I furnished it before handing the management of it over to my lawyers. They took money from my trust to hire a cleaning lady for the studio and attend to any necessary repairs.

I hope you had some contact with my brother Herman. I was so thrilled to find him; he is a fine person. My sister Irit died of a heart attack in 1955. She lived most of her life in Wales, a long way from Sydney. She had some psychological worries due to her early childhood. I visited her in the early 1930s, and it was meaningful for both of us. She identified her foster family, in which she was happy, as her true family.

I also hope you will support Beth as much as you can. She is a highly intense person, given to fanatical behavior. Despite her Jewish roots, she took to the Church of England. This conversion is a product of the schools we chose for Jodie and her. She is becoming a most devout Christian. I don't mind in the least. I am only worried she will become isolated with her zeal, as it will be hard to take for some people. I am so happy she has a regular job in a bank. That gets her out into society.

You were born into a volatile and concerning marriage. I hope you made it! Thank you for giving me hope, which is always the most critical asset.

Love,

Your Grandfather,

Feivel."

49

Music

Sometimes, it's a blessing to wait until much later in life to revisit a grudge, such as I had against Dalaigh over my musical education. I continued to play piano, strictly at a beginner amateur level like I do today. When I was in my early thirties, I heard on the radio, for the first time, the keyboard music of the composer William Byrd (1539/40 or 1543 – 4 July 1623). I was captivated by this composer, who has become my favorite. Many musicians play his keyboard music on the virginal, an instrument that's intimate and refined. Others play it on the harpsichord, which became my favorite instrument. I fell in love at about the same time with the interpretations of Louis Couperin (c. 1626 – 29 August 1661) by Blandine Verlet on the harpsichord. I realized that the music at which I would have worked so hard as an amateur child was not the music I would ultimately most like, as these composers are not typical of a generic repertoire for contemporary music education on the piano.

I would have been far too nervous, in any case, about performing to be a concert pianist. So, I can thank my father for freeing me up to find my true love in music as a mature adult without years of frustration playing compositions I could never wholly conquer and would like but not love.

My less classical musical tastes also expanded in my thirties. I found I loved Bluegrass and paid more attention to movie scores. My favorite composer for films is Dimitri Tiomkin. His most moving song, in my view, is *The Green Leaves of Summer*, from the movie *The Alamo* (1960). It is about young men fighting at the Alamo who have everything to live for but surrender their lives to give their co-combatants a military advantage.

The biggest news for me musically was rediscovering the piano recordings of the famous Canadian pianist Glenn Gould (1932-1982) when I was about thirty-five. I had some exposure as a teenager, but my mother had no recordings of him in her private collection. I first heard him play by chance on our radio when I was alone. His playing captivated me. I did not share this reaction with my mother, regarding it as too treasured to risk her possible criticism. He didn't play like any of the musicians she idolized. I put Glenn Gould to one side, promising myself I would listen to more of his recordings one day. That I acted on this resolve only twenty years later shows how engrossed I was in my mother's view of the world, including her musical landscape. Glenn Gould is famous for his performances of Bach, and he became my favorite pianist, even though Bach is not my preferred composer.

Music is an acutely important tool of mine to combat my schizophrenia symptoms. Let me focus on the example of Glenn Gould. His recordings help me deal with the linguistic suffering I endure from schizophrenia. This benefit has nothing in common with emotional release. At the heart of Glenn Gould's power to help me combat my symptoms is the lack of hierarchy, but not of an invitation to structure, in how he plays music. He ditches the dominance of one note over another for open structure, serving up the music as if to say, "I play every note without prejudice. Now, build a structure with these notes in your mind as the listener." He hints not at one structure but at many possible configurations. He gives just enough edifice within his playing to enable you to erect your own. His performances are like a kit, and it's up to you to put the pieces together. Glenn Gould encouraged the audience to view themselves as an artist. That invitation to a one-to-one relationship of artist player to artist listener, that outstretched hand , has helped me combat my linguistic and temporal confusion many times. Glenn Gould's recordings give me just enough structure to help me navigate the chaos of these symptoms.

Of all my senses, hearing has the most impact, and movement, which some say is also a sense, especially to music, comes a close second. Even though my ability to play piano is limited, my upbringing brought with it a love of music. The most influential musician in my life will always be Glenn Gould, who I have never met. I have a personal relationship with him that he sought for his audience, none whatsoever. My connection is purely to his music. My reaction to his playing is ever-changing, but always therapeutic.

50

Sarah: Overlife

overlive/ (ˌəʊvəˈlɪv) //verb/

: to live longer than (another person)

: to survive or outlive (an event)

Now that I am sixty-five, I can still hear the sounds of my childhood and teenage years. I can feel even now their powerful effect on my inner self growing up.

I occupy the Overlife of Jodie and Dalaigh in that I live after their deaths. The legacy of their Overlife, in that, what survives their end, is anchored in my vivid memories of them. I learned of my father's death at eighty-two from his lawyer. It was the year I turned fifty-two, in 2009. I never heard from him after my parent's divorce and never sought to contact him. I hope he was happy during those years away from Jodie and me. He left me nothing in his will. It would have been like him, and quite correct, to give anything he had to the friends close to him in his old age.

In a strange coincidence, Robert died at the same age as Dalaigh in 1994, when I turned thirty-seven. We had exchanged letters a few times a year but did not meet again after our chat over coffee in 1987 when I was thirty. To my joy, after Robert died, his lawyer sent me a package of Robert's incomplete and unpublished poems with his handwritten notes. What a wonderful gift to pass on to me! I treasure these poetic ideas and memos that reveal so much of his inner self. It's been fun to try to complete some of the unfinished poems.

When I turned fifty, Sasha passed away at ninety. He had maintained his phone friendship with me until he died, though we never met in person. When I look at my grandfather's watch, I see his generosity on its face. Sasha, who was part of my mother's legacy, was precious. Many times while I was struggling with the symptoms of schizophrenia, I called him to have a break and talk about something that wasn't my mental health troubles. Sasha always navigated the first few awkward *sentences by discussing his friendship with my mother. He then helped to deflect some of my anxiety with genuinely inspiring anecdotes about his artistic world and its inhabitants.*

I had an enjoyable relationship with my pen pal Uncle Herman, Feivel's brother, who died at eighty-four when I was twenty-three. I had a much closer pen-pal relationship with Beth, who passed away at the same age as Sasha, in 2013, from cancer when I was fifty-six. She was a wonderful aunt and never wavered in our frequent correspondence by handwritten letter. She shared many stories from her life that showed the good side of my ancestors. To have her cheering me along, as well as sticking up for my mother's side of the family, gave me self-confidence. Her continual reminders about following the ripe fruits of my conscience guided me through many difficult decisions I have made.

Looking back over my past, and appreciating the positive gifts of my now departed family and friends that extend into an Overlife as their survivor, is a powerful conditioning against self-pity.

Lucas and Enoch are still alive, Lucas in Perth and Enoch in Sydney. They have maintained a phone friendship with me that we still enjoy. However, I will only speak to them when I judge my symptoms are manageable. That state can be challenging to define correctly, but I have a lot of experience avoiding people unless the interaction is sure to go reasonably.

"Overlife" is a noun I made from the old-fashioned verb "overlive," whose meaning, quoted from the Collins English Dictionary (Copyright © HarperCollins Publishers), appears above, immediately following the title of this chapter. The living can overlive events that occur, and here I mean recovery, complete or partial, from significant incidents, including a diagnosis of a severe illness or the death of another person. The dead remain dead, but their legacy overlives their disappearance—those who survive the deceased weave together memories of their regrettable and good actions. In retrospect, the latter may transcend and shine brighter than the former.

I am happy to have had the family into which I was born. The bad times of that environment remain traumatic. However, it isn't just the bad times that are within me. All the positive attributes of my parents are also alive in my memory. I replay in my mind my mother's beautiful stories, like those about the ballet. Despite the overall torment of which they were *symptomatic, my mother's evolving fantastic narratives told a tale partly based on fact. She gained some relief by confiding them in me, and I gained vital knowledge of the progress of her mental illness. Actual events were the seeds my mother nurtured until they grew into trees of fiction sturdy enough to bear the leading players, of which she was one. Their branches supported her in the battle with her symptoms. They helped her forget her increasing disappointment in those who should have loved her. After the death of her parents, my love was the only totally committed one my mother knew. In following her mental path, I could support her. I was proud of that role. Not all the delusions my mother endured harmed her. Mixed in with her embellishments on the truth were enchanting stories that showed how much she loved certain people, like Wally, Robert, and Feivel. They had no bad associations in her mind and were part of the most exciting parts of her life. Though I knew that not everything she confided in me about them was true, her enthusiastic tales enriched her life and mine.*

My father, at his best, worried about the plight of poor people and genuinely identified with the working class. The year 1969 was significant for many people because it was the year Apollo 11 landed on the moon. Dalaigh was particularly excited about this achievement. It showed a side of him too often neglected in his marriage, that he had an active and focused intelligence. As a school child, I watched the first step onto the moon's surface in 1969 by Neil Armstrong in my classroom. My school did everything it could to ensure every one of its students witnessed this incredible feat. Sometimes, it's a warm feeling to be old enough to have lived a consequential moment of history.

My mental world is thick with these departed relatives and friends, still so full of life in my memory. I am privileged to be part of their Overlives, their enduring constructive legacies to me after their death.

I am not the only person to benefit from the legacies of my relatives. My mother could not attend the funerals of her parents in Adelaide, three days apart, as Dalaigh would not give her the money for the train from Sydney, where she lived at the time, to Adelaide. Although this wasn't Dalaigh's intention, the inability to make the trip may have saved my mother from added stress. The death of her parents deeply upset her, and the funerals may have only added to the tensions. Beth *called her on the telephone to report on the funerals. Edith's funeral drew only a small number of participants since she had withdrawn from the world in her last years. By contrast, Beth told my mother that many people turned up at Feivel's funeral. Some were friends and business associates that Beth knew. Of course, Herman and his wife attended. However, most of the people Beth didn't know.*

Who were they? Feivel never forgot that he made his living from the embers of abusive cruelty by his foster parents and total abandonment by his birth parents. Feivel also never lost sight of the fact that his subsequent success originated in the help he received as a teenager from some members of the Jewish community in Melbourne. The help was modest, but it was a first step up to a steady job. My mother told me that Feivel had a special place in his heart for the kids on street corners selling papers. It was hard work for little pay, and he often slipped them some extra coins when he bought papers from them. Beth told my mother that one of the mourners at Feivel's funeral approached her crying, saying that Feivel had given him money when he was so down on his luck that he was sleeping in the street. Feivel followed the fate of that man until he was sure he could manage financially. It turned out that Feivel's initial gift was enough to help this man get back on his feet, find a job, and go on to a financially secure life. The funeral drew many such people, and Beth heard from them, when they offered their condolences, lots of stories about Feivel's targeted generosity. They fit well with what my mother remembered of her father's feelings about poverty. To him, poverty was society's disgrace, and no one should shield their eyes from it. Jodie's family was never poor, but her father made sure he periodically walked his little girls through neighborhoods where people were not that lucky, where there were children with rickets. Feivel was at most comfortably middle class, but he knew even modest help to someone with next to nothing could have a significant impact.

My schizophrenia, and it is mine, just as anyone with schizophrenia has a unique experience, despite the common symptoms, did not disappear with age. At sixty-five, I have lived a sequence of Overlives as I survived and partially recovered from each downturn in my mental health. Since discovering Dr. Paige and Dr. Pearl, I have worked closely during each bad patch with a psychologist and psychiatrist I *trust, and that are heirs of a chain of recommendations beginning with those two initial doctors.*

I now live an Overlife that draws on the experience of all these previous ones. I still aim for the plateau, and my periods of good mental health have decorated that landscape with a life I genuinely want to lead. It only works because I am brutally frank with myself, remaining informed about my brain disorder yet appreciating but ignoring any current advice about schizophrenia that doesn't fit me as an individual. My ability to make and sustain friends is made much easier by modern technology, email, and social media. I have built quite an extensive array of "online" friends. I rely on medication and excellent doctors. However, these are not enough to fully cope with the paranoia, delusions, and linguistic torment that can still surface, especially under stress or a change in my routines. I am a mass of habits. They are simple and easy to achieve, providing me the comfort of predictability and valuable reference points as a backdrop to my symptoms.

When I am doing well, the main contribution of the medication is to aid my objectivity and regulate my sleep, which helps enormously. With that enhanced awareness, judging when I slip into unreality is easier. I then employ tools I have developed to help maintain an outward equilibrium while I turn myself back to a healthy path. Roughly speaking, I bring down the curtain on my social life, offline and online, contact my doctors, and lay low at home, partaking in my favorite pastimes, like listening to music and watching classic films. If I must go out for any reason, I imagine myself as someone else with conservative behavior. I act a part, but it avoids displaying the asocial behavior that may be begging to appear. If my health continues downward, despite these precautions, increasing my medication dosage attenuates significant symptoms like paranoia. It's a highly delicate business, and I rely heavily on my psychologist and psychiatrist to see me through such a stage. If I can keep focused, the outcome is usually good. Though I have had many alarming relapses, the medication and the doctors have enormously shortened my time in psychosis. They have helped me more rapidly advance to my now familiar plateau.

When I am in relatively decent health, I am not embarrassed when I reflect on my behavior that may have scared or offended others. To claim retrospective embarrassment is a lie that would only hinder knowing myself and thereby preventing a relapse into a place I seek to avoid. What counts for me is not the output but that I have, in the past, completely lost control of the mechanism responsible and had no clue how to regain societal normalcy. I became deeply invested as I aged in preventing such unfortunate lapses in my target behavior and recovering the socially conservative part of my personality that dominated the years before the numerous periods of decline in my mental health.

I am not embarrassed by the loss of control over my behavior, especially my verbal behavior, as it draws on my personal experiences. The challenge is to prevent that lack of embarrassment from clouding my judgment. All the self-expression that harmed my relationships originated in something I had heard other people say, people who are widely accepted and, at times, even celebrated. In my Australian upbringing, there was a lot of tolerance for British toilet humor. In addition, more contemporary media, for example, movies, including many celebrated ones, often contain highly offensive situations and profane language. The totality of my "bad language" would not even warrant a mention in this context.

What is crucial for me is that I would never, by choice, repeat profanities in public. Such behavior signals that I am struggling with my schizophrenia and a linguistic compulsion I cannot control. I believe that my lack of embarrassment in myself via such comparisons is a valid take on what I genuinely feel and that it is pretty correct. It's unfortunate that during my struggles with self-control, so many people ignored all the good things I was also expressing in a perfectly socially acceptable way, only focusing on the terrible stuff. I see it not in terms of good and terrible, but terrible is how they labeled what they chose to acknowledge. They passed over the worthy to justify dumping me. That's what they found most convenient.

My mother also lost control of her politeness as she aged and resorted to uncharacteristic language. In her case, these lapses concerned only her relationship with Dalaigh and her suspicions about his extra-marital affairs. That I had to listen to her and that she repeated herself to such an extent that she sought to brainwash me did worsen the control problems I would go on to have due to my schizophrenia. The memory of mental fatigue due to my mother's monologues did recur, along with other events that added to my PTSD from childhood experiences. For all that, when I had verbal control problems, I did not copy Jodie's script. My spoken and written words reflected what I wrongly assumed to be a current ambient and sanctioned shift in linguistic currency. In these periods of struggle with my schizophrenia, I often believed there was a global change in how the world treated me. What I perceived could not all be categorized as offensive. Still, there was often a significant slice of my perception invaded by profanities in word and gesture that I was convinced others were directing at me or sharing about me amongst themselves. In my relapses, there was always that backdrop of the conviction that everybody, or almost everybody, wanted me dead, and I had to fight the terror of that perception until it weakened as I improved.

It's instructive to ask whether I have been able, in bad mental health, to put myself in the shoes of someone who is on the receiving end of my departures from socially acceptable behavior. This technique has severe limitations. First, when in a paranoid state, I usually believe other people are behaving worse than me. In some sense, my asocial output is, in my mind, a response to their even more reprehensible behavior. Second, unsympathetic people often react to some aspect of my behavior that I don't consider a big deal. The torment, for me, is my lack of control over what I am dishing out. I fail to return to my former self and can only go forward in time, that illusive measure, in my quest to find ways out of my compulsive behavior. The reactions of people who barely know me touch me more than those of my acquaintances. At such a stage, I am usually disappointed in my so-called friends. If I upset someone I barely know, I feel concerned for this person with a walk-on part in the drama of my global paranoia. The question, "Did you feel bad when they reacted negatively?" is most often answered by me with a "Yes!". They hardly know me and owe me nothing, but I victimized them. Something is wrong. My most significant victories by the person I wish to be over the person I long to repress have emerged from such unfortunate encounters . My doctors are used to people with the type of problems I exhibit, and both are skilled at remaining my friend even through my most psychotic periods. This ability is crucial as the quest for stability passes through therapy and medication, at least for me.

I never returned to employment after being booted from the real estate agency for the second time in my thirties. My doctors supported my claims to stay on disability benefits, aided by my assets. This government assistance suffices for my daily expenses, and my grandfather's trust is there for emergencies outside my budget.

My interaction with other people is carefully measured. I have ditched concerts for listening to recorded music. I have an overpowering urge to move to all the music I enjoy, which is impossible at a concert. I participate in some pre-organized activities where I talk with others. Despite the bad experience I had with a book club when I was thirty-one, I am now a member of a Melbourne book club for women that meets once a month, and so far, no problems have occurred. The other members are serious readers, but they also enjoy the social aspect of the get-togethers. Similarly, despite the rejection by the food bank when I was the same age, I volunteer at one once a week, and, again, all is going well. In each case, the leader of the activity has an open mind. I informed them that I live with paranoid schizophrenia, which may lead me to fail to turn up at some of their events, and they insisted that wasn't a problem. Likewise,

I have made friends with the neighbors in my building, despite having "come out" to them that I live with a mental illness. My beloved dog, a Pomeranian named Chloe, is always with me and is a real charmer. Chloe is a certified, trained emotional support dog. There are, in any case, no restrictions on small pets in my Melbourne studio. I have provided for her welfare should anything happen to me. Often, she does all the talking for me.

I have volunteered at a local animal shelter. I have gained the respect of my co-volunteers. It was like walking on eggshells for a while, but the result is most comforting. I was upfront about my mental health diagnosis and that I may need to rest at home for periods. The volunteers are sweet, liberal people, supportive of my participation in the shelter. I see people every time I go shopping, to the bank, and to the mail. Although the exchanges with people during these activities are small and superficial, if they go well, I am immensely supported. Modern technology enables me to have more "online" friends than I would ever have thought possible before I partook in what's available via social media and email.

I am learning Welsh, something I have wanted to do since high school when I read "How Green Was My Valley" by

Richard Llewellyn. I attend monthly meetings of a Welsh club in Melbourne where participants speak only in Welsh. Most of us are beginners.

These interactions fared so much better than when I was in my thirties. I could discuss a specific diagnosis with people, even if the associated stigma may have frightened them. I spoke about my schizophrenia matter-of-factly and reassured these people that I would not show up if I were not doing well. Then, time without a nasty incident, and with my welcome contribution to their activities, had to pass while I established trust. I haven't repeated my thirties' error of showing up to these activities in an agitated and alarming state.

The advantage of pre-organized events, where I am not one of the organizers, is that they are independent of my participation. If I am having a terrible time with my schizophrenia, and I know it won't help to see other people in person, I can bow out while I work on my brain disorder with my doctors.

I am a deeply religious person, but I view religion as a strictly private matter in my case. I do not attend any church or temple. My primary interest is in Judaism and Christianity.

Nonetheless, from practicing meditation, I have gained insight into other religions.

I do participate in some support meetings organized by mental health advocacy groups. These support meetings, in my case, are not a good environment if I am relapsing badly. If I am paranoid, it's total; if I attended, I would be paranoid about the support group. Instead, I find them most useful when the doctors have brought me out of a slip in my mental health to a better place where I am confident I will cope. Then, being able to interact with others about their mental health challenges can be positive for them and me. I can bring something supportive to the meetings and feel supported. However, for other mental health consumers, using the support groups during their darkest times may work well, so I am not giving advice here, just reporting on my approach. Most mental health advocacy groups have resources online, like chat groups. If you don't feel you can go in person to a meeting, the online chat group may help you through that stage. The online experience can also allow you to participate in mental health advocacy groups in other countries.

When I was younger, I had some sexual relationships with men that mostly went well, even though each one did not last more than a few months. I never tried to involve anyone in my sex life while relapsing. I have gone long periods without a sexual partner. I enjoy the challenge of abstinence. The boyfriend era is in the past.

My relative social distancing has one aim, the ability to detach myself physically and mentally from every individual, except my doctors, if I feel I am slipping into another relapse. My experience has shown that attempts to continue contact with friends and relatives once the risk of a psychotic break is present lead more to misunderstanding than anything else. I worked hard to restore some online relationships with people who rejected me in the past due to my lack of self-control when sick.

I did find doctors in Melbourne as competent as the two excellent doctors I had in Sydney. Both these doctors inspired me with solid reasons to get well if I begin to develop psychosis. As some of these doctors retired, they recommended younger colleagues who were equally effective and whom I liked and respected. My only constraint was that I insisted on female doctors. I find the rapport with a doctor treating my mental health is better if they are female. It is terrific to have doctors who understand me and are competent at adjusting the dose of my medication, which, even at my age and despite my good intentions, is an ongoing and challenging task. Though treating me with medication remains difficult, I have been lucky with the drugs, though it took some time to get there. My psychiatrists found a working match that helps me cope with schizophrenia with few side effects. When new drugs come out, we must consider whether I should try them. With my current medication, the main challenge is finding the correct dosage to limit long-term side effects yet remain effective in mollifying my symptoms. Not everyone is so fortunate, which is a shame, as the proper medication can help immensely.

My grandfather's trust was a windfall, pure luck that most mentally ill people will not experience. Both the cash and stock portfolio parts of the trust are mainly intact. I used cash to upgrade my wardrobe, which boosted my morale, and bought some necessities for my studio in Melbourne. I also use some of the legacy to subscribe to various apps on my mobile phone, for example, those featuring movies and music. I have made a will with my favorite mental health advocacy groups as the main beneficiaries, apart from a share put aside for some animal rights groups. I want to show my support for these advocacy groups and all they accomplish by leaving them the bulk of my trust. They are trying, amongst other important goals, to erase the stigma of mental illness and save lives by helping those struggling with suicidal thoughts. As it says in the Talmud (Sanhedrin 37a): "Whoever saves a single life is considered by scripture to have saved the whole world." Of course, I may yet need some of my trust money for something else, like medical expenses, but I pray I don't. My goal is to continue my simple and inexpensive lifestyle.

There are Western social judgments that weigh on me more heavily than necessary, and here I criticize society, not myself. The ambient culture in which I live prioritizes youth. As a senior, many people view me as too old to matter. They feel I am too aged to aspire to anything more than what I currently have and do. Other cultures often view the elderly as valuable sources of wisdom for the younger and as people that are still evolving. I consider my life successful and still changing for the better. However, it is common only to recognize excess as success. Even if I now manage my schizophrenia well, if I am not also a genius, billionaire, or famous, some people ask whether my life was worth it. That is, given what I have been through and what may still await me. Such criteria are light years away from the best of what my parents passed down to me and from my values. We can also measure success by the ability to do without excess. Even more, a simple life with a small imprint, such as I lead, should help the planet rather than shame it. No life outcome makes schizophrenia "worth it" or "not worth it." Nothing makes "some schizophrenics more equal than others," to misquote from Orwell's novel "Animal Farm."

Then why is my life content though I live with a severe mental illness? A lot of my peace of mind comes from accepting that, through self-analysis, I can do a lot to make my symptoms unwelcome. The goal should not be to achieve some gold standard whereby I behave in a "normal" way. That would bore me, for a start. Instead, self-knowledge gives you the means to have socially acceptable and realistic standards. The tight control on my socializing is, in my case, a tool, not a symptom. My schizophrenia, like my mother's, is an alternate lens *through which to view the world. I see, and she saw, what happened around us differently than if we were not so afflicted. We both grew to love our uniqueness when we were lucky enough for it to coincide with a valid take on the reality that so often eluded us. It would be folly to deny the extreme downsides of paranoid schizophrenia that even lead some sufferers to suicide to escape the symptoms. Yet others are arrested and kept in prisons when they need anything but that. Many with clout and motivation are trying to correct these medical issues and societal wrongs. But, too often, no one talks about the upsides. In my youth, I was privately arrogant. My major crime against Dalaigh wasn't throwing a knife at his legs when he convincingly threatened to kill me but, despite his faults, undervaluing and disrespecting him. My illness has curbed my arrogance. I have become much more sympathetic to others struggling with some severe and chronic disorders. The people I've known for a long time, like Lucas and Enoch, and those who agree to stay "phone" friends with me, say I am pleasanter now compared to when they first met me. They can thank my schizophrenia for that.*

I am attracted to nostalgia. My studio has a corner dated around 1960, with no computer, mobile phone, and so on, where I write by hand and read the paper versions of books. Apart from providing an ambiance I enjoy, this space takes me back to my first memories of violence in our home in 1960, when I was three. I have fountain pens and high-quality paper on which I keep a diary of my thoughts, sometimes writing poems and short stories. I have some feather quills and use them dipped in bottled ink. I am old enough that I grew up using a school desk with an ink well. We had advanced past feather quills, but they are so romantic. The childhood traumas still haunt me, but confronting them in my 1960 place and going on to write with a feather quill is marvelous therapy. The set-up makes me feel that I can start over each day as a free adult and with the understanding of hindsight over many years. This process reminds me of a well-known quote from T. S. Eliot: "We shall not cease from exploration, and the end of all our exploring will be to arrive where we started and know the place for the first time."

It's sobering that two of my parent's "delusions" had an element of truth. Dalaigh thought I might be Robert's child and that Jodie suspected her father had "hidden money" he would manage in his way. From my perspective as a senior, these suspicions were powerfully confusing for my parents. It's a pity they did not find answers in their lifetime. Thinking about it makes me more sympathetic to their struggles to maintain an equilibrium in their marriage.

The mentally ill have doubts about certain matters, just as so-called sane people do. However, people can fail to acknowledge what may be their perfectly justified questions, putting anything not immediately apparent in the "crazy" category. This reaction leaves the mental health consumer feeling unsupported and frustrated when a conversation about their concerns might be enough to alleviate some of the stress caused by their worries.

Due to all that's available online, I have many resources for freshening the good memories of my upbringing: YouTube, Apple Music, and Amazon Music, to name just three. On YouTube, I can search for the humorous skits I enjoyed with my mother. Apple Music and Amazon Music cater to my musical tastes, which are still evolving. Then, there are all the excellent movie apps, like Criterion, Prime Video, and Netflix.

You can find almost all the comedy, music, ballet, and films I refer to in this book on one of these apps.

Despite my old-fashioned ways, I appreciate all that modern society has to offer, even if I only partake in a small part. I benefit from modern medicine. I have built a world of friends using email and social media. It can be great to get a fairly immediate response to a query by email. There is so much one can do independently online without dealing with a person face to face. That can be convenient and frustrating, but the former outweighs the latter.

In my case, after a sequence of bad relapses, I looked to discover more and more what was wrong in my approach to my schizophrenia between relapses. I gradually learned that, following a psychotic break, "getting back to 'normal'" or "how things were before" is an impossible aim that disguised the progress I was making both with my mental health and my relationships with other people. I have emerged from each period of struggle with my schizophrenia as a different person, wasting a lot of time and suffering emotional heartbreak mourning the person I would never be again. In my forties, I realized that, despite the horror of a schizophrenic relapse, one could emerge not so much as a better person but as a different person, someone better equipped to handle their disability and build a new future rather than attempting to reconstruct a lost past. Those who try to help someone with schizophrenia should not put too much emphasis on "returning to normal." Rather than such a return, rehabilitation can be an onward journey to a new yet happier place.

I believe in the quest for good mental health in a context that suits your personality and overall aims if those aims are harmless to society. There is every hope that someone living with schizophrenia, with the right support system and natural talent, should work successfully toward professional fulfillment. They can, with understanding friends, also enjoy a satisfying social life. However, we must consider the individual schizophrenic's personality, how their symptoms manifest themselves, and their upbringing. There are as many schizophrenias to understand as people living with schizophrenia. That plurality is one reason the scientific study of schizophrenia is so tricky, and predicting its prognosis for a given individual can be elusive. I live my schizophrenia in my way, without paying much attention to what I view as the narrow hallmarks of success as reported in the local newspapers, what my grandfather called "cheap notoriety."

Someone living with schizophrenia should have a say in their recovery. To warrant that, they mustn't fake their self-assessment. That social withdrawal is a common symptom of schizophrenia does not lead me anymore to try to take on more socializing than is comfortable for me to "please" or "show I am sane." My approach of low face-to-face contact with others when I am struggling, and need my doctor's help above all, is part of my solution. I am happy to have found this way to manage my life. I, of course, don't recommend it to anyone else because it is a personal choice.

Forcing a way of living on a mentally ill person can be distressing if they are not ready for that step or don't want that way of living. People are inclined to put the mentally ill under the microscope, looking for symptoms of "madness" in the most trivial deviations from a mundane way of life. Mentally ill people need to maintain the outlet of self-expression as long as they can keep it within bounds that avoid offending. At sixty-five, I have much experience maintaining my identity while not ruffling feathers. I am happier now about my behavior and its *intersection with the ambient society I live in than I was twenty to thirty years ago.*

A period of highly functional behavior doesn't necessarily mean the mental health consumer is healthy. Both my mother and I were able, in some situations that required work and understanding, to manage a difficult task while we sorted out the correct path, as long as this process did not take too long. It can be challenging for observers to understand such a highly skilled performance amidst a mental health struggle. To some, it made us look like we were coping better overall and should have been able to pull ourselves out of our psychosis. They didn't understand that free will played no part in our temporary remission. An important task was more like a shock that focused our attention for a while. It wasn't a cure. For example, my mother was always able to organize our many moves, even when she was struggling with paranoia. For example, she oversaw our move from Newcastle to Sydney and was canny enough to make sure we ended up in a picturesque suburban location.

I inherited an excellent education from my school, my father, and especially my mother. Repeated relapses have worsened my cognitive skills, but this learning has molded my interests and hobbies, making me grateful for my education daily.

As a youth and young adult, everybody told me my parents were ruining my life. Once I hit sixteen, most acquaintances and teachers urged me to leave home if I wanted to reach my full potential. Yet, even before Dalaigh left us, I was the only candidate for my mother's caregiver. I did it both out of necessity and out of love. The world my mother created during my childhood was beautiful. It was full of colorful characters, influential ideas, and laughter. She tried to tend to it even when she became alarmingly sick. I could still follow, having lived with her during the better years. She gave me so much in return for my caregiving, sharing everything she knew and loving me even during the dark times when she was so difficult. Would I stand by her if given a chance to relive my life? Absolutely!

Even at her most delusional, my mother passed on to me warped stories about my family that still contained an interesting grain of truth. I checked with Beth and Uncle Herman about the rumors concerning Feivel's childhood and the fostering of him and his siblings. Feivel used private *detectives and other means to search for why his parents left him and discovered next to nothing. Modern websites on genealogy finally brought limited knowledge. Though we still know nothing about what happened to Feivel's mother, his father walked out on his children in Ballarat and remarried in Sydney. While still in his early twenties, Feivel's father left for South Africa to work on the railroads and, soon after his arrival there, fell victim to a train accident and died. A photo of his headstone is available online.*

I play a part in Feivel's Overlife. His life started unhappily and ended in worry. He passed on a great deal of culture all the same to his two daughters, and they, in turn, cultivated me and told me stories that came directly from Feivel. His trust aimed at alleviating my financial worries has brought me closer to him, even though we only met before I could remember him. He believed in me, and I try to live up to that. I hope Feivel would have been proud of me, as I dreamed as a child.

Although I live my Overlife, that is, survival after the official diagnosis of my paranoid schizophrenia, with Hope, Fear is also my companion. My overriding Fear is that I will suffer another bad relapse or become lost in insanity like my mother. The terror of a relapse requires a lot of courage and energy to combat, and I am afraid the effort may ultimately fail. In my case, despite having had multiple relapses throughout my life, this Fear is offset by the increasing success I have had working with doctors and formulating my personal tools to deal with my periods of bad mental health. Therefore, at sixty-five, Fear has been a loser for quite some time, and Hope rules. I pray that this situation lasts my lifetime. The dream I had at age eleven with its huge face of death says to me now that the best way to approach a threat is to confront it and stare it down. I am not the only person who is afraid. In fact, we all have to live with some fear since life is finite, and we have limited ability to control our destiny.

When I was about twelve, a neighborhood dog blocked my path to school. I froze with fear for a good five minutes before I ventured further, and then the dog did bite me, a nasty bite but not permanently damaging. I continued to school, where the nurse there dressed the wound. On returning home at the end of the school day, I told my mother about the wicked dog across the street and showed her my injury. She remembered how, when she was thirty-eight, someone had complained about her *dogs. She didn't take the matter further than giving me advice. She told me, "A bully is always a coward, and their worst fear is that you will remain mentally untouched by anything they do. Tomorrow, stare the dog down, but without moving forward until it gives up, and it will. Look at the dog, and don't move your gaze until he retreats."*

Terrified, I tried her formula the next day when I saw the dog on my way to school. It took a full fifteen minutes to stare the dog down. He didn't bite me, retreated, and I never saw him again. My mother raised me to be tough. That's yet another gift she gave. This incident is a "don't try this at home," yet it worked for me on that particular occasion. It shows the times. This dog was a nasty canine of 1969. The attitude of my mother would not, in our neighborhood, at that time, have been considered uncaring. After all, the world of my future would contain greater perils than a possible second dog bite. My mother never doubted my courage. She told me, "When you were about three years old, you loved strong winds and would rush outside the home to meet them with your head held high. When the weather was even more severe, I had to lock the doors so you would not run outside to be in the thick of it. Therefore, you perched on the window sill to watch the weather enthusiastically!"

It takes extreme courage to battle schizophrenia, whether you are the mental health consumer or the caregiver. I am reminded of Job 39:19-25, and I quote,

"19 'Do you give the horse its strength or clothe its neck with a flowing mane?

20 Do you make it leap like a locust, striking terror with its proud snorting?

21 It paws fiercely, rejoicing in its strength, and charges into the fray.

22 It laughs at fear, afraid of nothing; it does not shy away from the sword.

23 The quiver rattles against its side, along with the flashing spear and lance.

24 In frenzied excitement it eats up the ground; it cannot stand still when the trumpet sounds.

25 At the blast of the trumpet it snorts, 'Aha!' It catches the scent of battle from afar, the shout of commanders and the battle cry."

The cruelest harm you can do to someone else's psyche is to tell them they have no hope. The stigma surrounding mental illness can engender precisely this assessment. Yet many people living with a severe mental illness can, under suitable conditions, lead lives as subtle and meaningful as someone not so afflicted. Even worse, many people evince no hope that the mental health consumer can change by ultimately improving their health and behavior. The simple question, "How can I help?" is seldom asked by a person learning that you have paranoid schizophrenia. They are afraid of the response. The tools of therapy and medication are underwritten by how others treat the mentally ill person. If that treatment deprives them of hope, that isn't on them but on others who don't want to miss out on all they feel life owes them. A severely mentally ill person needs kindness and encouragement. Suppose they are too sick to understand who wants to help them and who doesn't, then try to give them hope. Tell them they will soon have true friends and direct them towards activities that are non-threatening and that they can enjoy in their present state.

I believe that Oprah Winfrey once said something equivalent to, "The only courage you ever need is the courage to live the life you want." This attitude is critical for someone fighting schizophrenia. The goal shouldn't be to work towards a set of behaviors that will signal that the patient is "cured." While it is essential to help someone living with schizophrenia to behave in a socially acceptable way, the choice of lifestyle should be their own. Managing my interface with society, as I do, can lead me to keep to myself in times of struggle and should not be confused with the total social withdrawal that is commonly thought of as a classic "symptom" of schizophrenia.

One of the main challenges in looking after my mother was to keep her optimistic and to give her hope that her life would improve. I applauded all the parts of her behavior that were valid expressions of her originality at its best. I held her hand through the dark times, so she knew someone loved her. She gave me so much, from being a wonderful mother in my early years to opening up her intellect for me to enjoy. I feel my sacrifices for her sake were insufficient to repay her. I am pleased to have been born with such a mother and to have stood by her. I am proud of the fight I wage against my mental illness. My mother and I can both claim an Overlife. My mother lives on through me and my memories of her. I live, beyond the *diagnosis of paranoid schizophrenia, in what I consider the best way for my mental health and those around me.*

Many who care about the mentally ill, including those with a brain disorder like schizophrenia, strive to abolish stigma. The stigma against the mental health consumer is widespread and can be harmfully hysterical. I have been at the receiving end of such stigma. I had a double dose. As my mother's caregiver, I suffered because of the stigma directed at her, which left me alone with her mental health problems. I then suffered stigma aimed at me as a mental health consumer myself. In both our cases, many of the people who would have helped us in some other run of bad luck did not want anything to do with supporting us over a mental illness.

The mottos put forth to erase stigma should be accurate. Stigma is not a one-way street down which the prejudiced need to travel and do all the work before engaging with the mental health consumer at the other end of the road. It is a two-way street where the mental health consumer, if necessary with the aid of a caregiver, also tries their best to make such an encounter fruitful as they meet the bigoted partway. The mantra that mental health consumers are like everybody else *isn't true. Equally weak are statements saying that having a mental illness is like having a broken leg, except that the physical break is in the head. That analogy is absurd. What should be encouraged is a scientific way, accessible for the layperson, to view mental illness that relates to the latest research on the topic.*

Most people exercising stigma have never opened a decent recent scientific book for the general public on mental illness, though many such books have been published by now. There needs to be more communication about mental illness that is scientifically justified and underwritten by the experiences of the mental health consumer yet easy to understand and digestible. In relating to other people, the consumer of mental health should show pride in who they are and celebrate their difference. That individuality should not be confused with ignoring the extreme downside of their symptoms and acknowledging the difficulty many people have in compassionately viewing their manifestation. I have gained pride in myself. It is reflected in my love of music, sense of humor, online friendships with those who need one, and social involvement at a level I can adapt to my mental illness. My existence alone is a consequence of Jodie's. I talk about her often to people, letting her talents thrive now in memory. This pride was often impossible to find during the anguish of a psychotic break before I found medical support. The relapses I have since experienced, where I turned to my doctors early on for help and began to feel better, motivated me to handle my mental illness more successfully and practically.

It would help decrease stigma if more people understood that mental health consumers can be temporarily alarming to others but are mainly afraid at such times and not looking to harm anyone else. Often, they seek a way out of the worst aspects of their behavior or inner feelings. In the rare cases that a mentally ill person is physically threatening, it may be relevant to call the police, and this action is not necessarily an exercise of stigma. I have had the police at my door several times due to a lack of control over verbal symptoms. Yet, as soon as I reassured them that I was not a physical threat, they left me alone and told the person who called them to try harder to be nicer to me. I have been lucky. Some mentally ill people end up in jail for no good reason and receive no proper care. Mental health advocacy groups are working hard to abolish such abuse.

Stigma often says even more about the person exercising it than the person they reject. In my experience, most stigma originates in a fear people have that if they engage with someone who is chronically mentally ill, they will have to make some sacrifices. I have been incredulous when I have been combatting the stigma against my schizophrenia to observe how terrified so-called "sane" people can be about making any change in their carefully structured lives. My difference is a threat to them that goes beyond a reaction I may deserve because my symptoms make me temporarily scary and obnoxious. No outward behavior of mine, despite its, at times, unfortunate verbal manifestations, has been physically threatening, and I have always tried, once I feel better, to apologize and reassure people I may have alarmed when ill.

Stigma is, unfortunately, supported by the following frequent scenario. On learning that someone is severely mentally ill, most people they know immediately look for danger in every action of the mental health consumer, no matter how benign. On the other hand, the person exercising stigma has carte-blanche to behave as oddly as they like to cope with their fear of how a mentally ill person they know may affect their life. So often, the person exercising stigma behaves more madly than the person who lives with the mental illness.

Just as every person living with schizophrenia has their unique experience of it, so do they have a personal story to tell of the stigma they have encountered. I have not dealt with the experiences of inmates of a psychiatric hospital nor severe brushes with the police that can land some innocent mental health consumers in jail. The reason for these omissions is that I have no personal experience with them. I was never admitted to a psychiatric hospital. My minor clashes with the police force proved way more positive than the rejection of me by some people I thought were my friends. If you live with a mental illness or a brain disorder or are the caregiver of someone so afflicted, please write about it, for the world knows too little about you. Even your fellow mental health consumers may need education, as their experiences may differ from yours. Don't let anyone tell you that your age is a factor against revealing yourself. You are never too old or too young to have something valuable to say. Try to get a description of your remarkable life into the public eye. Mental health advocacy groups can provide resources for your self-expression. Above all, never seek to apologize for what you know is an undeniable and harmless part of yourself. It's a form of lying that will hinder others from identifying with you in a way that may genuinely help them. I have found that writing this novel uncovered much about myself that I had repressed, and this liberation is lighting my forward path. I hope the telling of my story is useful for others.

Never lose Hope. It's a crucial resource. When I was eleven, I had a nightmare in which I felt a strong force pushing me toward Death until I met the pull of Death itself. I stared down Death and looked to Hope though I was too paralyzed to move toward it. My life has led to accepting Hope as the main remedy for my recurrent paranoid delusion that everyone wants me dead. Unlike in my nightmare, I am now full of Hope, my most effective possession, and I have found ways to move towards it. Despite my age and mental health diagnosis, I feel a deep sense of purpose. I am a descendant of my mother and her father, both of whom worried about their legacy. I am a part of that legacy. That fact motivates me to do my best. I still have nightmares different from those of my childhood, but scary nonetheless, as the usual theme is that I am relapsing and that society is sentencing me to some awful fate. However, the daytime tools I have now to deal with such nights are powerful. I fill the day after with forward-looking activities I enjoy and do not seek to socialize unnecessarily, including on social media. I save a summary of my nightmares for my sessions with my psychologist and psychiatrist. Once I feel better, I remerge into my usual activities and social contacts.

So, I am happy with my Overlife. I have learned to negotiate the worst of my schizophrenia by having a strategy to deal with an impending relapse. My doctors help me identify when I am at risk, and self-knowledge goes a long way to picking up on what they may miss.

My main contribution to society now is, via social media, support groups, and animal welfare, to reach out to as many people and animals in need of a friend as I can. There are people in my small social circle who benefit from knowing me as I am now, just like the animals in the rescue center appreciate my love for them. I am a diligent citizen of the modest suburb in Melbourne, Australia, where I live in my studio. I am living a fortunate Overlife indeed! Even such a simple life as mine can be valuable for others.

I have placed emphasis on the meaning of *overlive* as surviving or outliving an event. However, it can also mean surviving or outliving another person. I am making a diary containing as much information as I can gather about the family I have overlived. By keeping their memory alive, I plan to advance an *Overlife* after death for Jodie, Beth, Feivel, and even Dalaigh.

Should I leave the door to my studio unlocked, and should someone enter unannounced, they may see me moving to music, just like Jodie, the dancer. It's a harmless form of self-expression and should not make anyone afraid.

About the Author

Diana Dirkby is a mental health consumer living with paranoid schizophrenia. Her mother also lived with this brain disorder. This affliction fractures the patient's relationship with reality and may cruelly trick the senses, causing hallucinations and the hearing of voices. These symptoms mix with acute paranoia. The quest to heal the fracture with the real world is arduous.

In writing this fiction novel, Diana Dirkby contributes an account of paranoid schizophrenia via a mother and daughter with this condition, describing its impact on their stories and those of their family and friends. The novel takes place in Australia, where Diana Dirkby was born and raised. By vocation, Diana Dirkby is a research mathematician who made her working life in academia before retiring in 2018. She continues to work on research mathematics. Diana Dirkby lives in the USA with her spouse, who was born in Brooklyn, New York.